THE SILVER ECLIPSE

THE OTHER CONTINENT

- BOOK 3 -

KRISTY DIXON

The Other Continent

The Silver Eclipse Book 3

Cover art by Miblart

Edited by Michelle Clark

First edition 2023

ISBN 978-1-960841-07-0 Paperback

ISBN 978-1-960841-08-7 Hardback

ISBN 978-1-960841-06-3 ebook

www.kristydixonbooks.com

For Reed

Chapter 1

Graham groaned as he rolled over onto his back. His shoulder ached, and he was freezing. He pried his eyes open and stared into the darkness. Where was he? Sitting up, he ran a hand over the cold, rough ground. The bumpy concrete scratched against his skin. Was he on the sidewalk? He held out his hand and tried to make a light. Nothing. A chill ran down his spine as he wondered where he could be and why he couldn't do magic.

"Hello?" he said, quietly. Only silence answered. He racked his brain, trying desperately to remember where he'd gone to sleep last night. The last thing he remembered was sneaking up to the castle in the Northern Kingdom with Wren and Tal. Had they gone to sleep in the woods? He shook his head. If he was outside, it wouldn't be this dark. There was no breeze or night sounds.

Pulling his knees into his chest and wrapping his arms around them to maintain some warmth, he listened hard and tried to still his breathing. After what seemed like an eternity, but was probably only a minute, he heard a light snore to the side of him. Graham sucked in a breath and raised up onto his hands and knees. He hoped the snore was from a friend. Crawling slowly towards the sound took all of his courage, and his heart almost stopped when he touched an arm.

"Wake up," Graham whispered, shaking the arm, and quickly crawling backwards, just in case.

"What?" Tal's groggy voice asked from the black nothingness. "Is it morning already?"

Graham sat back and sighed with relief. "Do you know where we are? I'm totally confused."

Tal yawned. "Are we in the woods? Where's the moon?"

"I think we're inside. I can't do magic."

"What?" Tal asked with a trace of panic in his voice. "Dang it. I can't either. Where's Wren?"

"I'm here," Wren's voice said from Graham's other side. "What's going on? It's so dark. Why can't we do magic?"

Tal made some shuffling noises. "Can anyone remember what happened last night?"

"Ahhhhh!" Graham yelled as something touched his arm.

"Sorry!" Wren apologized. "I didn't want to be by myself."

"I'm coming closer," Tal said, bumping into Graham's other side.

Graham ran a hand through his curls. His heart was pounding in his ears. The other two sat close to his side, and no one spoke. Graham ran his hand through his hair again and frowned. Something was wrong. Something besides waking up in the pitch black, not knowing where they were.

"The last thing I remember is sneaking towards the castle," Wren said. "I feel like I slept for a long time, though. I had some weird dreams and I couldn't wake up."

"That's all I remember as well," Tal said. "No dreams though."

"Something's really wrong," Graham said, still fiddling with his hair. "My hair's longer."

"What do you mean, longer?" Wren asked.

Graham tried not to panic. "My hair's longer than yesterday. Significantly."

"Whoa, so is mine," Tal said. "My bangs are past my eyes and it feels like I haven't shaved for a while."

"What does that mean?" Wren asked, linking her arm with Graham's.

"I don't know," he admitted. "Let's not freak out."

"Too late for that," Tal said. "What do we do? I can't see anything."

"We can't sit here in the dark forever," Wren said. "I'll stand up and walk slowly and feel around to see if there are any walls or anything."

"We shouldn't split up," Graham said as he grabbed Wren's hand. "Let's all stand up and we can walk carefully." He got to his feet and pulled Wren up. "Tal, grab my hand."

"No thanks," Tal said. Graham could almost see his lopsided smile. "I'll take Wren's other hand. I'm assuming you already have hers. Where are you Wren?"

"Here," she said, moving closer to Tal's voice. "Now what?"

"Tal and I will put our arms out straight and walk slowly. If we come to a wall, we don't want to hit hard."

"Okay, I'm ready," Tal said. They began taking slow, deliberate steps.

"I'm trusting you two to not run me into anything," Wren said with a nervous laugh.

Graham closed his eyes as he walked. Keeping them open was putting a strain on them. "Stop," he said as his hand bumped into something. It was cold and felt like metal. "It's a bar."

"A bar?" Wren asked.

"Bars," Tal agreed. "We're in a prison or something."

"Prison?" Wren squeaked. "How could we be in prison?"

Graham shook his head. He wished Tal was wrong, but that's what it felt like. He felt one bar, followed by another. "It makes sense. The bars, and the fact that we can't do magic."

"Do you think they captured us when we tried to get into the castle?" she asked.

"That's my guess."

"Let's turn around and see if we can find a wall," Tal suggested. "If we have to sit, at least we would be able to lean against something."

"Sit?" Wren asked. "Why would we sit? We need to get out of here!"

"There isn't a lot we can do," Graham said, steering them in the opposite direction. He put his arm out again as they walked. "Prisons aren't made to be easy to escape, and in the dark, we have no chance."

"Even prisons should have light," Wren mumbled as she allowed Graham and Tal to lead her. "And where are our cloaks? It's common decency to not let your prisoners freeze to death."

"What if we need to go to the bathroom?" Tal asked.

"Great," Wren muttered. "Thanks, Tal, now I'm going to need to go."

"Wall," Tal said, right as Graham's hand hit. "Let's sit and think." They released hands and Graham turned and sat with his back against the wall.

"Do you suppose someone's guarding us?" Wren asked, sitting closer to Graham than he believed she would be comfortable with. He wasn't going to complain. "We could yell or something."

"I'm not sure I'm ready to meet whoever might be out there," Tal admitted.

"What if someone's in here listening to us?" Graham wondered out loud. Wren linked her arm with his again and rested her head on his shoulder. If it was any other situation, he would be ecstatic ... actually, he might be even in this situation.

Graham searched his memories. He was obviously missing memories if his hair had had time to grow. There was nothing. He remembered leaving Flordillia with Wren and Tal. They'd gone to the other continent to look for a well that had special water they needed to make a silver eclipse. The Dark Cloud, led by their former gym teacher, Zalliah, had ruined the weather, and the silver eclipse was their only hope.

There were different steps to make the silver eclipse, and one was to get water from a well of Truth. Truth had been a man who had made a bunch of magical wells on the other continent. There were only two left, and both were owned by the kings on that continent. They split up and went to both kingdoms to save time. Graham, Wren, and Tal had gone to the Northern Kingdom, while Ming Li, Sen, and Austra had gone to the Southern Kingdom.

"I hope the others are having better luck than we are." Graham said.

"How long do you suppose it will take before they realize we're in trouble?" Tal asked.

"Who knows?" Graham said, shifting and putting his arm around Wren. He could feel the goosebumps on her arms. She cuddled in closer. "They probably know now if our hair has had time to grow."

A light burst into the room, blinding them all. Graham squinted at an outlined figure in the doorway. The figure walked forward and flipped a switch, flooding the room with light.

"Oh good, you're all awake," Governor Briggs said, sauntering up to the bars. Graham could barely make him out as his eyes worked on adjusting to the light.

"Seriously?" Tal growled, jumping to his feet. "You put us in prison?" He stormed over to the bars and glared at his father, who stood in a small hallway on the other side. "I should've guessed," he said, turning away angrily and spotting Wren and Graham behind him. His frown deepened. "Have you two been cuddling there the whole time?"

"It's freezing," Wren said, getting to her feet. Graham was right behind her. They joined Tal in front of the governor.

Tal gritted his teeth and looked back at his father. "Let us out."

Governor Briggs smiled smugly and rubbed his brown goatee. "Just like that? That isn't how I work."

"No, you lock your son and his friends up in a cell, in the dark, with no heat. That's how you work."

"Your cloaks are there in the corner," he said, pointing. Graham looked in the corner and rushed over to retrieve them. He handed them to Wren and Tal and put his own on. It was like ice. He hoped it warmed up soon.

"You couldn't leave a light on?" Tal asked, pulling his hood over his head.

The governor shrugged. "It was night. I can't help the lack of moonlight," he said, pointing to a barred window. It was completely black outside. "Unfortunately, I can't help the lack of sun, either. It's late morning right now."

"No," Graham said, walking to the window and looking out. "It can't be morning. I can't see anything."

"That's what the world has become, unfortunately. At least on this continent. The other continent isn't affected. The Dark Cloud has really outdone itself. There hasn't been a spark of natural light in over a month. We've been putting up lights all around Akkron, but honestly, the people are panicking."

"Locking us up is only going to delay the solution," Tal said, glaring at his dad.

"Yes, I know. I'm not sure letting you go is the best option, either."

"We're the ones that are chosen. We need to fix this."

"Yes? And how are you fixing it? By sneaking around on the other continent?"

"We're going to summon the silver eclipse. It will fix the weather."

"Tell me, Talon," the governor said, his eyebrows coming together. "How is sneaking around the other continent going to help anything?"

"We need a cup of water from a well of Truth."

"So why didn't you go directly to King Miadd? That would have been the best and easiest solution."

Tal looked at his boots with a scowl. "He might not have given it to us. He doesn't have the best reputation."

"So you thought sneaking around would work? Imagine my shock when Zera came pounding on my door demanding to know if I knew where the three of you were."

"She came to you?" Graham asked, rejoining them at the bars.

"Yes. I should have had her arrested right there, but that woman was angry. Zalliah told me Zera was part of your little rebellion. I know Zera and your group are trying to have me taken out of office. After I convinced her I didn't know where you were, she stormed away. Not a minute later, who should appear at my door, but a messenger from the other continent. He said the king had three children in prison and he found out one of them was you."

"We aren't children," Tal said, crossing his arms.

"His words, not mine. He held you in his prison for three months before he learned who you are and released you to me."

"Three months!" Wren exclaimed. "We lost three months?"

"King Miadd said he would gladly hand the three of you over to me, but only if he could erase your memories of being in his prison."

"How long have we been here?" Graham asked.

"Since last night. I find it ridiculous that you stayed in prison for three months and never told the king who you are, Tal. You could have saved yourself a lot of time."

"I can't tell you why we did what we did. We can't remember. Why are we locked up?" Tal asked, pushing his bangs to the side.

"Because that is the only way you will listen."

"We aren't the ones who need to listen," Wren protested. "And you need to stop listening to The Dark Cloud."

"I would never give them the time of day. Ridding the world of that group is at the front of my priorities right now."

"Zalliah is the leader of The Dark Cloud," Wren said.

The governor laughed. "Zalliah? That's ridiculous."

"It's true," Graham said. "She's enjoyed misleading you." Graham really hoped he would take them seriously.

The governor's eyes narrowed. "I can't afford to not believe you," he said, pacing in front of the bars. "If you are lying, you will be punished."

Tal grabbed the bars with both hands. "We aren't lying. You need to let us go."

"There are some things I have to check. I'll return shortly."

"No, let us out!" Tal yelled as his father disappeared through the doors. "He is so annoying!" he exclaimed, kicking the bars.

"Quiet," said a voice from the corner.

Wren jumped and looked to see a cloaked figure sitting in the corner. How had they missed him before?

"Who are you?" Graham asked.

"None of your concern," said a man's voice from inside the hood. "Let a person sleep."

Wren looked from Graham to Tal. They both shrugged. Graham motioned for them to follow him to the opposite corner of the man.

"Okay, criss-cross applesauce, and let's figure this out," Graham said, dropping to the floor by the bars.

"Criss-cross, huh?" Tal asked as he and Wren sat, making a circle with Graham.

"Nothing, it just means sit and cross your legs. It's something teachers say to little kids."

"That doesn't make a lot of sense," Wren said, trying to figure out how applesauce had anything to do with crossed legs.

"Let's keep it down so grumpy in the corner there doesn't hear us," Tal said. The cell was about twenty feet by twenty feet. With luck, the man didn't care enough to try to eavesdrop. It was creepy to think he had been in here with them all along.

"So, who knows how to play the piano?" Wren asked.

Graham scrunched his forehead. "The piano?"

"Yes. Remember my dad said the way to escape was to lick the bars to the tune of *The Old Troll in the Hills*?"

"Right," Tal said, looking sideways at the dirty bars. "How would we even know where to start?"

"Look, there are letters," Wren said, pointing towards the bottom of the bars. "They all have one. A, B, C, D, E, F, G, A, B, C. That makes it more helpful. I'm glad my dad came up with a way to get out of here when he designed the prison."

"It doesn't help if we can't play the piano, though," Graham said.

Tal sighed as he looked at the bars. "I play. Not by ear very well, though. It could take a million times to get it right, and those bars don't look sanitary."

Graham wrinkled his nose. "Even if we get it right, we have to go through the sewer. That doesn't sound fun."

"It's better than staying here," Wren said. "It's not like we're terribly clean at the moment as it is." She looked down at her dirty blue tunic and she held up a handful of red hair and frowned. It was disgusting. The king must not have allowed them many baths. She couldn't believe she'd put her dirty head on Graham's shoulder. She must smell terrible.

"Okay," Tal said, his mouth turning down, "Sing it and I'll try to figure it out."

Wren sang, "The old troll in the hills, he never pays his bills. The goblin came and stole his horse, which made him mad, of course. The old troll in the hills, he wasn't big on thrills. He would walk instead of ride, and in no one would confide."

"I can't believe that's actually a song," Graham said, shaking his head. "The tune sounds familiar, though."

"It goes on a lot longer, but the tune just repeats," Wren said.

"Do we have to go through the entire song?" Tal asked. "Since we won't hear anything, we won't know if we do it wrong until the end."

"I doubt it," Wren said. "I bet it's only the first stanza."

"Okay," Tal said, letting out a breath. "I'm going to say the first notes are E, B, C, C, C, C, C."

"So lick it," Graham said.

"Why do I have to figure it out and lick it?"

Graham sighed. "Fine." Looking slightly pale, he licked the bar with an E on it. "That's gross," he said, grimacing.

"Now B," Tal said. Graham shook his head, but licked the bar. By the time Tal was finished telling him the notes, Graham looked like he might puke.

"Nothing happened," Wren said, looking around the cell. "If we did it right, something on the floor should have opened."

"I'm not doing it again," Graham said. "Our chances are better waiting on the governor."

"We have to try again," Wren protested. "The longer we're in here, the longer The Dark Cloud is out there ruining Basura."

"Do you volunteer?" Graham asked. "Those bars seriously taste nasty, and this is coming from someone who can gag down my dad's cooking."

"That must be pretty bad," Tal said. "I can't even pretend to eat anything Brake cooks."

"So what do we do?" Wren asked.

"Oh, for goodness' sake," the man in the corner said, standing. He strode towards them, throwing off his hood.

"Professor Dovin?" they all exclaimed at once. Their old science teacher stopped in front of them and put his hands on his hips. His usually neat blond hair was a mess.

"I seriously don't understand how people become chosen anymore. So from what I overhear, you have to lick the bars to the right tune and the sewer opens?"

"Why would we tell you?" Tal asked. "We aren't helping a member of The Dark Cloud." Professor Dovin rolled his eyes and squatted, studying the bars. "Alright, I see. *The Old Troll in the Hills* was it?" Dovin pressed his tongue against the bars. He barely even hesitated. After a moment, a low sound rumbled in Wren's ears. She turned to see a piece of the floor pulling away.

"Whoa," Tal said as they walked towards the hole in the floor. "It's kinda deep. Do we jump?"

"It's not deep at all," Dovin said, looking down. "I'm assuming Drew didn't make this to stay open for a long amount of time. Jump." Dovin leaped into the dark hole. Wren heard a splash as he landed.

"Don't think about it," Graham said. "Just jump." Wren got down on her hands and knees and lowered herself into the enormous sewer pipe. Graham and Tal followed her lead. A horrible stench filled her nose, and she tried not to picture what she was standing in.

"Let's go," Dovin said, gesturing ahead. He walked forward, and they reluctantly followed. A rumbling above them signaled the hole sealing itself and putting them in the dark. An orb of light popped up in Professor Dovin's hand.

Wren held out her own hand and smiled when a light appeared. "We can do magic again." Tal and Graham immediately made their own lights.

"It was ingenious of Drew to come up with something like this," Dovin said, trudging along in front of them. "I wondered how I was going to get you all out. I have a bit of dynamite I planned to use on the window. They really don't search their prisoners well here. This is much better."

"Better?" Tal said, waving a hand in front of his nose. "I might puke. You know what we're walking in, right?"

"Nothing wrong with a little fertilizer," Dovin said.

"The smell is terrible," Graham said. "Why were you trying to get us out?"

"I know you haven't noticed," Dovin said, looking over his shoulder, "But I've been trying to get you out of trouble for a long time."

"What are you talking about?" Graham asked, sharing a look with Wren.

"Zalliah isn't the only person who can see auras around people."

"You didn't see an aura," Wren protested. "You saw me make a portal out of your office."

"Indeed, I did. I wanted to charge through after you to make sure you could make it back, but I had to get rid of Melly. I did not know where on Earth you would end up, so I couldn't follow you."

Tal almost slipped, but caught himself. "How would you know she went to Earth?"

"It was a good guess. Earth is bound closely to Basura. Our worlds cross all the time. It would have been pointless to try to find her. Earth is much bigger than our world, and since she went through a portal, she might not be at the time I would expect."

"What does that mean?" Tal asked.

Wren could take this one. "If you make a portal to a different world, you don't always move through time in a way that makes sense. You can lose hours. When I first went to Earth, it was noon. I only stayed a short time, but when I got home, it was night. It's not so bad when you go through a portal that's in the world you are already in."

"Exactly," Dovin said. "The next week I saw Graham in school and I was surprised to see an aura around him I had seen previously. An aura that I saw around a little baby years before."

Wren forgot about the cold, smelly sewage under their feet for a minute. "You saw Graham as a baby?"

"I did. I taught most of your parents, you realize. When I saw Brake and Zera's baby boy, I knew he was going to be one of the five who were chosen, just the same as I knew the first time I saw Wren, Tal, Ming Li, and Sen."

"This doesn't add up," Wren said as she walked through the sludge. "So you knew who we were, but what's your plan? You're part of The Dark Cloud."

"I have nothing to do with those people. I learned through a source that Melly wanted to join The Dark Cloud. They didn't need any more members, so I approached her, pretending to belong to their group. She believed me, so I sent her on a bunch of worthless missions to distract her."

"Wait," Tal said, "So you're trying to convince us you're a good guy?"

"I'll tell you I am a good guy, but I will not try to convince you. If you believe me, that's great. If you don't, you eventually will. I've been working for more years than I can count to figure out who the members of The Dark Cloud are. I have an extensive list at home. Years ago, I even helped Brake and his little group when they were first after The Dark Cloud. I didn't let them know I was helping, of course."

"Why didn't you join them?" Wren asked.

"I prefer to work alone. Those days are over, though."

Wren thought back to the conversation she'd overheard between Dovin and Zalliah. When she first heard it, she believed Zalliah was on their side and Dovin was Dark Cloud. Now that she knew Zalliah was bad, it would make sense from what she heard that Dovin wasn't on Zalliah's side.

"I've kept a close eye on all the people I've confirmed belong to The Dark Cloud, spending time here and on Earth. I waited years for the five of you to grow up and come together. Now I wonder if that wasn't wise. It might have been in the better interest of the world if I had slowly captured some of them."

"Did you know I was on Earth?" Graham asked.

"Unfortunately not. I didn't know what happened to you. There were lots of rumors, but nothing specific. I wish I would have looked into it more. I could have saved Brake and Zera years of heartache, since I can travel to Earth at will. I assumed your parents had hidden you. When I realized you knew Wren, and I realized how much you didn't know about our world, I went to Earth to see if you had been there."

"Why would that matter?" Graham asked.

"I wanted to know what your life had been like. I was planning to train you and I needed to know. The internet is a marvelous thing. I found out you were missing from a place called Missouri. I went and talked to your aunt. Not the most pleasant woman."

"Can you see auras around everyone?" Tal asked as they pushed forward.

"No, not everyone. Once things happen, there is no doubt what they meant. Unfortunately, that isn't always the case before they happen. It's hard to interpret auras. I usually only see them around people who are going to do great things. I knew what you were all capable of, the same as I know that someday, Graham's little cousin will come to this world and play an important role."

"Kaylee?" Graham asked, stopping for a moment. "I don't understand why Kaylee would ever come here. She isn't magic."

"That's not a worry for now," Dovin said. "It looks like the tunnel is sloping. Be careful." Dovin walked slowly at an incline, making sure his steps were carefully placed. Graham and Wren were right behind him, followed by Tal. Wren was getting used to the smell, which was nice, but also disturbing.

"Can't we teleport?" Graham asked.

"Too risky," Dovin said. "Magic leaves traces that some people can see. Zalliah and Gorbin can both see it. That's why I blocked all magic to the hotel that day you were on Earth."

"That was you?" Wren asked, watching her footing. "We thought it was Gorbin."

"I didn't want Gorbin to know you opened a portal. I didn't expect you to be so slow getting out. You should've gone."

"What about the lights? Can they see the magic from that?"

"I doubt it. Light is minor magic."

"Can The Dark Cloud block magic like you?"

Dovin shook his head. "No. That is something I thankfully didn't teach Zalliah."

"Did you teach her other things?" Wren asked.

"I did. A long time ago. I have a lot of guilt about that. It's my fault they can teleport."

"Whoa!" Tal yelled, slamming into Wren. She flew forward, knocking into Graham and Dovin. They all fell into the sewage and yelled as their lights went out and they were pushed down the pipe.

Wren struggled to keep her head up, and she kept her mouth shut as they blew out of the pipe and fell into deep water. She held her breath and swam to the top. Her head burst to the surface and she took a deep breath of air. Treading the water, she looked around. It was so dark. She held one hand out of the water and made a light appear. She saw Tal, Graham, and Dovin bobbing up and down. They seemed to be in a mellow river. Mellow, aside from the sewage blowing in.

"Is everyone alright?" Dovin asked.

"Fine," Wren said. Tal and Graham nodded. She swam towards the closest spot of land and hoped everyone else would follow. When her feet finally touched the ground, she scrambled to the shore. She untied her heavy water-logged cape and dropped it to the ground. The others followed her example.

"Graham, can you spray some water into the air so it'll come down like a shower?" she asked, shivering. "I don't want any sewage left on me."

"We just came out of a river," Tal said, holding a light. "That should have cleaned it off."

"We came out of a river that has sewage dumped into it," Wren protested.

"That's true," Tal admitted, looking at Graham.

Graham placed his light by his feet and raised his palms into the air, spraying water straight up. It fell back down, showering them all. The water wasn't warm, but it wasn't as cold as the river either. Wren rubbed her hands through her hair and over her face. It was going to have to do for now. Graham put his hands down and wiped water from his stubbly cheek.

Wren concentrated on heating herself the way Sen taught her, and she quickly dried. She kneeled by her cloak and held out her hands, trying to dry it. Nothing. She still couldn't make the heat leave her hands.

"You're trying too hard," Dovin said, picking up Wren's cloak. He twirled it around his arms and handed it to her. It was dry.

Wren looked at Tal and Graham as she put on the warm cloak. Tal was dry, but Graham was still soaked. He had his arms folded, and he was trembling.

"Didn't Sen teach you to dry yourself?" Wren asked him.

His teeth chattered. "I can't do it."

"I thought you could do everything."

"Sen thinks I can't do it because of the ice. He's under the impression that people can't do cold and warm magic."

"That's probably true," Dovin said, holding his hands out towards Graham. Graham turned in circles as Dovin dried his clothes. "I guess that means the rumors about you shooting ice are true. I've never heard of anyone in our lifetimes who could do that.

"It's so dark," Wren said. "I never realized how much light the moon gave off."

"I don't suppose any of you have your dragon scales?" Dovin asked. They all shook their heads. "I didn't imagine you would sit in the dark if you had them."

Professor Dovin taught some of his classes to boil dragon scales and make them glow. The glow was a lot brighter than a simple orb of light. Wren hadn't made one because only the grade ahead did them. Graham's had been useful a few times.

"Well, I guess we should get out of here. It won't be long before the governor misses you."

CHAPTER 2

"Where are we going?" Tal asked as they walked down a slope through the dense woods. "If we keep going down, we're going to end up right in Akkron."

"I haven't decided," Dovin said, leading the way.

Tal grabbed Wren's arm and put a hand up to stop Graham. "Why are we following him?"

"No idea." Graham stopped and pictured Brake in Flordillia. *"Dad, we're okay,"* he whispered.

"Do you suppose the others are still with the trolls?" Wren asked.

"Where are you?" Brake's voice asked, filling his head.

"Akkron, with Dovin."

"Talk to Ming Li."

"He told me to talk to Ming Li," Graham told them. Graham, Wren, Tal, Ming Li, and Sen could all talk to each other telepathically, with no consequences. Others who sent messages like this got headaches. Dovin still hadn't noticed they weren't following him.

"Graham?" Ming Li's voice pierced his head, blasting louder than was comfortable. *"Brake wants to know if you're safe and why you're with Dovin."*

Graham placed his fingers to his head and concentrated on Ming Li. *"Dovin helped us escape from prison. He said he's not part of The Dark Cloud."*

"Brake said not to bring him to Flordillia."

"We weren't planning to."

"Brake said to meet him where the old meeting house burned down, and to bring Dovin with you."

"Alright."

"What are you doing?" Dovin asked, walking back to them.

"Brake wants us to meet him somewhere."

"I can open a portal," Wren offered. Dovin nodded. "Brake is going to want a detailed confession from me, I'm sure." Wren opened a shimmering silver portal, and they jumped through.

Brake was standing in front of the remains of the old meeting house, holding a light. He held out his arms when they came through and caught Graham up in a hug. "Dryson, we've been looking for you for months. Ming Li said you were in prison?" Dryson was the name Graham had been born with. He'd thought it was his last name until just recently.

"We don't remember most of it," Graham told him. "We woke up in Governor Briggs' prison today and he told us we were in prison on the other continent for three months. They erased our memories."

"Interesting," Brake said. "I wonder what they didn't want you to remember."

"It might be a good thing we can't remember," Wren said with a shiver.

Brake put one arm around her and the other around Tal. "Are you both alright?"

"Yes," they answered.

"I guess we didn't search well enough," he said, shaking his head. "Austra had an audience with King Miadd and asked him if any teenagers had come by looking for water from the well and the king said he hadn't heard from any. The king has a horrible reputation, but we didn't have reason to believe he would lie."

"He didn't know why we were there," Tal said. "At least that's what we assume. It's hard to know since we don't remember."

"Well, let's not dwell on the past. I want you all to go to the place we were at last," he told them, looking towards Dovin. "There are a lot of people that want to see you. I'll catch up to you after I talk to Dovin."

Wren didn't have time to breathe after they stepped into the mansion in Flordillia. After her dad and Ming Li stopped embracing her, Brog wrapped them all up in a group hug. Wren had never seen the giant show affection before. Hamble gave them all a pat on the back and even

Austra hugged her. That was awkward, since Wren was still upset her dad was in love with the snooty woman. They all stood in the entryway by a fountain and two curved staircases.

Zera had Graham locked in a hug and she didn't look like she was ever going to let him go. It was nice he finally had parents. Tal's mom, Valeena, was looking him over for injuries, and Sen and Hedder were watching all of it like detached spectators. Wren smiled to herself when she tried to picture Hedder hugging anyone.

"What's our next move?" Graham finally asked. "Did you get the water from the well?" he asked Ming Li and Sen. They shook their heads.

"Next move?" Zera asked, crossing her arms. "You should rest for now. We have been looking for you for months and I am not ready to let you go again."

"Have you seen it outside?" Graham protested. "It's pitch black. Nothing is going to grow, and this continent can't rely on the other continent forever." Zera frowned, but Wren could tell she didn't have an argument for that.

"The governor seemed to believe we could walk right in and ask the king for the water," Wren said. "I don't see that happening since he had us in prison for three months."

"He didn't know who I was back then, though," Tal said, sitting on a step. He ran his fingers through his brown waves and sighed. Valeena sat beside him and rubbed her hand over his back.

"You think he'll give us the water because of your dad?" Graham asked.

Tal shrugged. "Among other things."

"What other things?" Ming Li asked.

"I don't want to talk about it."

"I'm sorry," Valeena said quietly. "It probably is the best way, though. I would have told you to go directly to the king if I'd known you would try to sneak in."

Tal sighed. "I've heard enough about King Miadd to know he doesn't do anything without a price. I didn't want to chance it. I thought we could be in and out without anyone knowing."

"The king is a hard, manipulating man, but he still might have done it for you."

"I want to know why the king had our memories erased," Graham said. "I wonder if we saw or overheard something."

"King Miadd has always been secretive," Valeena said. "I never understood why Briggs insisted on making deals with him."

"Because he only cares about himself," Tal growled.

"Wait, a second ..." Ming Li said, lighting up. "I know you were out of your mind when Sen captured us, but some of what you said might have been true."

"Ming Li," Graham said, shaking his head.

"No," she said, "Everyone keeps saying no more secrets. When Talon was crazy on ailam powder, he said he didn't want to marry the princess. Is Talon's arranged marriage to King Miadd's daughter?"

"Arg!" Tal exclaimed, jumping to his feet and stomping up the stairs.

Valeena watched him with a frown. She twisted one of her perfect blond ringlets around her finger. "I didn't want to make the match, but Briggs was insistent. He couldn't resist the prestige that would come from having his son marry royalty."

"What's she like?" Ming Li asked.

"We've never met her. King Miadd wouldn't allow it."

"She's probably ugly then," Ming Li said. Wren poked her friend. "What?"

"You should've kept quiet," Wren said. "Now Tal's upset."

"Yeah, but now we understand what we're dealing with. If the king's reasonable at all, he should give Tal one little cup of water. If we explain the situation, he should be happy to help. This continent is in complete darkness, and it could spread. He wouldn't want it to happen in his own kingdom."

"I'm going to go talk to Tal," Wren said, starting up the stairs.

"I'm not sure that's a good idea." Graham said. "I should go."

"Why isn't it a good idea?" Wren asked.

"Because the thought of his arranged marriage is making him upset ... and having you come to comfort him might do the opposite."

"I'm not that bad at comforting people," Wren said, looking around at the others for support. "Why would he have an easier time with you than me?" Hedder, Drew, and Brog studied the floor. Zera and Valeena were frowning, and Hamble was smiling. Wren shook her head. What was wrong with everyone?

"He doesn't have a crush on Graham, so he might be more willing to talk to him," Hamble said, when nobody else offered an answer.

Wren shook her head. "Tal doesn't have a crush on me."

Ming Li snorted. "I don't know how long you're going to be in denial. Didn't we already have this conversation?"

Wren knew Ming Li thought Tal liked her, but she didn't think it was true. "Is that what everyone thinks?" There were several nods. She sank down onto the step, resting her elbows on her knees, and covered her face in her hands.

She remembered back to the time Graham looked like he was going to kiss her and how angry Tal had been. Was it possible? Maybe everyone was right. There was also the time he told her Solia was jealous of her because of the way he talked her up. When she looked up again, everyone was gone except Drew. He was sitting next to her on the step. She wondered what kind of awkward motioning had been going on to get everyone to disappear.

"So what do I do, Dad?" she asked. "I just ignore my friend that needs help?"

"You don't ignore him," Drew said. "But right now, someone else might be the best one to talk to him."

"I doubt Graham is the best one."

"Graham didn't go. Valeena did."

"Oh," Wren said. "That's good. He needs to realize she cares."

"Graham would have been a worse option than you."

"Why? They're best friends."

Drew shook his head and put an arm over her shoulder. "Tal's upset because he doesn't get to choose who he marries. Graham doesn't have an arranged marriage, so he can't understand the feelings Tal must be having. I probably should have talked to him. I understand only too well."

Wren pondered about that for a minute. She never really took time to think about how hard it must have been for her dad to marry someone when he was in love with someone else.

"It would also be hard for Tal to talk to Graham because Graham is closer to having what he wants than he will ever be."

"If you say it's me, I'm going to puke."

"I won't say it, but you know it's true."

"Why does everyone assume something is going on between us? I can't believe you told Brog to watch us. Nothing's ever happened."

"But it will."

"You don't know that."

"But I believe it. That's why I had that talk with him a while back."

"Why do you do stuff like that?" Wren asked, rubbing her eyes.

"It's my job. You're almost sixteen. I've been sixteen, you know."

"It's not like I'm old enough to be planning on running off and getting married or something. I know we're still kids. They locked us up for three months and Graham and

Tal still can't grow facial hair worth bragging about. Can't you tell Brog he doesn't need to watch us anymore?"

"I'll think about it," he said, smiling. "And you shouldn't judge their facial hair. They're doing a lot better than Professor Hedder."

Wren smiled. That was true. Poor Professor Hedder.

"I've got something for you," Drew said, digging into his pocket. He handed her a ring. Wren studied the gold band with a red gem on top. It was pretty.

"Thanks. What's it for? It's not a holiday," she said, slipping it on her finger.

"It belonged to Magnalee," he said, staring blankly ahead. "She would've wanted you to have it."

Wren looked closer at the ring and tried to swallow the lump in her throat.

"I'm sorry I haven't ever been eager to tell you about your mom. The truth is, we didn't know each other well."

"I know you had an arranged marriage," she said, linking her arm with his.

"I wondered if Hamble would ever let that slip." He smiled, but it didn't reach his eyes. "Magnalee was a good person. We just never had a great connection."

"Not like you and Austra?" Wren asked.

"I'm not talking about that now. That ring isn't an ordinary ring. It's magic."

She raised her hand and let the light reflect off the red gem. "What can it do?"

"It can reverse magic. It only works once from what I understand, and then it's just an ordinary ring."

"Reverse how?"

"If someone throws a spell at you, it will rebound and hit them. Magnalee wanted to save it for a special occasion and she never wore it for fear of accidentally using it when she wasn't ready. I sometimes wonder if she could have saved herself, if she had been wearing it." He shook his head. "No, it wouldn't have mattered. She was pushed. That isn't magic. I want you to wear it. Don't save it for something that might never happen."

Wren nodded. "Thanks Dad."

"So, we just walk confidently down the road, and no one's going to arrest us?" Sen asked.

"That's the plan," Graham said, fastening the clip on his cloak. "Valeena said if we walk confidently and don't look suspicious, it will go better for us. She said the only reason they captured the three of us last time was because they found us sneaking around."

Tal kicked the dirt with his black boot. "I don't know why they had to erase our memories. That means they have an advantage. We've lost three entire months! Anything could have happened in that much time."

Graham looked down the dirt road. There was nobody out today, so they had the road to themselves. It was nice to be in the sun again, and trees shadowed most of the road, so it would be a pleasant walk.

"I wonder if it was a good idea for all of us to come," Ming Li said. "We really need to make a silver eclipse, so we should probably split up."

"After last time, the adults thought it would be safer if we were all together," said Wren.

"Well, if we all end up in prison, I don't see that being helpful. Do you know how long those three months felt to us? The adults were out everyday trying to find you and we were stuck with whoever they decided was our babysitter for the day. It was so boring! It was also stressful because we had no idea where you were."

"I'm sure it was rough on you, but we were in prison," Tal said. "I'm sure we had it worse."

"Yeah, but you don't remember, so it doesn't count. We still remember the stress. Your parents were all crazy worried. They were all starting to look like zombies."

"It was pretty intense," Sen agreed.

Ming Li shook her head as they began walking. "I don't know why the adults don't help us more. Our entire continent is in chaos and they are leaving it up to the teenagers."

"We were chosen, though," Sen said.

"Still," Ming Li protested, "If your world is in chaos, you don't just leave it up to someone else to fix it all."

"They did at least look over the steps to the silver eclipse this last month," Sen protested. "That was helpful."

"Did they figure anything out?" Wren asked.

"The step that says something about amber with eight sides. Hamble thinks he knows that one." Sen pulled a paper out of his pocket. "I brought this, just in case." He unfolded it and showed them a picture that was torn from a book. It showed five pieces of what must be amber, and each of them was shaped like an octagon. "There was a legend about a woman with five children. She left them all one of those pieces of amber. She put some kind of spell on them so they would always bring the bearer good luck."

Tal took the page from Sen and studied it. "Did Hamble have any idea where we could find one?"

"No, he said they were all lost. No one even knows if they really existed."

Tal handed the page to Graham, and he studied it. "It looks really familiar, but I'm not sure why."

"Did they figure out any of the other steps?" Wren asked.

"No, but we're getting pretty close," Sen said, pushing his black hair out of his eyes.

"I still think they could help us more," Ming Li muttered.

"The adults are trying to fix the government," Graham said. The road curved, and a castle appeared in the distance.

"Yes, but if they all put effort into figuring out the silver eclipse steps, we might be done by now. If Austra had even just read the steps, she could have told us what a well of Truth meant."

Graham nodded. "My dad said this is our quest. He said they are there if we need help, but it's up to us."

"Their priorities shifted," Wren said. "I remember when we first started. They said it was their goal to destroy The Dark Cloud."

"It was their goal until we were chosen. Then they moved on to another problem." Graham watched the castle get closer. It was the first castle he had ever seen, but it looked a lot like Tal's house. The draw bridge was open, so they didn't need to worry about that. Guards stood in a line across it.

"I remember hearing that people didn't actually live in castles," Ming Li said. "Castles were for battle and palaces were to live in."

"Here, they're used for both," Tal said. "There haven't been a lot of wars."

"I hope we get to see Talon's princess," Ming Li said. Graham shook his head.

"Come on Li," Tal said, with a lopsided grin. "I'm sure she's so smart and pretty it will make everyone jealous."

"Is that what you tell yourself at night?"

"It is now. I've been dreading it for so many years. I can't see any reason for a king to make a deal like this with the governor of a far-away city. What's the benefit for him? I figured she must be ugly and unpleasant. Ugly I can handle, but I need someone I can talk to. I'm trying to tell myself she's going to be perfect for me. It's the only way I can go on."

Ming Li looked at him from the corner of her eye. "What's her name? You can tell a lot about a person by their name."

"Princess Lesandri."

She wrinkled her nose. "I hope she has a nickname, because I'm never going to remember that."

"I just hope she isn't there. I'm not in the mood to meet her today."

"Well, I want to meet her."

They walked up to the castle, and a guard dressed in armor stepped forward. "What is your business?"

"We've come to speak to the king," Tal said, taking the lead as they had agreed.

"Who are you?"

"My name is Talon." Tal barely paused over giving his complete name.

"Talon? We were told to admit you at once if you were to come. Follow me." The guards made an opening, and the five followed.

The guard led them into the castle. It was cool inside and made entirely of stone. There was nothing in the sizable area they entered. The man led them up a spiral staircase and into a large throne room. It had bright tapestries on the walls that showed scenes Graham was unfamiliar with. There were lots of pictures of dragons and trolls. A large red carpet covered the floor and at the head of the room was a large red throne. It had gold around the edges and on the armrests. It looked stiff and uncomfortable.

"Wait here," the guard said. He exited swiftly, and they all stood examining the room.

"So, will you be king someday?" Ming Li asked.

Tal grinned. "No way. Lesandri has an older brother. That's another reason I'm surprised the king agreed to our match. He should've been trying to pair her with the prince from the other kingdom."

"Yes, I should have," a deep voice said, entering the room. "But that isn't why we are here, is it?" If Tal's theory about a person looking evil was true, King Miadd definitely had the look. He was giving off a Tim Curry vibe with his dark brown hair and goatee. There was something similar about him and Governor Briggs. He was wearing light armor and had no crown. Nothing but his superior expression marked him as king. He went directly to his throne and sat. "Now, why are you here?"

"We're here for a favor," Tal said.

"Oh? This should be interesting. You want money? A title?"

"No," Tal said, shaking his head. "We want a cup of water from your well."

"Is that why you were sneaking around here before? You were all tight-lipped about it. I had my suspicions when that woman came looking for teenagers that were looking for water. I sent her on her way, because I was tired and not in the right frame of mind to deal with you."

"You knew someone might be looking for us and didn't tell her we might be in your prison?" Tal asked. "There were a lot of people worried about us."

"I had more important things to worry about, and nothing was harming you."

"You could have saved people a lot of stress," Graham said, disliking this man for causing his parents unneeded worry.

"Other people's stress is not my concern. No need to give me a lesson on compassion. I have none, so let's move on, shall we? When I finally learned your identity, I assumed you were trying to get a peek at my daughter. Now, tell me. Why would you want water?" he asked, rubbing his thumb over his goatee.

"We're gathering things to make a silver eclipse. The weather has gotten worse and worse in Akkron. Actually, on our entire continent. It's cold and dark. If we don't fix it, it might spread here."

"I've heard of your triumph at Meegore. I was relieved. Until then, I was worried I had attached my daughter to someone worthless."

Graham frowned as he noticed Tal clenching his teeth. He hoped he could remain civil.

"You look a lot better now that you have all cleaned up."

"That reminds me," Graham said, taking a step forward. "Why did you erase our memories?"

"I had you in my dungeons for three months. Do you really imagine that's something you want to remember?"

"So you erased our memories for our benefit?"

"That's part of it."

"What's the other part?"

He flashed his white teeth. "If I told you, I would have to erase it again, wouldn't I? Trust me. You should thank me for the service I did for you. If I hadn't done it, I seriously doubt you would all be friends right now."

"What's that supposed to mean?" Wren asked.

"Yes, the pretty redhead would like to know that, wouldn't she? I don't believe you were in on the fighting, but you get credit for being the cause."

Graham and Tal shared a glance. Had they been fighting?

"Three months is a long time to be cooped up with anyone," Graham said. "I would imagine a lot of people would get into an argument here and there."

"An argument?" The king's smile looked big enough to break his face. "An argument would be pretty mild from the way I heard it. The prison guard had to blast you both with ailam powder to get you to stop swinging fists."

Graham frowned. He'd never been the type of person to fight. Tal looked from Wren to Graham, but Graham couldn't read his expression.

"I was called down to the dungeon when young Talon had a bizarre reaction to the ailam powder and the guard thought he might have said something significant."

"Those ailam reactions are embarrassing things to witness," Ming Li said. Tal shot her a frown.

The king kept his smile. "Until that point, we didn't know who you were. You gave us your names, but it wasn't until you were out of your mind that you said your name was Talon and we made the connection. I contacted your father immediately."

"Why do people give me ailam powder?" Tal muttered.

"It was the most entertaining thing the dungeon has seen in years. All the prisoners and guards enjoyed it. They enjoyed the fight as well. It's good to see you are still friends. You owe that to me."

"Can we talk about the water?" Tal asked, crossing his arms.

"The crystal at Meegore chose you and you entered the cave. That is something I would love to see. Perhaps we can make an exchange."

"Not regarding the cave," Tal said. "We aren't taking anyone there."

"That's unfortunate. I guess you'll have to try your luck elsewhere. The Southern Kingdom, perhaps?"

“If we don’t fix this problem, people will start dying. It will move over here.”

“I guess we’ll see, won’t we?” The king smiled and stood. “You have three days to change your mind. If you don’t, don’t bother trying to come back.”

CHAPTER 3

Wren sat on a log and threw a stick into the fire. They were going to spend the night in the woods near the castle to come up with ideas. They all gathered around the flames as they ate their dinner of homemade bread, cheese, fruit, and cookies. Ming Li's mom didn't like to be involved in magic, but she was always kind enough to send food.

"I can't think of anything we can do except take the king to Meegore," Sen said. "We need to have that water."

"We can't let anymore power hungry people into the cave," Tal said, stuffing a cookie into his mouth.

Sen tilted his head. "But if we tell Padmire first, he can make sure he gets something stupid, like Zalliah."

Padmire was a bungle that had been created to protect the cave. He was the one that decided what magic people who went in would get. When Zalliah had manipulated her way into the cave, Padmire gave her the power to secrete mucus that glows in the dark. She probably hated them for that.

The light from the fire caused eerie shadows to fall across the camp. Wren tried to ignore the uneasy feeling of being watched from the trees. Sometimes she was paranoid.

Tal leaned back on his elbows and sighed. "He's not even my father-in-law yet and I already can't stand the guy."

"He's annoying, but he gets points for looking like the guy on *Muppet Treasure Island,*" Ming Li said.

"That's exactly what I thought," Graham said, smiling.

"Maybe we should try sneaking in again," Wren suggested.

"Nah," Tal said. "They know what we're here for, so they're going to guard the well a lot closer."

"We should ask Padmire if invisibility is a power he could give one of us," Ming Li said. "That would come in handy right now."

"I hate going in the cave," Wren admitted. "I don't want to go again unless I absolutely need to."

"So, what do you suppose you two were fighting about in the dungeon?" Ming Li asked, glancing from Tal to Graham.

Graham and Tal both looked at Wren and then away. She frowned. Why couldn't Ming Li let anything be?

"Since we have no idea what happened, I don't see any reason to dwell on it," Graham finally said.

"It's probably good we can't remember," Tal added. "Three months in a smelly dungeon is enough to make anyone go crazy. We can't blame anyone for something in those conditions, especially since we don't know what happened."

"I wish we knew how to teleport to Earth," Ming Li said. "We could go really fast and get some marshmallows."

"Is that something important?" Tal asked. "If it is, Wren could always go."

"Yes, but portals don't always bring you back to the same time," Wren protested. "I don't want to come back and have to find you."

"It's not important, just awesome for a camp out."

"Everyone, drop your weapons!" someone called from inside the trees. They all jumped to their feet and turned towards the voice. "You are surrounded!"

A girl stepped into their small clearing and pointed a crossbow at them.

"We don't have weapons," Graham said, holding his empty hands in the air. The other four followed his lead. Wren scanned the girl and wondered how many others were out there, if any. The girl looked about their age. She was wearing all black, from her cloak to her boots. Her light brown hair hung over her shoulder in soft ringlets.

"Put your weapon down," Graham said. "We aren't armed."

"Then you shouldn't be the one making demands!" she growled, pointing her crossbow at him.

"I think you're alone," Tal said, looking at the surrounding trees.

"Perhaps, but I still have the crossbow," she said.

"So, are you robbing us or what?" Ming Li asked. "We really don't have time for this."

"I'm not robbing you. I've come to make a deal with you."

"We try not to make deals with people holding weapons on us," Graham said.

"Do you see the pouch hooked to my belt?" she asked, not lowering the weapon. They all nodded. "It's full of water from the well of Truth."

"And you couldn't just come peacefully?" Ming Li asked, putting her hand on her hips.

"I don't know you," the girl said. "You could be dangerous. All I know is you are the five people everyone is talking about. The five who opened the cave at Meegore."

"So what?" Ming Li asked. "You want the same thing as the king? You want to give us the water in exchange for taking you into the cave?"

"No. The last thing I want is to go into the cave."

"Then what do you want?"

"I want to get out of here. I want you to take me to Boztoll."

Wren raised her eyebrow. "Boztoll? Why would you want to go to Boztoll?"

"I'm the only one who gets to ask questions," the girl said, motioning to the crossbow with her head.

"Okay, well, here's the thing," Ming Li said, taking a step towards the girl. "You scared us for a second, but weapon or not, the only reason your face isn't smashed into the dirt right now is because we're too polite. You want to go to Boztoll and you have a weapon. To me that screams 'I'm not magic.' We might not have weapons, but we could take you out with magic in a second flat. How about you set the crossbow down and we sit and talk?"

"I'm not dropping it. Ahhhhh!" she screamed as Sen grabbed her from behind. He knocked the crossbow out of her hand and had a knife against her throat before Wren could blink. She hadn't even realized Sen was moving.

"Good job, Sendo," Ming Li clapped. "And that seemed totally fair, since he didn't use magic."

"Let me go!" the girl whimpered.

Tal picked her fallen weapon from the ground and sat, placing it on his lap.

"Are you going to behave?" Sen asked. She nodded. "Sit on that log." The girl sat and began sobbing into her hands. "Don't try anything. I'm standing right behind you."

Wren sank down and looked between Tal and Graham. She couldn't tell what they were thinking. "If all she wants is to go to Boztoll, is it really terrible? I don't see an easier way to get the water."

"Please!" the girl said, dropping her hands to her lap. "I can't stand living here another minute! People can be so cruel when you aren't magic!"

"Boztoll isn't the best place to be right now," Graham said, sinking down beside Wren. "The entire continent is in almost complete darkness."

"I don't care," she sniffed. "Anywhere would be better than here! At least in Boztoll there would be others like me."

"Don't you have parents or family that would miss you?" Tal asked.

The girl stared at her hands. "They wouldn't miss me. I'm an embarrassment to them."

"What's your name?" Wren asked.

"Amry."

"We can't just dump you in Boztoll," Sen said. "That wouldn't be safe. It's pitch black there and members of The Dark Cloud are all over the place. You wouldn't have anywhere to live."

"I have money. Is there an inn?"

"No. It burned a while ago."

"I already snuck away! It's not like I can go back. I've been waiting to get away for so long. If I return, I'll be punished for taking the water."

"How did you get the water?" Wren asked.

"My parents work at the castle."

"You're lying about something," Tal said. "I just haven't figured out what."

"I don't lie!"

"You said we were surrounded. Definitely a lie."

"I agree," Sen said. "We can't take her back with us. She can't see where we're staying until she proves she's trustworthy."

"I don't care where you take me! Just please take me away from here!"

Tal and Graham looked at each other. Ming Li braided her long hair over her shoulder and watched the girl suspiciously.

Amry whipped her eyes with her sleeve. "If you won't take me off this continent, take me to the Southern Kingdom. Please."

"We probably shouldn't stay here whatever we decide," Wren reasoned. "People might come looking for her."

"I'm not willing to take someone we don't trust to our hideout," Graham said, shaking his head. "We've trusted people too easily before, and it didn't go well."

"Why don't we go somewhere in the Southern Kingdom until we decide what to do next?" Tal suggested. "I'd rather plan in a place that isn't dark all the time."

Wren pulled out a map and studied it. "We could go to these woods in the other kingdom," she said, pointing. "We can camp there until we decide what to do."

"Sounds good to me," Ming Li said, and everyone else nodded.

"Don't make us regret taking you," Tal said to Amry.

"I won't!" the girl sniffed. "Thank you."

Graham gave up on sleep. It was close enough to call it morning. Night felt like an eternity. Even though the weather seemed nice, it was still cooler than was comfortable after the sun went down. They had set up camp somewhere in the Southern Kingdom's forest. Before they went to sleep, Sen teleported and took the water from the well to Austra so she could put it somewhere safe.

Graham couldn't see the sun yet, but it was getting lighter. He stood and staggered to the fire. Tal already sat in the dirt, staring into the flames. Everyone else must still be asleep. Graham dropped to the ground next to Tal and yawned.

"Too cold to sleep?" he asked.

"No," Tal said, shifting. "Thinking too hard to sleep."

"About the silver eclipse?"

"Nah. I was wondering what happened when we were in King Miadd's dungeon." He looked sideways at Graham. "You know, we were fighting about Wren."

Graham stared into the fire. "Probably."

"I've decided to change the way I think. I have to marry Princess Lesandri, so I shouldn't be dreaming about anyone else. It's a bad habit of mine to daydream about what if situations. What if the law changed, and I could marry who I chose? What if she decided she didn't want to marry me, and her parents broke the contract? Well, I'm done with it. No more daydreams."

"It's not bad to hope for something different," Graham said, unsure how to proceed.

"Yeah, well, even if I didn't have to marry her, Wren likes you more anyway."

Graham shook his head. "I don't know about that."

"It was you she was cuddling with in the prison."

"That wasn't cuddling. That was just because of the cold."

"Yeah? But who leaned on who first?"

Graham shrugged. "She did, but she was cold."

"And I was as close to her as you were. She chose you."

"It was dark. She might not have even remembered who was where."

"Graham," Tal said, clapping him on the shoulder. "Knock it off. I don't know how we ever got into a fight when you act like this. You like Wren. Why are you trying to talk me into having hope? Just take what I'm giving you, okay?"

Graham nodded. "I'm still not sure she likes me."

"Well, whether she does or not, I'm done thinking about her that way. I've said similar things before, but this time I mean it."

"It looks like Amry didn't run off in the night," Graham said, changing the subject.

Tal looked at the sleeping figures. "Yeah, I kinda hoped she would. I can't think of where we could take her."

"She's pretty," Graham said, raising his eyebrow.

Tal playfully shoved him. "No girls except the princess, remember? I need you on my side."

"I am."

"Hey guys," Ming Li mumbled as she plopped down beside them. "Why are you just sitting here? You should warm water for hot chocolate. That's what you do when you're camping."

"I'll do it," Graham said, jumping up. Wren had brought back better camping supplies when she took the well water to Austra. He grabbed a pot and the container of chocolate powder and stared at the fire. How did one make hot chocolate over a fire?

"I've got it," Ming Li said, taking the pan from him. "Haven't you ever been camping?"

"Once."

"Is it already morning?" Wren asked, stumbling towards them with a blanket draped over her shoulders.

"It's getting there," Tal said. Wren sat in the dirt, and Amry and Sen joined them. No one looked well rested. Sen had weird blanket marks on his face and Amry's eyes were bloodshot.

"Thanks for bringing me," Amry said. "I realize it's been an inconvenience for you."

"We still don't know where to take you, though," Tal told her. "We can't just leave you somewhere, but we can't take you with us either."

"I won't get in the way," she said. "I'll do everything you say."

"We've made poor decisions about who we've trusted before. We can't afford to do that again."

"I understand," she said, pulling her cloak tightly around herself.

Graham unfolded the book page with the amber shapes. Why did they look so familiar? It would be nice if they knew how big they were. Ming Li ladled hot chocolate into cups and handed them around.

Amry looked suspiciously into her cup and sniffed it. "What is this? Coffee?"

"It's called hot chocolate," Ming Li told her. "It'll warm you up."

She took a small sip, and then another. "It's good. I've had nothing like it before."

"Li's mom comes up with some great recipes," Tal said.

"Well, she doesn't really come up with them," Mind Li admitted. "It's just nobody here has had it before."

An image flashed through Graham's mind. "My basketball coach had an earring that looked like this," Graham said, holding up the page. How had he forgotten? "It doesn't seem possible that it would be what we're looking for, but he always wore it."

"We should go check," Wren said. "We don't have any other leads."

"Not all of us," Graham said. "Last time you all became T.V. zombies."

"You could've let us leave the room," Tal said. "What else were we going to do?"

"I'll have to go to open the portal," Wren said, drinking her chocolate.

Tal nodded. "If Dovin really is on our side, he should teach us to teleport to other worlds."

"There's someone that can go to other worlds?" Amry said, with wide eyes. "That sounds so dangerous. You never know what type of monsters you might find in a different world."

"Most worlds aren't any more dangerous than here," Wren said.

"I've heard terrifying stories." Amry shivered. "I would never chance going to one myself. My mother said there are worlds where monsters eat you if you don't obey your parents. Big monsters with horns and huge yellow teeth."

Ming Li snorted, and the others shared looks.

"That sounds like the kind of story parents tell their kids to trick them into behaving," Tal said.

Amry frowned. "Are you saying my mother would lie to me?"

Tal shrugged. "I don't know your mother, but it sounds like a lie to me."

"How old are you?" Ming Li asked. "You seem too old to still believe in the boogie man."

"I'm sixteen, and there actually is a boogie man. He comes out from under your bed if you try to get out before morning."

Tal and Ming Li both laughed, and Graham and Wren shared a look. Wren shrugged. She wasn't sure it was her place to tell this girl her parents were lying to keep her obedient.

"What do you do if you need to use the bathroom at night?" Ming Li asked.

She tilted her head and looked at Ming Li. "I never drink anything after the noon meal, so that isn't a problem."

"You've never had to leave your bed at night? Not in your entire life?"

"There was once. I stood on the bed and jumped as far as I could. I bolted from the room and spent the rest of the night in the hallway."

"It sounds like your parents were trying to scare you into behaving," Tal said through his smile.

"Is that what you all believe?" she asked. They all nodded. "What about the goblins that watch you to make sure you behave with your tutors?"

"Nope," Tal said. "There are goblins, but they couldn't care less about whether you're behaving."

Amry sighed and took another sip of her drink. "I guess I shouldn't be surprised."

"Didn't your friends ever tell you those things weren't real?" Ming Li asked. "I wouldn't let my friends go on believing stuff like that until they were sixteen."

"I'm not allowed any friends," she said. "They make you weak."

"Another lie," Tal said. "Unless, of course, you chose your friends poorly. Good friends strengthen you."

She frowned into her cup. "I feel like I know nothing. How am I going to survive?"

"We can take you back home," Wren offered.

"No!" she said with wide eyes. "My father would never forgive me. I can't deal with his punishments."

"You know some things," Ming Li said, sitting cross-legged with her own hot chocolate. "You can use a crossbow. That's awesome. I would love to own one."

Amry looked into her cup. "Uh, yeah, well, I don't actually know how to use it."

"What?" Tal asked. "You were pointing it at us and you didn't know how to use it? We should've been more scared."

"My parents don't really like me to do many things. They wouldn't even let me learn to cook."

"We could take you to my mom," Ming Li said. "She might let you stay. She doesn't enjoy being alone."

"I'm willing to stay there," Tal smiled. "I would get so fat. Her food is soooo good."

Ming Li grinned. "You're not invited, Talon. At least not for more than a quick visit."

Amry's face went pale. "Talon? Your name is Talon?"

"Yeah, but my dad and Ming Li are the only ones that call me that. Tal is what I go by. If you frown any harder, it's going to hurt," Tal told her. "It's a dumb name. That's why I go by Tal."

"You should tell people your entire name to begin with!" she said angrily, slamming her cup into the dirt.

Graham raised his eyebrows and then understood. "What did you say your name was?"

Amry looked at him, still frowning. "It's ... uh ... it's Arm, er Emry."

"You said it was Amry," Sen said.

"I bet it's Lesandri," Graham said.

"What!" Tal yelled, jumping to his feet. He walked five steps away and then came back. He ran both of his hands through his hair. "Are you Lesandri?"

The girl clenched her teeth and nodded.

"Oh man," Tal said. "You said you didn't lie?"

"I don't ... usually. I didn't see any other way to get away."

"Let's just dump her here and leave," Tal said, looking at Graham for support.

"You can't dump me here!" she said, getting to her feet. "At least take me to a city."

"We aren't going to dump you anywhere," Wren said, glaring at Tal.

Tal pointed at the princess. "I knew my father would make me this kind of match. She believes in the boogie man! I can't work with that."

"Well, part of my running away was also getting out of that ridiculous contract! Arranged marriages should be done away with."

"At least we agree on that," Tal said, pushing his bangs to the side.

"I've begged my parents to break the contract, but they refused."

"Yeah, your dad doesn't take me as the reasonable type."

"I've heard enough about your own father to know he isn't either."

"I'm not denying it."

"Let's walk," Graham said, getting up and grabbing Tal's arm. He led him away from the group.

"I know what you're going to say," Tal mumbled when they were out of earshot.

"Really?" Graham asked. "Because I hadn't decided yet."

"This is so annoying. I can't believe she's the princess. And she's running away! Not just from her family, but from me!"

"Shouldn't that make you happy?"

"I'm just saying it's rude. If I don't marry her, I can't marry anyone, whether or not she disappears. She should at least have the decency to try to get the arrangement canceled."

"It sounds like she already tried."

"Yeah, but she still had years to do something."

"Maybe you can come up with a plan together."

"I don't believe she's big on ideas. You would think it would cross your mind at sixteen that you aren't being spied on by goblins."

"I'm sure she has good qualities."

"Being pretty doesn't count for much."

"Just because she's a little gullible doesn't mean she doesn't have good qualities. Her parents kept her ignorant. That's not her fault."

"I guess. But she lied to us."

Graham put a hand to Tal's shoulder. "Come on, even you can see why she did. She just wants to get away from her crazy life. I can forgive that."

Tal raised his brow. "That's because you don't have to marry her."

"Be nice to her. It sounds like she's had a hard life."

"I'll try, but I'm not promising anything."

They turned and walked back to the group. Lesandri was sitting again, and she glanced up at them as they came near.

"Do you want some more hot chocolate Dree?" Ming Li asked.

"No, thank you," the princess said, not taking her eyes off of Tal.

"Dree?" Tal asked.

"She can't go by Lesandri if she's trying to hide," Ming Li said. "Dree will be easier for everyone to remember since it's part of her name, but it's different enough it won't stand out to someone looking for her."

"Okay, whatever." Tal said, sitting. Graham sighed.

"So, what's our plan?" Wren asked. "Are we going back to Earth?"

"I guess," Graham said, relaxing next to her. "I can't be sure Coach William's earring is really the amber we're looking for, but since we don't have any other leads, we should try."

"Graham and Wren should be the only ones that go," Ming Li said. "We should drop Dree off with my mom and the rest of us should go try to figure out the next step."

"I'm not sure that's a good idea," Tal said. "There's a good chance my dad or The Dark Cloud is watching your mom."

"But she's been sending us supplies, so someone is in contact with her," Wren said.

"My dad pops in and out," Graham explained. "No one would see him because he doesn't go outside."

"Well, we could take her right into the house," Ming Li said.

"But she would have to stay in the house all the time," Tal argued. "That would be hard on her and Mali."

"Can't we just take her inside our hideout?" Ming Li asked. "She won't know where we are."

"That's probably fine," Graham said. "Take her to the kitchen or something and don't let her leave until one of the adults decides it's safe. If not, they can lock her up."

"Do you believe I'm a spy or something?"

"Don't take it personally," Ming Li said. "We've been tricked before."

Tal leaned back on his elbows. "I don't think you're a spy."

Dree raised her eyebrow. "You don't?"

"No, you don't have enough knowledge to pull off being a spy."

"Are you saying I'm stupid?" she asked, narrowing her eyes.

"Not out loud."

“Tal!” Wren scolded. “Why are you being so rude?”

“Sorry,” he said, looking down. “It’s my dad I should be mad at, not you.”

“Start over?” she asked, holding out her hand. He sat up and took her hand.

Tal had the decency to look ashamed. “I really am sorry. I’m not usually like this.”

“I understand the feeling.”

“Okay, so should we go?” Graham asked.

“I’m ready,” Wren said.

“So we’re starting the day off on a stomach full of hot chocolate?” Ming Li asked. “I’m glad I’m going to the hideout. I’m starving.”

Chapter 4

"I love this thing," Wren said, pulling at the gray replacement cloak Graham bought for her when they got to Earth. He said it was called a hoodie. It was so snug. It was too cold to run around without something, and their cloaks would make them stand out. The jeans were already becoming a favorite, but she'd worn them a few times before.

They'd ended up shopping longer than they wanted to, because they'd needed to wait until school was over so his team would be practicing. The bonus of that was Graham bought her a hotdog. Those things were amazing.

"Hoodies are really popular with teenagers," Graham said as they walked towards his old school. He was wearing a black hoodie and dark blue jeans. Wren had to admit it was a good look on him.

"Your school is so fancy!" she said as they neared the doors. It had a mixed color of bricks that were shades of red and brown. It looked a lot neater than her school, which was a sad gray. There was a big concrete letter E that was taller than she was near the entrance. The windows were outlined in brown, which was a nice touch. Akkron could take notes from this place.

"I never thought of it as fancy until I went to Akkron."

Graham led her through long hallways that were filled with colorful posters advertising dances and something called assemblies. They weren't professional looking, but they made the school feel inviting and fun.

They went into a large gym, and she looked around. It appeared similar to the gym back home, except there were weird lines on the floor. A bunch of guys were bouncing balls and throwing them in hoops. She had learned that much about basketball. They were all wearing the funny short pants Graham had worn the day she met him.

"Dryson!" One of the boys yelled, running towards him. "Where you been, man? You can't even imagine the rumors going round 'bout you." He wiped sweat from his forehead. Everyone stopped what they were doing and came rushing over.

"Hey Boone," Graham said. The two grabbed each other's hands and used the other hand to slap each other on the back. The team surrounded them. Wren stood up straight and tried to look confident. She had never seen this many hairstyles in her life! One guy had little tiny braids all over his head. She wondered how long that would take to do. Another one had blue hair. Blue!

"What happened to you?" Boone asked.

"It's a long story."

"The police was looking for you, and they questioned all of us," the blue-haired boy said. His hair was the color of his eyes. Wren found that fascinating.

"Ya know Boone had to pull a D+ all on his own?" someone else added. "Without you, he was almost off the team."

"But I pulled it off, so no worries," Boone smiled. "And who is this?" he asked, motioning to Wren.

"This is my friend Wren."

"Nice to know you, Wren," he smiled. She smiled back.

"And where have you been?"

"It's complicated. I need to talk to Coach."

"He'll be here in a minute. Are you back?"

"No. I just need to talk to him."

"So, did you run away or what?" Boone asked, raising his eyebrow. "Your aunt called my mom like fifty times a day."

"I didn't run away. I actually found my parents."

"What? I thought they was dead."

"So did I, but it turns out they weren't.

Boone scratched his short black hair. "So you been with them?"

"A lot of the time I have."

"You know your aunt is a millionaire or something these days?" the blue-haired boy asked. "She been livin' up in the classy neighborhood. When we ask 'bout you, she just acts like she's all too good to be talkin' to us."

"She's a millionaire?" Graham asked, raising an eyebrow.

"She, like, came into some money or somethin' like that. She got a nice car and put a down payment on a fancy house and then she ended up marrying some rich dude from India."

"I hear he's like a surgeon," Boone added. "Kaylee don't like him though. I seen her at the donut shop and she had a lot to complain about."

"Dryson? Is that you?" A man walked into the gym. He must be the coach. He had a whistle, just like Coach Zalliah. He was a tall man, with impressive muscles. Something about him reminded her of Brake. "What are you doing here? I thought you were gone for good."

"I need to talk to you," Graham said, stepping towards him.

"You want me to put you back on the team?"

"No. Can we talk in private?"

"Sure," the man said, glancing quickly at Wren. "Follow me. Everyone else, keep practicing."

They followed him to the back of the gym, to an office with big glass windows. He opened the door, and they went inside. He motioned to two chairs, and they sat. He went around a dark brown desk and sank down into a chair. He put his elbows on the desk and locked his fingers together, resting his chin on them.

"Sorry, I didn't call ahead."

"What's up?" the coach asked. "There have been a handful of rumors about you these days. Each one is stranger than the last."

"I'm sure," Graham said, nodding. Wren looked at the coach's ear. Sure enough, he had something in his ear that looked like the amber they needed. "I don't even know where to start."

"Just spit it out. You know you can talk to me."

Wren wondered if Graham knew he was wringing his hands.

"I was wondering about your earring," Graham said.

"My earring? You disappear for almost a year and come back to ask me about my earring? This is my lucky earring. I never take it out."

Graham let out a heavy sigh. "That's going to make it more difficult. Can I buy it from you?"

His eyebrows bunched together. "You want to buy my earring? That's the weirdest request I've ever had. It's not for sale. What in the world would you want with my earring?"

"It's complicated. It's amber, isn't it?"

"Yes."

Wren looked at the coach's arm. There was a picture on it. It looked like a sword in a flame.

"You like my tattoo?" he asked Wren, when he noticed her staring.

"Is a tattoo that picture on your arm?" she asked. "Did you draw it yourself?"

"I'll tell you about it later," Graham said to her. She nodded. Coach Williams was looking at her funny. She shouldn't have said anything.

Graham took the picture of the five amber shapes from his pocket and unfolded it. He handed it to the coach. "We need it for a type of experiment."

Coach Williams stared at the paper, and then looked at Graham. "What's going on, man? Don't tell me it's complicated. Are you getting mixed up with something shady? Did someone try to talk you into getting it from me?"

"No, I saw the picture and recognized it."

"Where did you get that picture?"

"From a book."

"Yeah, I get that. That's not from a book you find at the public library. That's from a book you shouldn't have access to."

"Maybe we should go," Wren said, softly. "We can find another one."

"Do you see how small that is?" he asked, pointing at the earring. "It's a miracle I knew where that one was."

"Where's your friend from?" Coach Williams asked.

"Um ..."

Coach Williams leaned forward. "Akkron? Curmain? Boztoll? The Other Continent?"

Graham and Wren looked at each other.

"I guessed it, did I? Now why do you need the amber?" he asked, with a fixed stare.

"We need to create a silver eclipse," Graham said, leaning back in his chair.

The coach whistled. "A silver eclipse? That hasn't been done in a long time."

"How do you know about all this?" Graham asked.

"I was wondering the same thing about you. I'm from Akkron. I left with my parents when I was sixteen. My mom was from Earth and she wanted to come back. Now what does Akkron have to do with you?"

"I found out my parents were from Akkron. That's where I've been."

"Wow. Someone right from my own school, and I didn't even know it. I should have guessed immediately when I saw your friends hair."

"My hair?" Wren asked, pulling it over her shoulder.

"The water over there is a lot better than here. Everyone's hair is super shiny and healthy. I suspect that's why they live longer ... not because they have shiny hair, because they have better water." He leaned back in his chair and let out a slow breath. "A silver eclipse. Hm. A silver eclipse was only called on when things got pretty desperate. At least that's the way I remember hearing about it. My dad used to tell us stories about it."

"It's getting desperate," Wren said. "The whole continent is in darkness. Nothing can grow. People are going to die."

Coach Williams removed his earring and held it out to Graham. "I don't suppose it's going to survive this?"

"I don't know," Graham said, taking it. "If it does, I'll bring it back."

"Thanks."

"Do you know a man named Brake?" Wren couldn't help asking. They looked so similar.

Coach Williams studied her. "I have a cousin named Brake."

"I knew it!" she said, grinning at Graham. "That makes him your uncle!"

"Uncle?" he asked, turning his surprised gaze on Graham. "Brake is your father?"

"Yes," Graham said, his eyes wide.

"This is a lot to take in. My star athlete is my nephew, and I never knew it. Is Zera your mom?"

"Yes."

"Good, good. I always hoped those two would stay together. They're a little older than me, but we were in school together. Now tell me how you ended up here to begin with?"

Graham gave him a brief rundown of all he had been through since meeting Wren.

"Wow," Coach Williams said, leaning back in his chair. "I wish I could help more."

"We could take you back if you want," Graham offered.

"No. I like it here. I've been here for longer than I lived there. I don't miss anything but my cousins. I don't have magic, so I don't really fit in there."

"Hopefully that will change soon." Graham said. "We aren't going to stop until the non magic are just as respected as anyone else."

"Good on you," he said, reaching out and shaking Graham's hand. "I don't know if it's possible, but if anyone can do it, it's you."

"Graham Dryson? I thought you were gone for good!"

Graham gritted his teeth and turned. "Hi Olive," he said to the tall thin girl standing with her pack of friends. They had almost gotten out of the school. "It's a little late to be at school."

"Cheer practice," she said, looking Wren up and down. She tossed her little black braids over her shoulder and smiled.

"We're just leaving," Graham said, holding onto Wren's elbow and trying to lead her around the cheerleaders.

"Aren't you going to introduce us to your friend?" she asked. "Is she your girlfriend? Did you finally find someone who will let you kiss them?" She laughed, and so did her friends. Graham told himself to keep walking.

"Sorry bro," Boone called, running down the hall. "I was going to warn you Olive was, here."

"What do you mean, warn him?" she asked, narrowing her eyes.

"I mean, warn him so he doesn't have to deal with your sassy old mouth."

"Well, I was just going to warn his friend here that he's the worst kisser on the planet. He even got voted ugliest kisser." She smiled as the girls giggled.

"Ah, no. You didn't bring up junior high," Boone said, getting into Olive's face. "And don't you mean you both got voted the ugliest kiss? You were on the other end of it. The only reason Graham got more garbage over it was because you started saying what a horrible kisser he was. He's too classy to say the same about you!"

Graham didn't dare look at Wren. He didn't want to see the horrified expression that was probably on her face.

"It was obviously Graham," Olive said, pushing Boone back a few steps. "Nobody has complained about my kissing since!"

"Well, you get enough practice," Boone said with his hand on his hip. "There ain't nobody on the football team you haven't kissed. Don't you even got standards?"

"I hate you Boone. Go away," she said, dismissing him.

"Why do you hate me? 'Cause the basketball team is smarter than the football team, and none of us is gonna kiss you. And I saw all you other girls drooling every time Graham walked by. You all just scared of Olive. Puppets. There ain't one of you here who wouldn't go runnin' like a love sick pup if Graham called to you."

Graham tried to take another step away, but Wren was anchored to the floor. His face was burning, and he was ready to run. He turned to her, but he couldn't read her expression. She almost looked amused.

"I can't imagine Graham ever being called an ugly kisser," she said, tapping her lip. "I mean, look at him. He's gorgeous. The first time I saw him, I stared at him for a solid five minutes." Some of Olive's clan nodded.

"Looks can be deceiving," Olive said, tossing her hair again.

"As for his kissing, I would say he's pretty skilled. If there was something wrong when you kissed him, I imagine it was all on you."

"Oh burn!" Boone laughed. "I like your girl, Graham."

Graham just nodded and pulled Wren away from Olive and her gaping mouth. Graham half dragged Wren out of the building and across the parking lot, where they left a bag of hoodies for their friends. He couldn't imagine what was going through Wren's mind. He hoped she didn't think he went around kissing snotty girls like Olive all the time. Olive was actually the only girl he had ever kissed, and it was on a dare.

Wren grabbed the bag and turned to Graham. "I guess there are Solias in every world."

"Probably," Graham said, thinking about Tal's stuck up former friend. "Thanks for lying for me back there. I've definitely learned to never take a dare. Kissing Olive was the worst mistake ever."

"I try not to lie," Wren said, handing him the bag. She looked around to make sure nobody was looking, and threw her arms open, making a silver portal. "I did stare at you for five minutes the first time I saw you."

"You said that was because you hadn't ever seen a game like basketball before."

"I did say that. It was true, but you know I don't care about sports. As for the kissing part, I said I would *say* you were skilled. I didn't say you were. Besides, I'm hoping you're going to prove that skill to me someday." Without looking at him Wren disappeared into the portal. Graham stood staring after her. Did she just say what he thought she did?

Wren made sure Graham made it through the portal before she shut it and ran up the stairs at the troll house in Flordillia. She couldn't believe she had just admitted to

Graham that she hoped he kissed her someday. What was wrong with her? She was going to have to hide forever. How would she ever look at him again?

She slowed down when she saw her bedroom door open. She peeked around the corner and saw Ming Li, Sen, Tal, and Dree sitting on the floor in a circle looking at the paper with the silver eclipse items.

"Wren!" Ming Li said, looking up. "It took you long enough. It feels like we've been waiting forever. Dree knows what the last two items we need are!"

"Really?" Wren asked, joining them on the floor.

Dree nodded, her ringlets bouncing. Graham entered the room and sat next to Wren. She kept her focus on Dree. She didn't want to see his expression.

"I hope it isn't hard. We did get the amber," Graham said, holding up the earring.

"It all depends on what stories are true or myth," Dree said. "The sand where sad love turned to peace is in my kingdom. I've never been there because it's in the middle of nowhere in the desert. There are some complications I believe you will run into."

"Of course there are," Tal said, wrapping his arms around his legs.

Dree pushed a ringlet behind her ear. "No one goes to the desert. There isn't a reason. The exact place is unknown."

Graham sighed. "Oh, man. Please tell me it's a small desert."

"As far as deserts go, it isn't huge, but it will feel huge searching by foot. I don't know if you need dust from any part of the desert or from the specific area."

"We don't want to risk having the wrong thing," Wren said, chewing her bottom lip. "We better find the right spot."

"How will we know it's the right spot?" Tal asked.

"There's a small wall that surrounds the area," Dree explained. "There is also a statue. It was built as a memorial, though I've never heard of anyone who's actually seen it. Nobody wants to deal with the desert. There are rumors of monsters that guard the area."

"Monsters?" Tal asked, rolling his eyes.

"These monsters might be real," Dree said, frowning. "I heard about it from my tutor, not my parents."

Ming Li shook her head and looked at the ceiling. "I don't do monsters."

"There is something worse," Dree added, fiddling with her ring. "Magic doesn't work in the desert. We don't know why. It's another reason we avoid it."

They all groaned, and Tal dramatically threw himself onto his back and covered his eyes. "Why are there places that block magic? It's so annoying."

"I am coming," Brog said from the doorway. "It is not open for discussion."

"I'm in favor of that," Wren said to the giant. The others nodded.

"Should I come?" Dree asked, twisting a ringlet around her finger.

"I don't see why you would need to," Tal said, sitting up. "If you don't know where it is, you'll just be in the way. You don't really have fighting skills."

Dree nodded. Wren would have been offended, but the princess looked relieved.

"Your dad said Dree can stay here," Tal told Graham. "Since she left a note for her family, he doesn't think the king will believe we had anything to do with her disappearance."

"What's the other item?" Sen asked. "Should we split up and finish faster?"

"The heart of Nalum is in a cave. It's also in my kingdom."

"Every time I read that, I hope it's not a real heart," Wren said with a shiver.

"I'm confused," Tal said, his brows knit together. "These items we have to find have all been pretty specific. If it's the heart of something, wouldn't there only be one? If the silver eclipse has been summoned at least three times before, wouldn't that mean some of these things wouldn't be there anymore? Sure sand and water are eternal. I can even believe multiple people could get a golden tear, but not a heart."

"It's not a literal heart," Dree explained. "It's actually a rock formation inside the cave, and there is more than one. They are supposed to look like a heart and have a reddish hue to them. They are all over in the center of the cave. I believe you must break them from the cave."

"That doesn't sound too bad," Graham said, drumming his fingers on the carpet.

"Any monsters?" Ming Li asked.

Dree shook her head. "The only problem I see here is that its illegal to enter the cave. It's blocked off for safety reasons."

"Is it guarded?" Sen asked.

"Not that I know of."

"I should go to both places," Brog said.

"I've never been to the cave, but I hear it's small. I remember hearing it was a tight fit."

"Then I suppose I should go to the desert."

"I'll go to the cave," Ming Li said. "I'm small and I'm good at climbing."

Sen nodded. "Me too."

"I'd rather go to the desert," Wren said. "I hate caves, and I don't want to be in a claustrophobic one."

"You would fit better than Graham or Tal, though," Ming Li argued. "And if the desert is going to have monsters, it might be a good idea to send them with Brog. The cave doesn't sound dangerous."

"I know I can be a wimp, and I'm working on it, but it was scary when I was trapped in the cave at Meegore."

Sen leaned forward. "Ming Li and I could go to the cave alone. If it's blocked off, we might have to sneak in. I'm good at sneaking, and it would be easier with only the two of us."

Wren wrinkled her nose. "But that puts four going to the desert and only two to the cave."

"Yes, but the cave doesn't sound dangerous," Ming Li said. "And if something does happen, we can use magic, and Sen and I are both good at fighting. Well, I assume Sen is because he is fast with that knife."

Sen's knife appeared out of nowhere and he smiled. It was strange to see him smile. Wren wasn't sure if she'd seen him do it before.

"Do we know what ever happened with Professor Dovin?" Wren asked. "Did Brake ever say?"

"Yeah," Tal said. "It turns out most of the adults had doubts about Dovin belonging to The Dark Cloud in the first place. Don't ask me why they never told us. I guess Dovin spent a lot of time in Boztoll helping the magic teenagers learn to do magic. Like the kind of stuff he taught Sen. He was worried about Boztoll and thought they would need an advantage there."

"It always annoyed us because he ignored the non-magic," Sen told them. "I guess it makes sense, though. He couldn't teach them anything."

"Dovin's family has passed down forgotten magic for years. His parents made him learn it. They kept it secret. I get it. If my dad knew someone could teleport, he probably would have them arrested and force them to teach him."

"Your father. I forgot," Brog said. "I came up here because Brake needs to speak to Tal immediately. He is in the kitchen."

"To me?" Tal asked, gesturing to himself.

"Yes. I believe it has something to do with your father."

"Dang. No way this can be a good thing."

"Do you want me to come?" Wren asked as he stood.

He winked. "Sure. Moral support is always appreciated."

"Should I come?" Dree asked, tilting her head.

"Nope, we're good," Tal said, pulling Wren to her feet and almost dragging her to the door.

"You should be nice to her," Wren said as they walked down the hallway.

"I know," he said, clenching his fists. "I keep telling myself she isn't to blame anymore than I am in this whole mess. Seeing her is a constant reminder."

"She seems nice."

"Yeah, but she's useless. She doesn't know how to do anything. I thought princesses were better trained."

"She's not useless," Wren said as they clomped down the stairs. "Sure, she doesn't have a lot of survival skills. You like adventures. Just imagine how much fun you could have showing her things she's never seen? It sounds like she's been pretty sheltered. You could take her to so many places."

"That's true. I never thought of that. It's still weird to try to make yourself like someone."

"I bet." Wren was glad her parents hadn't arranged her marriage. That would be terrible. They wound around the main floor until they came to the kitchen. Brake sat at the table. He had a plate of cookies in front of him. It must be bad. He was rubbing the black stubble on his chin.

"Ah, Tal," he said as they entered. "Sit. You too Wren. Have a cookie."

"I need a cookie?" Tal asked, grabbing one and sitting. "What's my dad done this time?"

Brake cleared his throat. "It's not what he's done. It's what we've done."

"Did you capture him?"

"Zera interrupted a meeting with the governor and the fleet. She told them the governor needed to be taken out of office. Every fleet member agreed, but Fleetman Petral. Before the governor could react, he was voted out."

"Good. It's about time something went right."

"Briggs tried to get the guards involved, but with the fleet voting against them, they held the power. This happened yesterday, and he hasn't been seen since."

"So, now what?" Tal asked, biting his cookie. "Is there going to be an election? Is Zera going to run?"

"Yes, to both of your questions. The election will be held this month. Zera will be running against Fleetman Petral."

"Ugh," Tal said, dropping his cookie to the table. "Petral was like my dad's little lap dog. If he ends up in office, it will be almost as bad as my dad. He's less competent though, so it could be worse."

"Zera was always one of the most popular fleet members," Wren reminded him. "Petral wouldn't stand a chance against her."

"That's true," Tal said. "Does my mom know?"

"Yes," Brake said. "She's taking it well. She knew it needed to happen. She's a little worried about not knowing Briggs whereabouts. He could be up to anything."

"He doesn't have any resources, though. Can he really cause too much trouble?"

"It's hard to say."

"Where's Zera?"

"She's staying in Akkron for now. She's helping supervise the lighting project. They're putting lights on all the streets. Similar projects are going on all over the continent."

"Flordillia got their lights up fast," Wren said. "It's not even scary out there."

"Hopefully we make the silver eclipse soon, and we won't have to worry about it any more," Tal said, picking up his cookie. "Why don't you tell Brake about the last two items and then he can tell us our plan is bad?"

"I don't always disapprove of your plans," Brake said with a small smile. "They just usually need some tweaking."

Chapter 5

The Dark Cloud wasn't interfering on the other continent, that was for sure. Wren blew out a breath as she looked around at the sand. Lots and lots of sand. The sun beat down relentlessly, and there wasn't a cloud to be seen. She could feel it cooking her skin, and they hadn't been here for more than a few minutes. She pulled her light blue hood over her head, hoping it didn't just lock in more heat.

Graham, Tal, and Brog were looking around just as hopelessly as she felt. She should have volunteered for the cave. At least it wouldn't be so hot. She glanced down at the sword in her hand and shook her head. Graham and Tal both had similar swords and Brog had one that was three times bigger. Without magic, they might need something. The other three had theirs sheathed at their sides, but Wren felt funny trying to walk with hers hitting her in the leg. She must be doing something wrong.

"Your arm's going to get tired if you hold it the whole time," Graham said.

"It keeps bumping my leg. It's going to trip me."

"You're wearing it funny," Tal said, helping her adjust the sheath. "There. Now try."

Wren awkwardly sheathed the sword and took a few steps. It was better. It was still pretty heavy. She really hoped she wouldn't need to use it. She would probably hurt herself.

"How do you know so much about swords?" Brog asked Tal.

"I took fencing lessons for years. Those swords were a lot lighter. I don't know how I'll do if I actually need to use it."

"This is the first time I've touched a sword," Graham admitted. "I should've taken Dree's crossbow. Pushing a lever is probably easier."

"If anything happens, I get in front," Brog said. "If anyone gets in front of me, there will be consequences."

Tal gave the giant a lopsided smile. "Oh yeah? What will they be?"

"First, I will tell your mother."

"Ouch. Come on Brog. Don't be inhumane."

"I will also tell your betrothed."

Tal grinned. "Did I just see your eyes sparkle? Are you teasing me?"

"Perhaps. Dree would probably be happy to see you injured. I should not have threatened you with her. If you get in front of me, you will end up dead and that should be enough incentive."

"I doubt there are monsters. It's probably something Dree's parents had her tutor tell her to go along with the boogeyman."

"So, where do we start?" Wren asked.

They had waited two weeks at the adult's request. In that time, everyone had researched the sand where sad love turned to peace. There was a story about two young people who fell in love and were forbidden to marry. They ran away and ended up in the desert. When their families found them, there was a fight. When half of the people were dead, they realized how ridiculous the whole thing was and they made an oath of peace.

There were rumors about the exact location, but nothing solid. Austra had used some of her resources and gotten them a map of where some people thought it might be.

"I guess we walk," Wren said, looking down at the map. "I can imagine how easily we could get lost. A map isn't really helpful when everything looks the same. I wish we could take alicorns."

"Alicorns can't take this kind of heat," Tal said, adjusting the strap on his bag. They made sure to bring plenty of food and water. If the map was right, it shouldn't take more than a few hours. "If we walk straight, we should hit it, right?"

"We should hit a large tower, and then we should turn right," Graham said as they started.

"It's going to be hard to walk in a straight line," Wren said. "We'll never know if we aren't going straight."

"I can go straight," Brog assured them. "Giants have excellent direction."

"Excellent direction and excellent hearing?" Graham asked, smiling.

"Yes. You would all be blushing to your toes if you knew some things I have overheard you say."

Tal laughed. "I believe it."

Wren could feel heat creeping up her neck as she pondered over what he could have overheard. She wondered if he heard Ming Li tell her Brog was her backup backup crush. The thought of that made her smile. It was going to be hard not to fall. With each step, her boots sank deep into the sand and she had to lift her leg high to step out. It was going to be a long day.

Graham's eyes stung, and his sunburned face was going to blister. It was miserable wearing a cloak in the desert, but they had to keep the sun off. It felt like they had been walking for hours, but he wasn't really sure how to gauge time. Everything was so bright. A hot wind had started a while back, and so they trudged forward in silence, not wanting to get sand in their mouths. It was dying down, but they were exhausted. Brog was the only one that seemed unaffected. The hot sand didn't even seem to bother his bare feet.

Wren looked like she might fall on her face and not get up. Tal looked determined, but the lines around his eyes were getting more defined. Probably from the squinting. His face was really red. Graham needed to create some type of sunblock. They had applied a goopy gel Brake had given them, but it was proving ineffective.

"Up ahead!" Wren said, pointing. "That has to be the tower."

"Yes, I spotted it a few minutes ago," Brog confirmed.

"You should've told us," Tal complained. "It gives us a goal. We can do this."

"How far do you suppose the actual monument is from the tower?" Wren asked, stopping to drink some water.

"It looks closer than the distance we've come," Graham said, studying the map.

"Good."

"You are all doing well," Brog told them. "I expected more complaining."

Wren smiled, but it didn't reach her eyes. "Yeah, but you can't hear the complaining in my head."

"Exactly. I'm pretty sure I would cry, but it would hurt my sunburn," Tal said, grinning.

"You wanna race?" Graham suggested.

"Noooooo!" Wren protested as she started walking. "I'm just telling myself to keep my legs moving. That's all I can manage."

Graham walked. And walked. He wouldn't mind The Dark Cloud bringing in a little cloud cover right about now. Of course, magic didn't work here, so that was a pointless daydream. The tower was getting close. He felt like his face might crack if he changed expressions too fast.

The tower was about five feet wide and twenty feet tall. As soon as they reached it, they all stood on the side that was shaded.

"That's nice," Wren said, pulling her water out of her pack. She pushed her hood off and took a sip. Red hair was pasted to her cheek. Graham pushed his own hood down and enjoyed a pleasant wind against his sweaty head. He pulled his water out and took a long drink.

"What if we just stay here?" Tal asked, leaning against the stone wall.

"We can't stop for long," Wren protested. "The longer we wait, the harder it will be to get our legs going again."

"I'm wishing I'd gone to the cave," Graham said. He wondered how Ming Li, Sen, and Hamble were doing. The adults had agreed to the plan, but insisted an adult go with them. They decided on Hamble because he was smaller than Brake or Drew, and Zera and Austra were busy.

"AAAAAH!" Wren screamed. Graham spun towards her. She was bending over, pulling on something at her ankle. "Something's got me!" she yelled as she kept trying to pull. Graham and Brog dropped to the sand and looked down.

"It looks like a huge hand!" Tal exclaimed. Brog grabbed at the hand and tried to pull it off of her.

Graham couldn't decide what to do. He put his hand to his sword as another hand popped out of the sand and wrapped around Tal's leg, knocking him to the ground. Before he could react, more hands popped out of the sand.

"What's going on?" he yelled, stomping on the hand closest to him. An enormous arm came up and anchored itself to the ground. A large creature burst from the ground and growled as sand fell from its body. Graham pulled out his sword with an unsteady hand.

In less than twenty seconds, ten of these creatures emerged from the sand. They were tall, with cloth masks over their faces. They looked human, but they were almost as tall as Brog. All of them had four sandy braids and were wearing armor. Their feet were bare, and they all held a sword or knife.

"Face me!" Brog called, pulling his sword from the sheath. They all turned to inspect him and then paused.

"Who are you?" a woman's voice asked. One figure pulled down her mask.

"They're giants," Wren muttered, next to Graham.

"You are giants," Brog said, lowering his sword. "How did you come to be here?"

"We are in command here," she said, shaking sand from her black braids. "You will answer what we ask. Where are you from, and why are you here?"

"I am Brog from Meegore. We are here because the other continent is in trouble. We need some special sand to help create a silver eclipse so that we can fix the weather and save humanity."

The giant tilted her head as she studied Brog. "We have heard of the troubles on the other continent. We remain hidden, but we listen. Are there others like you?"

"Giants?" Brog asked. She nodded. "Yes. We are few on the Island of Meegore, but we are strong."

"There are other men?" another giant asked.

"We are almost all men."

One giant squealed, and Graham raised his eyebrows. He never would've expected that sound to come from a ten foot tall giant. It sounded like a teenage girl.

"Control yourself, Nalisha," the leader said.

"But they have men!" said a smiling brown haired giant. It was really weird to see an armor covered giant bouncing up and down.

"Please excuse Nalisha. We've had no men in our group in over ten years."

"You live in the desert?" Brog asked, his eyes wandering to Nalisha.

"Under the desert. We are sand giants. We used to boast large numbers, but those days are over. My name is Vronika."

"How do you breathe under the sand?" Tal asked. The giants all turned and looked at the three of them.

Vronika frowned. "You travel with humans?"

"Yes."

"We avoid them unless they come into our desert."

"So you're the reason people say that monsters live here?" Tal asked.

"Monsters?" Nalisha giggled. "That's funny. I'm glad people picture us as monsters." She held her hands up like claws and growled at the giant at her side. The giant took a step away.

"We don't mean to intrude on you," Graham said, "But we really need that sand. If we don't get it, people will starve."

Vronika narrowed her eyes. "I suppose you mean sand from that silly square that has been walled off. Long ago people used to come because they thought the sand there was special. We will let you take the sand, but only because of Brog. We wish you to leave as soon as you have what you need."

"That's fair," Graham said.

"Can't we make a deal?" Nalisha begged. "We give them the sand, and they give us Brog?"

"Nalisha, you must stop talking," Vronika said, shaking her head. "We live directly under this tower. We can travel anywhere under the desert. Do you know how to enter the sand?"

"No," Brog admitted. "It is something I have never heard of."

"We will take you. As you are unused to it, it will be unpleasant. I suggest you all close your mouths and eyes, and we will take you down." She pointed to three of the giants. "You all take one of them. I'll take Brog."

A giant wrapped her arms around Graham and told him to relax. Relax. She was about to pull him under the ground, and she wanted him to relax. He closed his eyes and mouth and felt himself being pulled downwards. When he hit the sand, it blasted under his closed eyelids and into his nose. It took all of his concentration to keep his mouth shut.

When he felt like he might pass out from lack of air, they landed hard. The giant released him and he fell to the ground, gasping for air. Blinking was painful. The sand scratched his already sensitive eyes. He sat back on his knees. Someone handed him a handkerchief, and he tried to blow the sand out of his nose. The squishy cave sounded better and better.

"Drink this," someone said, handing him a cup of purple liquid. He took a swallow and a burst of berry juice slid down his throat. It was good. He blinked some more and looked up. Tal was spitting into a handkerchief and Wren was sitting on the ground, looking miserable. Her eyes were red to match her sunburn. She was holding a cup, but didn't appear interested in it.

"Drink that," he said, pointing to her cup. "It made me feel better." She nodded and lifted it to her mouth.

"I've got sand in places I didn't know I had," Tal said, shaking sand from his head. He glanced around. "This place is impressive. Who would've thought all of this was under the desert?"

Graham inspected his surroundings. He could almost believe they were outside. There were trees and plants. The only thing that made it look like they weren't outside was the sky, or lack of sky. It was bright, but instead of a sky, there was a sandy-looking ceiling.

Wren stood and looked up. "How is the sand staying up there?"

"This land is enchanted," Vronika said. "Our ancestors created this place with some of the finest magic. Our people have been living down here for generations. It's the safest place for us when our numbers are small."

"How many of you are there?" Brog asked. He didn't seem to be affected by the sand the way the rest of them were.

"Thirty-five."

"And all women?"

"Yes."

"It seems so strange that most of the giants at Meegore are men and here it is all women."

Vronika studied Brog. "Why are there so few women? We have no men because they kept fighting each other."

Brog's eyebrows came together. "They fought each other? Where I come from, giants are peaceful towards each other and only fight others when necessary. We are not sure why there are so few females. We wonder if it has something to do with the island we live on. Ever since our people moved there, most of the babies born have been male."

"How strange," Vronika mumbled. "I don't believe you came here by coincidence. We believed we were the only giants left. This was meant to be."

"It would honor me to take you to Meegore," Brog said, with one of his rare smiles. "I feel that destiny is involved here. It could be the means of saving our population."

"Perhaps we could have our people move between places. It may be the end of us if we all unite and only have male children."

"I don't like where this conversation is going," Tal said, standing. "How about someone directs us to the sand we need, and Brog can stay here arranging marriages with Vronika?"

Brog shook his head. "I cannot let you go without my protection."

"But now we know there aren't monsters, we don't have to worry," Graham told him.

"I can take them," Nalisha said, spinning a knife in her hand. "There really isn't anything dangerous down here, but if there was, I would protect them."

"Nalisha is capable," Vronika assured Brog. "And I believe we have a lot to discuss."

"Alright," Brog agreed. "How long will it take them to get there?"

"It isn't far when you aren't in the desert. They could be there and back in three hours."

"Come on, Brog," Tal said, with a smirk. "Aren't you the one who told us we trust too easily? Now you're going to send us off with some giant we don't know?"

"Giants do not lie," Brog told him. "It is not in our nature. Giants are not all good, but they will tell you that themselves if you ask them."

"Ming Li and Sen need help," Wren said from her place on the ground.

"Are they okay?" Graham asked, brushing sand from his pants.

"Yes. Ming Li said they found the right place in the cave, but they need another person to help them. She said Hamble wouldn't fit all the way, so they need me."

Wren looked sick. Graham kneeled by her and looked her over. "Are you alright? You don't look so good."

"I'll be okay," she said with a shaky smile. "I have a headache and my legs hurt, but it's not terrible."

"Here," Graham said, pulling a bottle out of his pack. "Take a swig of this. I'm not sure if you should go by yourself."

"If Hamble didn't fit, you and Tal won't either," she said, swallowing the medicine. She sighed and smiled. "That's so much better."

"You already look better," he said, pulling her to her feet. "I always carry the medicine. Just let me know if you ever need any."

She smiled. "Thanks." Her smile fell. "I'm nervous about going through the desert by myself."

"Do you not have any helpful magic?" Vronika asked.

"Yes, but we were told we can't use magic," Wren said.

"That's only up above. You can use it down here."

"Alright," Wren said with a relieved smile. "I guess I'll meet you guys later." She held the medicine bottle out to Graham.

"Keep it with you," he said, closing his hand over hers. Her eyes really were an amazing color of green.

Tal sighed. "She didn't hit her head, so I'm guessing you aren't checking for a concussion."

"No, I was just thinking that green is my new favorite color."

Wren smiled, and Tal snorted.

Graham pulled out all his courage and kissed Wren's clenched hand. "Be careful and send a message if you need us." She nodded and disappeared into a portal.

Tal put a hand on Graham's shoulder. "Smooth. I'm proud of you."

"Knock it off," he said, shrugging him off.

"That was so sweet!" Nalisha cooed. "If a giant kissed my hand, I would die of happiness!"

Graham smiled. The armor and knife really didn't seem to fit Nalisha's personality.

"Should we start now, or did you want to rest?" she asked.

"Might as well be now," Tal said. "The sooner we finish, the sooner we can make sure the others are alright."

"Follow me," she said, glancing at the place Vronika and Brog were talking.

Graham wished he could shower first. Everything about him felt gritty. He forced his legs to follow Tal and Nalisha as he wondered how he had gotten sand in knee-high boots.

"How do you get things to grow down here?" Tal asked.

Nalisha looked over her shoulder. "Giants can grow things anywhere. Put us on an iceberg and we'll grow you some of the best moakberries you ever tasted."

"That's crazy. Is it magic?"

"Yeah. It is pretty useful. You'll never find a hungry giant."

The grassy path looked like it stretched on forever. It wasn't nicely clipped grass, but long, wild grass. Graham wasn't going to complain. Grass was preferable to sand, and the temperature down here was cool, but not cold. There were wildflowers all over and the occasional tree. Berry bushes were littered here and there, and Graham was pretty sure he heard a bird. It was too bad Wren only got to see the sandy part of this quest. It was pretty down here.

Nalisha took big steps, so they had to move their legs fast to keep up. For being so tall, she had a bounce in her step.

She twirled her knife in her hand as she walked. Graham wondered if she even knew she was doing it.

"So," she said, looking sideways at them, "Are all the giants on Meegore as handsome as Brog?"

"Um ... I don't know if I really ever thought about it," Graham said, shrugging. "They all dress the same."

Tal smirked. "I'm not sure we're qualified to judge a giant's good looks."

"Oh, please," Nalisha said, shaking her head. "Anyone can see Brog is good looking. Even a human. Although I suppose you are preoccupied with that redhead girl. I can excuse you from noticing something in front of your face," she said, nodding to Graham. "Do you have a girl preoccupying you as well?" she asked Tal.

"Tnarg is pretty good looking," Tal said, ignoring the last question. "He's strong too. He's one of the guards on the island."

"A guard? Hm. I'll have to meet this Tnarg."

"If you think Brog is handsome, you could just go after him," Tal reasoned.

"Haha. You don't understand giants. Vronika is our leader. She'll be married to Brog before the end of this day."

"Nah," Tal disagreed. "Brog isn't one to jump into something like marriage that fast. He likes to ponder on things."

"Oh, believe me. You don't know Vronika. She gets what she wants."

"Wouldn't she want to see all the giants at Meegore to see which one she likes best?"

"Brog must be the best. Vronika likes adventure. It kills her to stay underground. She was excited when we sensed you today. She was itching for something to happen. It's nice down here, but it's boring. Brog is obviously an adventurer. That will draw Vronika to him. You noticed none of the others said anything? Everyone already knows how it will be. They are all scared to make her mad."

"You weren't scared to talk."

"That's because Vronika's my sister. She has to deal with me."

"I still don't believe Brog can be talked or scared into a marriage. What do you think, Graham?"

"No. Brog's too careful."

"What are the women giants like that are on Meegore?" she asked, raising an eyebrow. "Are they pretty?"

"We've only met one, and she is super old," Tal admitted.

"Vronika is young and pretty. Trust me. They'll be married when we get back."

Graham just smiled. He wasn't sure he would call Vronika pretty, but to be fair, she was wearing armor and covered in sand. It was hard to say what she really looked like.

Nalisha's eyes twinkled. "You both look skeptical. Do you want to make a wager?"

"We don't really have anything valuable with us," Graham told her.

"What do you have?"

"We have some water, food, and medicine."

"What type of medicine?"

"I have something that helps with burns and one for cuts."

"How well do they work? We don't have medicine here."

"Graham has healing power," Tal explained. "When he makes medicine, it works really well."

"If Vronika and Brog aren't married by the time we get back, I'll give you my knife. It's a good knife, she said, spinning it. If they are, you give me your medicine."

"Deal," Tal grinned.

"We don't need a knife," Graham told him.

He shrugged. "No, but it makes life interesting."

"And you are going to lose," Nalisha said, spinning in a circle. Graham couldn't help thinking she would be better suited wearing a long, flowing dress than in armor. "I know my sister."

Tal's eyes sparkled. "And we know Brog."

Chapter 6

Wren gazed inside the cave. The opening was smaller than the one at Meegore. She wondered where Hamble was. The cave had been blocked off with boards, but there were some that had been pulled away, leaving a space a person could slide through. She opened her pack and placed the medicine Graham gave her inside. She looked down at her hand and smiled. He'd kissed her hand. Shaking her head, she walked into the cool cave. It was nice after the desert sun. There wasn't time for daydreams.

She pulled up an orb of light and looked around the cave. Her light bounced off the close stone walls. It was a good thing she wasn't too claustrophobic because the pathway was much more narrow than Meegore. She kept her ears open for any wild animal sounds, but so far all she could hear were her own feet. "Just go forward," she muttered, walking deeper. She hoped it wasn't far. There really wasn't anything to be scared of. Ming Li and Sen were here somewhere.

She stopped and closed her eyes. *"I'm in the cave,"* she transmitted to Ming Li. *"How long until I reach you?"*

"It's not far, but it takes a while to climb," Ming Li answered.

"Climb?"

"You can do it. It's not bad."

"Great," Wren said, walking on. It was a good thing she'd taken Graham's medicine. If she hadn't, there was no way she would be able to get through anything that involved climbing. Up ahead, she could see a light and a person.

"Wren, is that you?" Hamble's voice echoed through the cave.

"Yes," she said, moving faster towards his voice. The closer she got, the brighter it was. Hamble was holding two orbs of light, illuminating a small cavern. The light bounced off his face, giving him an eerie appearance.

"I understand why you don't love caves," he said. "I keep waiting for bats to fly into my face or something equally horrifying."

"There aren't any bats at Meegore," Wren said as she reached him. "This cave feels creepier because it's so tight."

Hamble rubbed his bald head. "If you think this is tight, just wait. You see this hole?" He pointed at an opening down low on the cave wall. It wasn't any bigger than three feet wide.

"Please tell me I don't have to go in there."

"Yep, that's it. And it gets tighter. You have to start out crawling and then, after a minute, it goes up. Once it started going up, I couldn't fit. I had to back out."

"I can do this," Wren said under her breath. "I don't want to do this, but I can do it. How will I crawl and keep my light? Without light, I won't be able to climb."

"When we climbed in, we levitated the light in front of us. Try to feel a connection with the light and put it about two feet in front of you. Connect with the distance and the light and you can keep it going without giving it much thought."

Wren focused on the light and levitated it in front of her. She moved forward, and the light moved with her. "That's convenient."

"How was the desert? Any monsters?"

"No, but we found a group of female giants."

"Really?" he chuckled. "I had heard stories about giants living on the other continent, but I didn't imagine they were true. I bet Brog was excited."

"It's hard to tell what goes on in Brog's head. I had a hard time paying attention. They pulled us under the sand. They live under the desert. I was so hot and tired I couldn't concentrate."

"You do look like you had a fight with a sand monster. Will you be alright going in there?"

"Yes. Graham gave me some medicine. I'm feeling a lot better."

"You should go. They've been waiting in there for a while."

Wren took off her cloak and sword and dropped them to the dirt. She placed her pack on top of it. She didn't need it getting in her way.

"Good luck," Hamble said, watching her get down on her hands and knees.

Flashbacks to being stuck in the other cave entered her mind as she crawled along the rocky floor. The light stayed steady in front of her and caused spiderwebs to sparkle. Ming Li and Sen probably got the webs in their faces. She was glad she wasn't the first one coming in. Her knees were going to be bruised and her hands were probably getting torn up. The cave started sloping upward at a gentle incline.

"Are you coming?" Ming Li's voice filled her head.

"I just got to the incline." It was getting steeper. The rocky bottom made it easy to move, but not comfortably. Going back was going to be rough. There was no way she could slide back down. This was painful. A movement in front of her caused her to pause. She moved slowly towards it. It was only a lizard. She could handle lizards, but it was pretty tight in the tunnel, and she didn't know how to get around it without squishing it.

"Come here," she cooed at the little brown reptile. She put her hand out, and it ran to the ceiling. She ducked down low and crawled under it. Sweat trickled down her neck. Her head kept scraping on the top now and it was starting to feel less like crawling and more like climbing. She didn't even want to think about how she was going to get back down.

"I can see your light!" Sen called from above. "You're almost there!"

Wren looked up and saw Sen and his light. She was close.

"Be careful when you get here. It drops down."

"Of course it does."

"It isn't hard to levitate to the bottom. Li said you can levitate now?"

"Yes," she said, grabbing something rocky and pulling herself forward.

"Okay, grab my hand and pull yourself up next to me. Be careful, it's not a big ledge."

She grabbed his hand, and he helped pull her to where he was sitting. "Oh, wow," she said, looking down. "This is really high." Ming Li looked small down below. Okay, that was an exaggeration, but still. It was high.

"Are you good at levitating?" Sen asked, cocking his head.

"I don't know. I haven't had the ability for long, and I haven't had a reason to use it much. I'm assuming I should be okay since I got the power at Meegore. I've never tried it on myself."

"I'll go down first and if you have any trouble, I'll catch you. I lowered Li down. I guess she's pretty scared of heights. Don't tell her I told you. I'm surprised she was able to lift herself so high when we were in Boztoll. That was higher than this. She must have been really focused."

Wren swallowed hard and nodded. Sen easily lowered himself through the air and landed gently below. She focused on lifting herself from the small ledge. It was a strange, unnatural feeling, but she felt stable. It was like holding herself up. She concentrated on lowering herself slowly. Wren wanted to close her eyes, but she wasn't sure if she would lose her focus. She watched Ming Li and Sen get closer. Placing herself gently on the ground, she let out a breath of relief.

"You did that so smoothly," Ming Li said, grinning.

Wren looked around the large cavern. It wasn't as light as she would like, but it wasn't terribly dark with Sen and Ming Li's lights hovering in the air. "What did you need my help with?" she asked, looking down at her sore hands.

"Do you see the hearts?"

Wren inspected the cavern closer. There were several areas where stalagmites and stalactites came together, with a reddish rock connecting the two. They were about twenty feet from the ground. "I'm guessing those?" she said, pointing.

"That's what we figure."

"How do I help?"

"The hearts are connected to the stalagmites," Sen said. "Like really connected. I tried to levitate up there and pull one off, but I couldn't. I also tried to kick one out, but I couldn't kick hard enough and levitate at the same time. We both levitated up, and I held onto Li while she kicked one. It came loose, but then it fell to the ground and broke. We tried a few times, but it happened every time. We can't levitate ourselves and the heart at the same time."

Ming Li handed her a piece of red rock. "We didn't want to keep trying and ruining them."

"So you want me to levitate the rock after you kick it out?"

Sen nodded. "That's what we were thinking. You'll have to be fast."

"Okay. I'm ready when you are."

"Actually, what if you go up with Sen and I catch it?" Ming Li asked.

"You can kick better than I can."

"Yeah, but it's higher than I want to be."

"Alright. Let's go." Wren raised herself up to one of the hearts. It felt like flying, but in slow motion. Sen was right next to her.

"I'm going to hold on to your shoulders," Sen explained. "You kick the stone. I can hold us both steady, if that's all I focus on." He moved behind her and clamped onto her shoulders. He had a good grip. "Okay, kick it." Wren kicked the stone. It wasn't hard enough.

"Come on Wren!" Ming Li called up. "Pretend it's Solia!"

Wren rolled her eyes. She didn't like Solia, but she didn't want to kick her. "I'll try again." She focused all her energy into the kick and the heart broke free. Before it could fall too far, Ming Li levitated it down. Sen and Wren slowly followed.

Ming Li turned the heart in circles. "This heart of Nalum isn't as exciting as it should be."

"What do you want it to do?" Wren asked, looking at the rock.

"I don't know. I just keep wondering about this whole silver eclipse thing. Most of the items aren't that exciting. I mean, the golden tear was definitely cool, but sand? Water? This rock? The amber? I just wonder if someone made it all up and we're going on some wild goose chase."

"I guess we won't know until we try," Wren said.

Ming Li wrinkled her nose. "And what do we do when we have all the ingredients? I keep picturing us all throwing stuff into a boiling cauldron and cackling like witches."

"Do witches cackle?" Sen asked, looking confused. "I thought chickens cackle?"

"It could be an Earth thing."

"Earth witches cackle?"

"Yes. No. Witches are mostly just in stories. I've never heard of a real one on Earth."

"Can I see it?" Wren asked. Ming Li handed it to her. She turned it around in her hand. It felt like any rock, except there was something she couldn't quite place. She wrapped both of her hands around it and held it tight. It was pulsing. She shoved it into Sen's hands. "Hold it still and tight."

Sen's eyebrows came together. "Is it beating?"

"What?" Ming Li asked. "What do you mean, beating?"

"It feels like it's beating." He held it out to Ming Li. "Hold it again, but hold still."

"No," Ming Li said, backing away. "That sounds creepy. Why would it be beating? It's a rock, right?"

"It must be magic," Wren reasoned. "Maybe that's why it's part of the silver eclipse."

"I'll put it in my pack," Sen said, opening his bag.

Wren tried to open a portal, but it didn't work. "I'm not excited about getting out of here," she admitted, gazing up at the hole they had come through.

"I'm less excited," Ming Li muttered. "Can we teleport to Hamble?"

"I'm pretty sure you can't teleport in a cave. The rock is too thick. I'll lift you up," Sen offered.

"I can do it. Up seems better than down. Last one up is a stinky rednax."

"We're here," Nalisha said, looking up at the sandy ceiling. "If we go straight up, we should be right next to the monument and inside the walls."

"How do we get up?" Graham asked.

"I'll have to hold on to you. Prepare yourselves, because it's a lot worse going up than down."

Tal grimaced. "Down was pretty bad."

"Yes, but falling through the sand is easier than pushing up through it. It's even worse here because we don't come up here very often. The sand is more solid. Just close your eyes and mouth and I'll do the rest."

Graham shut his eyes and sighed as Nalisha grabbed him on one side and Tal on the other. She jumped and Graham clenched his teeth together, trying not to scream. They were going fast. They hit the sand with tremendous force and he tried to hold his breath. It felt like they were flying through the sand for an eternity, but it was probably only a minute. When they burst through the surface, he fell to the ground and gulped air.

Tal coughed next to him. "That was terrible," he managed. "But, I would say down was worse. I didn't get a mouth and nose full of sand this time."

Graham shook the sand from his head and clothes. "It felt longer though," he said, trying to ignore the gritty feeling all over his body. He looked around the hot desert. It was the same as everywhere else, except this small area was fenced in and there was a sand covered monument in the middle. It looked like it might have been two people at one time, but it was old and the sand had eroded it into an unidentifiable mass.

"Let's grab some sand and go," Tal said. "It's too hot to wait around too long."

Graham pulled a container out of his pack and filled it with sand. "Alright, should we go?"

"What's that?" Nalisha asked, pointing up at the sky. Graham and Tal shaded their eyes with their hands and followed her finger. Five creatures were flying in a circle above them.

"Dragons," Tal said. "And they aren't happy to be out in the heat."

"They're a lot bigger than Ben," Graham said. "What do you think they're doing?"

"They have riders on them."

Nalisha pulled out her knife. "Riders? Do you know them?"

Tal shook his head. "I don't know. I just know the dragons aren't happy about this trip, and they aren't happy with their riders."

"How do you know that?"

"I have a magical connection to animals. I can sense their thoughts."

"Wow. Can you ask them if they are here peacefully?"

"I can try. We communicate more through feelings than words, so it isn't always easy."

Graham watched the dragons get lower. One was a golden color. Two looked silver, and the other two were blue. "Can't we just sink back into the sand?" Graham just barely got over his fear of small dragons. These were huge.

"I need to see if they're a threat," Nalisha said, keeping her eyes focused on the sky.

Tal shook his head. "I can't get a feeling for why they're here. I can only tell they're grumbling."

"I thought we couldn't do magic in the desert," Graham said. "How can you sense the dragons?"

"This is the only spot where magic can be performed," Nalisha explained. "This whole squared off area is magic. That's probably why you need the sand from this spot and not just anywhere."

"Can big dragons breathe fire?" Graham asked.

"Yeah," Tal said. "Not for very long, and they don't like to do it. These dragons are probably thirsty, which would make it hard for them. Don't attack them or anything. They don't seem terribly attached to their riders, so I can probably keep them from attacking us."

The golden dragon landed, its wings blowing dust into their faces. Graham covered his face and waited for the sand to settle. When he looked up, it was to see Zalliah climbing down from the dragon.

"What an interesting place to run into you," she said, smiling. She wore a black tunic and pants. Her makeup was darker than usual, and her brown hair was falling down her back in soft curls.

"You know her?" Nalisha asked.

"Yes, keep your knife out," Graham said. He thought about taking out his sword, but if they could do magic here, that would be more practical.

Zalliah threw back her head and laughed as she grabbed a handful of sand and placed it in her pocket. "Yes, keep your little knife out. It's sure to stop me." The other dragons landed outside the wall. "Getting close to the silver eclipse?"

"Why are you here?" Tal demanded.

"No small talk? You want to jump right to the threat?"

"Yes, that would be preferable."

"That's because you don't know what it is," she said, flashing her white teeth. "I'm afraid this one is aimed at you, Tal."

"Lovely."

"Should I capture her? Kill her?" Nalisha asked. "She's puny. It wouldn't be hard."

Zalliah smiled. "But then you wouldn't get to hear my demands. You might want to hear those first."

"We don't care what your demands are," Tal said. "We aren't giving in to anything you have to say."

"Warm out here, isn't it?" she said, looking over her shoulder to where the other dragons and their riders were waiting. "Bring the hostage!" she called.

"Great," Tal said under his breath. "It better not be my mom."

Graham was trying to focus on too many things at once. It was hard to look away from the dragon. If anyone attacked, he wasn't sure who he should go after first. The dragon or Zalliah. Zalliah seemed a little scarier at the moment.

Gorbin walked through the opening in the gate, pulling Briggs with him. Gorbin was smiling as he yanked the ropes on the former governor's hands.

"Really?" Tal asked. "My dad? You're threatening us with my dad as a hostage?"

"You might not have the best relationship, but he is your father," she said, smiling as Gorbin came closer. Briggs' hands were tied together and his cape was torn in several places. Briggs was strong, but Gorbin was huge.

"Tal, don't do anything for these people," Briggs said as they reached the group.

"I wasn't planning on it."

"Oh, I think you will," Zalliah smiled, pulling a five-inch knife from somewhere in her cape. "I want to go back into the cave at Meegore."

"We could have guessed that," Graham said.

"That isn't all. I want good magic. I know your little bungle messed with the magic I got last time. Believe me, he will pay for it."

"You don't like making your own glowing mucus?" Tal said with a lopsided smile. "I thought it looked good on you."

She frowned as she pressed the knife up to Briggs' chest. "You will take me to the cave and you will tell that obnoxious little bungle to give me what I want. Are we clear? If you don't agree, your father is dead."

Briggs narrowed his eyes at Zalliah and turned to Tal. "Tal, I know you might not believe it, but I love you."

"Oh, isn't that sweet?" Zalliah cooed.

"Tell Valeena I love her. I always have. I would have loved her even if she was ugly. She won't believe it, but tell her."

"Come now, Briggs," she said, rolling her eyes. "Do you really believe Tal is going to let you die?" Tal was shifting nervously from one foot to the other.

"I know I haven't always made the best decisions, and I am self-serving, but I know that The Dark Cloud cannot win. I'm at peace with this. I believe in you, Tal. Don't let her win."

The golden dragon roared and made a beeline for Gorbin.

"Stop!" Zalliah yelled at the creature, holding her hand up. The dragon ignored her and plowed into Gorbin, knocking him and governor Briggs to the ground. Graham shot a bolt of ice at Zalliah, slicing her arm.

Nalisha grabbed Zalliah and threw her to the ground. "Are we going for capture or kill?"

"Capture, if you can," Graham said, "But they have to be stopped."

Nalisha spun her knife. "No problem."

Zalliah sat up and brushed sand from herself. "Silly me," she said, looking unconcerned. "I avoided the jungle so that Tal couldn't fight, and then I brought worthless animals for him to control." She stood as Nalisha moved in closer. She reached into her cape and pulled some powder out of her pocket and threw it in Nalisha's face. The giant blinked and fell to the sand.

Briggs was struggling to get up, and the dragon was sitting on Gorbin. All Graham could see was his black hair. He wondered if he was alive.

"It looks like it's just me and the two of you," Zalliah said, smiling. "I know it's not a fair fight, but you'll do your best, I'm sure."

"I can make the dragon eat you," Tal said, pointing at her.

"Dragons don't eat people, silly boy. Why don't we stop playing around and go to Meegore?" she suggested. Briggs unsteadily got to his feet. He glared at her and plowed forward. Right when he would have made contact, she moved out of the way and he fell into the sand. "I don't have time for this. Take me to Meegore now. I brought extra dragons you can ride."

"Don't take her," Briggs said, struggling to get back up.

"This is your last chance. Take me now."

"Never," Tal said as Graham shot more ice at her. She dropped to the ground, and it flew over her head. She rolled and smoothly stood, plunging her knife into Briggs' stomach. His eyes widened, and he fell to his knees. Graham tried to shoot more ice, but nothing happened. It must be too hot.

"I can't do ice," he told Tal. Tal rushed Zalliah, but she put her hand out and he flew backwards, smashing into the ground.

"I can't show you all my tricks at once," she said. Graham ran towards her and smashed into an invisible barrier. "You do seem to want to see them all, though. Next time I see you, you will know I mean business. Think about what you just cost yourself," she said, pointing towards Briggs.

Gorbin pulled himself out from under the dragon. Blood ran down his face, but he was going to be alright. Graham couldn't get off the ground. Something was holding him down. Gorbin stood and limped towards Graham.

"I never got a chance to deal with you well enough after you stole Fria," he growled. Gorbin pulled his fist back and punched him in the face. Graham rolled on the ground and got up, wiping blood from his lip. That was going to leave a mark. That was much worse than being slapped by the man when they had been at Meegore.

"Enough," Zalliah commanded. "We will meet again soon, and I hope next time you remember what happened here." They turned and ran in the direction of the dragons outside the wall. They left the golden dragon there.

"Get them!" Tal said, pointing at the retreating figures. The golden dragon turned and ran after them.

Graham stumbled over to Briggs. Tal was crawling towards him, his sword dragging a path in the sand.

"I'm sorry you have to live with this," Briggs said, sinking lower into the sand. "But you made the right decision."

He coughed. There was too much blood. "You need to stop that woman. I know you will. I'm proud of you."

"Graham can heal you," Tal said. Graham opened his pack. It was hard to concentrate past the throbbing in his cheek.

"This can't be healed." Briggs fell backwards into the sand. His breathing was labored. He closed his eyes. "It's alright. I needed to go out this way."

"Let Graham try," Tal said, leaning over his father. Briggs let out a rattling breath and went limp. "Dad? Dad?" He shook his shoulder. "He's dead."

Graham leaned in and checked the man's pulse. Nothing. "I'm sorry."

Tal bit his lip and nodded. "Now what do we do?" he asked as he looked at the sky and watched the golden dragon chase the others.

"Do you need to take a minute?" Graham asked, glancing quickly at Briggs and away.

"No," he said, standing and brushing off his clothes. "I honestly don't know what I'm feeling right now. We need to get Nalisha help. Who even knows what they did to her? Hopefully it's just ailam powder."

"I don't know how we can get back under the sand," Graham said, getting to his feet.

Tal grimaced. "Your face doesn't look too good. It's pretty swollen."

"It's not important right now," Graham said, bending over Nalisha. "Her pulse is strong. I bet it was ailam powder."

"I'm too late," said a voice from behind Graham. He spun around to face Dovin. The man was wearing a leather jerkin and a black cloak. He was going to be hot. His eyes were fixed on Briggs. He bent down next to him and felt his neck.

"He's gone," Graham said softly.

"Blast you Briggs!" Dovin growled, sinking down in the sand. "You had so much potential. Why did you make the decisions you did?" A tear ran down Dovin's face. Graham and Tal shared a confused look. "What happened?" he asked, wiping his cheek.

"Zalliah captured him. She brought him here to threaten us," Tal said, looking at the sand. "I didn't really think she would do anything. She stabbed him."

"Zalliah did this?" His lip trembled. "I knew she was coming after you. I should have come faster. I didn't ever imagine she would actually do something like this herself. I know she isn't innocent in so many things, but this is past what I ..." he put his head in his knees and his shoulders shook.

Graham felt helpless and more than a little dizzy. Tal was staring anywhere but at Briggs. He wiped at his eye and took a few steps away.

"I'm sorry," Dovin said standing. "Briggs was one of my favorite students. He was so bright and optimistic. He let power get the best of him, but I don't believe he was as bad as some believe. And Zalliah ... Who is the giant? Is she alright?"

"They got her with ailam powder."

"We need to get back," Tal muttered. "I don't know how we contact Brog. We can't just leave him alone down there."

"If we can do magic here, and under the sand, maybe we can teleport down there."

"What happened to your face?" Dovin asked, looking at Graham's cheek and lip. "Zalliah?"

"No, that was Gorbin."

"It doesn't look good."

"It doesn't feel that great either."

Dovin raised an eyebrow. "Was he wearing a ring?"

Graham rubbed his cheek. "I don't know."

"We need to get you somewhere. Fast."

Tal's eyes were wide. "What's happening? That doesn't look normal."

"What?" Graham asked.

"There are weird veins going up your face and down your neck."

Graham felt his face. All he could feel was the swelling.

Dovin studied Graham closely. "He must have poisoned his ring."

Graham let out a slow breath. He couldn't heal himself. Sweat poured down his face and things were blurry.

"Tal, touch the giant and grab Graham's hand," Dovin commanded. "I'll hold on to your father and get Graham's other hand. Wherever Brog is, he'll have to wait."

Chapter 7

"It's good we brought food this time," Ming Li said, sitting cross-legged in the dirt as she searched through her pack. Wren sat in the reeds next to the cave and stretched her arms above her head. Getting out of the cave had been worse than going in. It had been hard to get down without slipping.

"Graham should give us all a bunch of different medicines," she said, inspecting her scraped hands. "It would be nice to have some of that lotion that helps scratches."

Ming Li bit an apple. "My hands are okay, but I'm so tired."

"I'm sorry I couldn't help more," Hamble said, leaning against a tree. "I wasn't useful on this trip."

"That's alright," Sen said. "It wasn't bad once Wren came."

"Hopefully, the others got the sand. It didn't sound like it would be too hard," Wren said, taking a drink of water.

"Do we go help them, or go back to Flordillia?" Ming Li asked.

"I would say Flordillia. It would be easier than trying to find them in the desert."

"True, but not as fun."

Wren cringed. "Believe me, it's not fun in the desert. It was way too hot and there was a terrible dry wind. It would be hard to find them unless the giants sensed us or something. I don't really know how that works."

"If they aren't in Flordillia, we can make a plan after that," Hamble said.

"Then why are we hanging around here?" Sen asked. "Let's go."

"Sometimes it's hard to remember we can just teleport wherever we want," Ming Li said, hopping up. "I guess I'll see you all there." She waved and disappeared.

Wren stood and grabbed her pack. It would be nice if the others were already back. She was ready for a nap. Everything swirled as she teleported to the troll house. Tal sat on one of the enormous staircases in the entryway. He was still covered in sand and he looked tired. He stared at all of them with no readable expression.

"Did you get the sand?" Ming Li asked him. Sen and Hamble appeared beside her.

"The sand?" Tal asked, hoarsely.

"Yeah ... The sand you and Graham went to get?" Sen prodded.

"Oh right," Tal said, shaking his head. "We got it. Who even cares, though?"

"What do you mean, who cares?" Wren asked. "We all care. We need it."

Tal swallowed hard and looked down at his hands. "I don't care right now," he said. Wren felt uneasy. This wasn't Tal. What could have gone wrong?

"Are you okay?" Ming Li asked, sitting down next to Tal.

"I don't know," Tal admitted. He looked up and tears spilled down his cheeks.

"What happened?" Wren asked, sitting on a step below them.

"Zalliah came," he whispered. "She killed my dad."

"Oh, no!" Wren exclaimed. Ming Li wrapped her arms around Tal, and he put his head on her shoulder.

"That's not the worst part," Tal said, sniffling. "Gorbin cut Graham with his ring. It poisoned him or something. He's got weird vein things all over the place and he passed out when we got back. We don't know if he's going to be alright."

Wren stiffened, and her heart pounded in her ears. "Where is he?" she asked, leaping up. Tears threatened to fall.

"In his room with his parents."

Wren took the stairs two at a time. Graham couldn't die. They needed him. Without him, how would they summon the silver eclipse? Even if they didn't need him for that ... she needed him. She knocked on the bedroom door and Zera opened it. Her eyes were red and puffy. She gathered Wren into a hug, and they both cried.

"I've got him stable," said a gravelly voice. Wren looked up and saw a troll leaning over Graham. He was big, with black hair that looked more like porcupine quills than hair. "I don't know what will happen, but he's breathing normally. Give him some of this medicine every hour. I'll be back tomorrow, but call on me if anything changes. I will send something to ward off anything evil."

"Thank you," Brake said, taking the bottle from the troll. He must be a healer. He packed up a bag and slowly shuffled out the door.

Wren crept closer to the bed and wiped the tears from her eyes. If it weren't for the weird veins running all over Graham's face and neck, it would be easy to think he was just sleeping.

Brake came to her side and patted her on the back. "We'll figure this out. We have to." Wren nodded and tried to believe him.

"Where's everyone else?" Wren finally asked.

Zera blew her nose and sat down on a chair by the bed. "Valeena took Briggs' body home. Tal did not wish to go, so I am not sure what he is doing. Someone should probably check on him."

"Ming Li, Sen, and Hamble were with him when I came up."

"Good. Everyone has been running around trying to make sense of anything, and I am afraid he might have been overlooked. Austra is taking care of the giant, and your father and Hedder are off talking to different healers to see if any of them might have an idea about what we can do."

"Is Dree still here?"

"She's in her room," Brake said, looking at the ceiling and shaking his head. "I guess her parents raised her in a way to scare her into keeping safe. She's afraid Graham might spread whatever he has to her. Tal wasn't very impressed with her reaction."

"What did the troll mean about warding off anything evil?" Wren asked, wiping her eye.

"Trolls are superstitious. They imagine there is evil everywhere. All the trolls believe this house has bad luck. I had to pay him a lot to come here."

"Right. I remember hearing that. What can I do? How can I help Graham?"

"I'm not sure there's anything anyone can do right now. You should all get cleaned up and eat something, and things might not seem so bleak."

"I should stay here. I want to be helpful."

Brake shook his head. "Everyone will be most helpful if they are feeling well. Go take a shower and eat. Then come and Zera can put something on that sunburn."

Wren raced to her room, took a quick shower, and pulled on some clean clothes. Ming Li was in the kitchen when she got there, eating stew.

"How's Tal?" Wren asked, getting her own bowl and scooping some stew from a pot on the stove.

Ming Li shrugged. "He's going to be fine. He's really worried about Graham, of course. By the time he went up to his room, he was mad at his dad again. It really irritated him that his dad waited until he was about to die to tell him he loved him. He thinks it was just a jab at him to make him feel worse."

"I'll never understand the way Governor Briggs thought or did things," Wren said, sitting at the table.

"How's Graham? I was going to go up there, but I figure there isn't anything I can do right now."

"He looked bad," Wren said, looking into the stew. "A troll healer said he's stable, whatever that's supposed to mean." She took a bite of potato and sighed. It felt good hitting her stomach.

"Do you remember all those stories I told you a long time ago?" Ming Li asked. "The fairy tales?"

"Some of them."

"Remember how in some of them the princess was in a deep sleep and the only way to wake her was with a kiss?"

Wren shook her head as she chewed. "I hope you aren't saying I should kiss Graham while he's unconscious and hope he wakes up."

"True love's kiss. It's the most powerful thing on Earth."

"We aren't on Earth, and who has ever said anything about true love?" She shoved more stew into her mouth as she watched her friend.

Ming Li shifted in her chair and looked thoughtfully at the ceiling. "But what if it worked?"

"Fairy tales aren't real."

"I grew up believing magic wasn't real, and guess what?"

"They made fairy tales up for children."

"What if there's some truth behind them?" She took a bite and pointed her spoon at Wren. "What if that was all it took, and you didn't do it because you didn't think it would help?"

"Kissing someone isn't magic."

"I bet it is if it's the right person," Tal said, coming into the room. He looked better than when they came in.

"Sit down and I'll get you some stew," Ming Li said as she jumped to her feet and grabbed a bowl. "And while you're sitting there, tell Wren she should kiss Graham and see if it wakes him up."

Tal raised his eyebrow as he sat next to Wren. "Why would kissing someone wake them up from something like that?"

"Don't you guys have any fairy tales here about true love's kiss? It's supposed to heal everything." She put a bowl of stew in front of Tal and sat back down.

"Well, I don't see what it could hurt," Tal said, digging in. "This is fantastic."

"See? Tal agrees. You're outvoted. You need to try."

"You can't vote that I have to kiss someone. It doesn't make any sense."

"Neither does snapping your fingers and having something appear out of nowhere."

"That's different."

Ming Li tilted her head and studied Wren. "Okay, if you say so."

"I'm going upstairs. I'll check on Graham, then I'm going to rest." Wren stood and stretched. She really couldn't concentrate when she was tired. She took her bowl to the sink and rinsed it.

"Just give him a little kiss when you check on him."

Wren rolled her eyes. "Yeah, right in front of his parents. That would make it a hundred times weirder."

"It would make it more memorable, that's for sure," Tal said with a lopsided smile that didn't reach his eyes.

Wren shook her head and left the kitchen. She trudged down the hallway and up the stairs. Ming Li was crazy. Fairy tales were so odd on Earth. She knocked on Graham's door and then slowly opened it. Brake and Zera were gone. She sank into the chair by his bed and looked at him.

"Blast you, Ming Li," she muttered under her breath. What if Ming Li was right? What if it worked, and she didn't try it because it was too easy and silly? Would she be able to live with herself if she didn't try it and Graham died? The veins on his face made him look almost scary. His breathing was raspy, but at least he was breathing.

Someone could come in any second. If she was going to do it, she needed to hurry. She wrung her hands as she watched him. She could only imagine how awkward it would be if she kissed him as someone walked in. How could she explain kissing an unconscious person? She wasn't a weirdo.

Wren stood and pushed a stray lock of hair behind her ear. Her heart was pounding obnoxiously loud in her head and she was sweating. She sat on the edge of the bed and tried to make her body stop trembling. This was ridiculous. Did it have to be on the lips? She couldn't remember the stories very well.

She popped up and dashed to the door. She wasn't risking someone walking in. After bolting the door, she returned to her spot on the bed. She could do this, and if it didn't work, nobody had to know it happened.

Leaning down, she closed her eyes. She didn't want to see Graham's eyes pop open if it worked. She pressed her lips to his, and she immediately felt something flow from her hand and up her arm until her whole body was warm and twitchy. Her mom's ring! The ring was using Graham's healing power and bouncing it back onto him. She kissed him for a few more seconds for good measure and when she felt him move; she jumped up.

Wren put a hand to her chest and watched as Graham rubbed his eyes. The veins were gone and so was the raspy breathing. She looked down at her ring and it was white instead of red. It must have worked. Why hadn't she thought of it in the first place? His eyes fluttered and then opened.

"Wren? What happened?" he asked, sitting up.

"We thought you were going to die," she said, with a new set of tears running down her cheeks. Great. Now she was crying in front of him.

"I actually feel great," he said, standing up. "Like, better than usual." He opened his arms and Wren threw herself into them, crying into his shirt. He rubbed her back. "It's okay, I'm really fine. Why am I fine? Did you do something?"

Wren stopped crying and went still. She stepped away from him as someone began pounding on the door.

Graham touched his lips and frowned. "Hey, did you ..."

"Someone's at the door!" Wren said, rushing away from him. She opened the door to find Zera, Brake, Tal, and Ming Li.

"Why was the door locked?" Brake asked, entering the room. "Graham!"

Zera pushed her way in. "You are awake!" she exclaimed, rushing to him and wrapping him in a hug. Everyone filled the room and started talking at once. Wren backed up to the wall and hoped her face wasn't as red as she was sure it was. It felt so hot she was surprised her hair wasn't on fire.

"What happened? You look great," Zera said.

"I don't know. I just woke up and Wren was here," Graham said, motioning towards her. Everyone turned and looked at her. If she thought her face was hot before, it was nothing compared to the inferno that was now consuming her. "I don't know how I got better."

"It was my mom's ring," Wren blurted out, holding out her hand. "I touched him and the ring used Graham's power and healed him. See how it turned white?"

"I thought it was silly that Magnalee wouldn't wear the ring," Zera said, still holding onto Graham. "Now I'm glad she saved it for you."

"So what did you do?" Tal asked, the sparkle back in his eyes. "Just touch his face or something?"

Wren really wished she could kick him. "Yes, I touched his face." Tal chuckled and Ming Li smiled and gave her the thumbs up sign. Graham rubbed his lips again and was looking at her with a strange expression she couldn't read.

"Thank you Wren," Brake said, walking over and putting a hand on her shoulder. "We appreciate you sacrificing the ring for him." She nodded.

Drew burst through the door and stopped when his eyes landed on Graham. "Graham! You're healed! That's a relief. I was getting worried. I couldn't find any healers who had any ideas on how to help. Are you alright, Wren?"

"Fine," she said, feeling a new wave of heat. She could feel everyone's eyes on her. Why did her face turn red so easily? With hope, everyone would blame the sunburn.

Graham followed everyone out the door. He hadn't felt this good in a long time. It was hard to believe he had been near death only a few minutes ago. He had been having a really bizarre dream about Padmire, the bungle who lived in the cave at Meegore. Suddenly, he'd felt something warm on his lips and he'd woken up to Wren.

His lips tingled, and he was almost a hundred percent sure she had kissed him. If the strange sensation on his lips wasn't the only sign, Wren's face was a dead giveaway. She looked like she might pass out of embarrassment at any moment. It figured he was out when it happened.

"We need to get some food into you," Zera said, dragging him away from the others and into the kitchen. "I wish you could be done with these dangerous things. I am not sure how much more I can take. You need to be more careful."

Graham sat at the table and decided it was best not to remind his mom that she had been doing dangerous things since she was his age. "I'm not hungry."

"You should eat anyway," she said, placing a bowl of stew in front of him. "Your body needs it."

He took a bite of the cold stew and cringed. He missed microwaves.

"Is it cold?" Zera asked. "I can warm it."

"I'll just have a banana," he said, pulling one from the bunch on the table.

Tal entered and sat across from him. "I'm glad you're alright."

"I'm sorry I couldn't help your dad," Graham said.

Tal shrugged. "It's not your fault. I'm more relieved that you're okay. I feel guilty about my dad, because we really didn't have a relationship, and I should have tried harder, but I'm fine, because, like I said. We didn't have a relationship."

Zera patted Tal on the shoulder. "Let us know if you need anything. We all care about you."

"Thanks," Tal said, turning red.

A knock sounded on the front door. Nobody ever came that knocked. Graham and Tal rushed from the kitchen and into the entryway. Zera was right behind them, and Brake was opening the door, with Ming Li and Wren beside him.

"Oh, my!" Brake exclaimed at the head of the group. He stepped back as a cow pushed its way into the house. A group of trolls herded a bunch of cows and chickens into the entryway. No one protested, because they were all too stunned.

"Whoa!" Drew said from the top of the stairs. "What's going on?" There were at least ten cows and fifteen chickens. The trolls left, shutting the door behind them.

"Gross!" Ming Li exclaimed. "Look at what they are doing to the floor! That's nasty!"

"Yes," Brake finally said, "But you have to admit, it's *egg-citing*."

Graham looked sideways at his dad. He had a gleam in his eye.

"And thankfully there isn't any carpet down there, so there isn't a lot at *steak*," Drew said, descending the stairs.

Brake grinned. "Exactly. Let's just take *stock* of the situation."

Drew nodded. "It's strange to be sure. In fact, it's *utterly* ridiculous."

"What is ridiculous is the two of you," Zera said, smiling.

"So you're going to *hen-peck* us?" Brake asked, winking at Zera.

Drew grinned. "Yeah, come on Zera. That's a *yolk* that will put you in a good *mooo-d*."

"I believe the two of you are just *milking* this for attention," Zera said, wrapping her arm around Brakes.

Graham smiled. He hadn't seen his parents like this.

"Those were terrible puns," Ming Li said, shaking her head.

"My dad can go on forever," Wren warned with a small smile. "I've learned to tune him out."

"Why would they do this?" Tal asked.

"Trolls believe livestock bring good luck," Brake said. "I bet the healer had them sent over."

"What do we do with them?" Graham asked, going up a few steps. Some cows were enormous!

"Whoa!" Hamble exclaimed, entering from the opposite hallway. "Well, this is a *fowl* bit of *a-moooos-ment.*"

Ming Li, Graham, Wren, and Tal all moaned, and the adults all laughed.

Ming Li put her hands on her waist. "I don't know how you can laugh. Who's gonna clean this up? Do you see what they're doing on the floor?"

"It's just good, clean fertilizer," Hamble said, patting the spotted cow nearest him. "We can scoop it up and let Zera use it in her garden."

"That's a good idea," Zera said, tapping her chin. "Do we have a wheelbarrow?"

Ming Li snorted. "I can't imagine Zera scooping up cow manure. This I've gotta see."

"Oh, you will not see me scooping it," Zera said, batting her eyelashes innocently. "But I will make sure you all get a nice, warm shower when you are finished."

Chapter 8

Wren yawned and rolled over in bed. She heard someone clomping around the hallway, so it was probably morning. It was hard to tell these days. Three weeks had passed since they'd gathered the last few things to make the silver eclipse. They were so excited to have everything they hadn't stopped to remember that they didn't know what to do with the things once they collected them. They had spent their days looking through books, hoping to find something they might have missed.

Briggs' funeral had taken place a few days after his death, and they all attended to support Tal and Valeena. There was a large turnout, even though Briggs had fallen out of favor with a lot of people. It was nice to see so many people supporting their family.

Graham seemed to have more energy than usual. It must have come from the ring healing him. He was up earlier than the rest of them, starting on research.

Graham and Tal's giant friend, Nalisha, had recovered and returned home. Brog hadn't been around because the giants were all planning on joining their two groups and it was taking all of his time. It sounded like both groups were excited to merge, but couldn't decide where their ultimate dwelling place should be.

Ben jumped on the bed and nuzzled into Wren's cheek. She rubbed his head and sat up.

"I know. I'm up. What are we going to do today?" she asked him. He tilted his head and studied her. "Do you suppose anyone remembers it's my birthday?" Ben licked her face. "Probably not. We've been too busy. Dad won't forget. Sixteen is a big deal."

The door creaked open and Ming Li peeked in. "Awesome, you're awake." She pushed the door open and Graham and Tal came running in, throwing small, colorful pieces of paper on her head.

"Happy birthday!" Ming Li exclaimed.

Wren tried to smooth her hair down as they continued throwing handfuls of the colorful scraps. Couldn't they wait until she got out of bed?

"What is this stuff?" she asked once they stopped.

"Homemade confetti," Ming Li said. "And it took us a LONG time to cut it all out. You're welcome."

"Who gets to clean it up?" Wren asked, looking at the mess on her bed and floor.

"We don't worry about that right now," Tal said, sitting at the foot of her bed. "It's present time!"

"Can't you guys wait until I get dressed?"

"We tried," Graham said, grinning at her. "But you sleep forever."

"Where's Sen?"

Tal rolled his eyes. "He's not much into partying. He's teaching Dree to use her crossbow."

"My present first!" Ming Li said, handing her a sloppily wrapped blue present. "Open ours first, because you aren't going to care what we got you once you see what your dad has for you."

Graham covered his ears as Wren let out a shriek. "An alicorn!" she yelled. She snuggled her face into the big white beast. "I can't believe it!"

"I knew you would have earned one by now if things were different," Drew said, smiling. "I decided it was time." They all stood in the trees at Meegore. Now that they could teleport, it made things a lot easier.

"She's beautiful! Thank you." She threw her arms around Drew and gave him a tight squeeze. Graham thought she was beautiful. But he wasn't thinking about the alicorn.

"So, does she have to keep it here?" Ming Li asked.

"I'm afraid so," Drew said. "It's only temporary. Once things get better, we'll take her home."

"It has been nice to see animals on the island," Brog said. "Walter and Zebra make all of us happy. We are only too glad to help with the alicorn."

Wren rubbed her hand over the alicorn's back. "How tame is she?"

"Very," Drew said, patting the animal. "You can ride her. She's trained."

"We haven't seen much of you," Tal said, grinning mischievously at Brog.

"I have been busy."

"I imagine. Thirty-five new giants to get to know. Thirty-five *female* giants."

"Yes, it has been interesting for all of us."

"That reminds me. Where's Nalisha? She owes us a knife."

Graham snickered, and everyone else looked confused.

"Why would she owe you a knife?" Brog asked, his brow raised.

Graham grinned. "She bet us you would be married to Vronika that first day you met her. We told her you were too careful for something like that." Everyone laughed, and Brog cleared his throat nervously.

"Oh, no! Brog!" Tal exclaimed, raising one eyebrow. "You didn't marry her, did you?"

Brog looked up at the sky, then down at Wren. "Are you going to test the alicorn?"

"You did! You married Vronika!" Tal smacked his knee and chuckled.

"She is very persuasive," the giant said, as they all laughed.

"Congratulations," Drew said, reaching up to clap him on the shoulder. "I hope you'll be happy."

"I think we will," Brog beamed.

"That's so adorable," Ming Li said. "Brog deserves happiness."

Brog's grin stretched from ear to ear. "It has been an adventure so far. Our groups have different fighting styles. We have been sparring, and we have all learned a lot."

"Can you beat Vronika in a fight?" Tal asked.

"I do not see what that has to do with anything."

Ming Li snorted. "I take that as a no."

"The desert giants have different ways of doing things," Brog said. "I don't want to say they have no standards when they fight, but they come close. In my opinion, we at Meegore are more disciplined. We do not fight dirty. With the desert giants, there are no rules."

"What does Haltina think about the desert giants?" Drew asked.

"She is polite," Brog said, studying his feet, "But I do not believe she enjoys their company. She sees the necessity of joining our groups. Haltina is a sensible woman."

"I still can't believe you got married just like that," Tal said. "I was sure Nalisha was wrong."

Graham nodded. "That means we owe Nalisha some medicine."

"You boys really shouldn't be betting," Drew scolded, still smiling. "It's a bad habit to get into."

Tal grinned. "We didn't think we would lose."

"Nobody ever does. Are you going to take the alicorn for a ride, Wren?"

"Yes," Wren said. "It will be nice to be up in the sky. The non-cloudy sky. Does anyone want to come with me?"

Graham froze. Getting on animals was not his favorite thing, but he would be with Wren. Tal bumped his shoulder into Graham's and motioned to Wren with his head.

Wren looked away from the alicorn when no one answered. "Nobody?"

"I will," Graham heard himself say. Wren beamed. She mounted the animal and waited.

Drew grabbed Graham's arm and leaned into him. "When I said Wren could date when she was sixteen, I meant seventeen," he whispered so only Graham could hear. Well, Graham and Ming Li, if the snort from Ming Li was any sign.

"There's no crate to stand on," Tal smirked. "I bet Graham can't get on." Graham side-eyed his friend and walked up to the enormous creature. Before he could decide how to get on without his friends making fun of him, Brog lifted him up and put him on the alicorn.

"Uh, thanks," Graham said, ignoring Tal's grin.

"Are you ready?" Wren asked, excitement dripping from her voice.

"Sure," Graham lied. Wren prodded the animal, and it ran through the trees. Graham's heart pounded in his chest. This wasn't his first time on an alicorn, but he was still shaking. He hoped Wren couldn't tell.

"Here we go!" she called as they left the ground. Graham closed his eyes. He was pretty sure he left his stomach on the island. "This is so great!" she exclaimed.

"Great," Graham mumbled, keeping a tight hold on her waist.

When they got higher than was probably necessary, they leveled out and Graham's heart started to beat normally. Sweat dripped down his forehead.

"Takeoff is my favorite," Wren said.

"Yeah, it's great," Graham said.

Wren laughed. "You don't sound convincing."

"It's like a rollercoaster. It's terrifying, but fun at the same time."

"What's a rollercoaster?"

"Once we finish with all this Dark Cloud business, you can come with me to Earth and I'll take you on one. You'll love it."

"Sounds great," she said as they dove. Graham closed his eyes again and clamped his mouth shut. He would not give Tal the privilege of hearing him scream. They landed and Graham realized he hadn't left his stomach behind on takeoff. If he had, it wouldn't be tumbling like it was.

They trotted toward the others. "That was short."

"Yeah, well, we have things we need to do. We can't just forget about the world because it's my birthday."

Graham smiled. That was one reason he liked Wren. She cared about others.

"That's a beautiful animal," Tal said as they reached the group. "It makes me miss Lazreelle."

"Graham looks like he's going to puke," Ming Li said, watching Graham slide from the alicorn.

"I'm thinking about it." He walked around for a minute, waiting for his stomach to settle.

Ming Li tilted her head. "Sen just sent me a message. He said that Brake wants to talk to everyone in Flordillia."

"I'll take the alicorn," Brog said. Wren nodded, and they teleported back home. She could finally see the sense in teleporting. She still liked making portals, but they were more dangerous and unpredictable.

Graham landed at the troll mansion and followed the others to the kitchen. It had become the unofficial meeting place. Brake and Dovin sat at the table laughing. Sen and Dree were standing next to the counter.

"What's going on?" Drew asked, sitting at the table.

"We've had a glorious victory today," Dovin said, eyes shining. "They elected Zera governor."

Everyone cheered. Graham was happy for his mom. She would be a great governor.

Brake nodded. "Not only that, but she passed a law that a person can run for the fleet even if they are from the other continent. Austra is running to fill one of the open positions."

"Why didn't we know the election had already happened?" Tal asked.

"You all have a lot on your minds," Brake said. "We didn't want you to feel more stress until it was over."

Sen let out a long sigh. "All I have on my mind is the silver eclipse. What if we never figure out how to make it? I thought we would have done it by now."

"Even if you figure out how to do it, now isn't a good time," Dovin said, tapping the table.

"Why not?" Graham asked.

"If you make the silver eclipse and fix the weather, what is to stop Zalliah from messing everything up again? You need to wait until after you defeat The Dark Cloud."

Everyone was quiet. He had a point. It wouldn't be easy to get all the ingredients they needed again.

"So what do we do?" Graham finally asked.

"We need to go after The Dark Cloud," Dovin said, rubbing his temples. "They need to be stopped. Zalliah needs to be stopped."

"Our mission should get easier," Brake said. "You realize that with Zera as governor, she has control over the guards and soldiers in Akkron. She is making it known to everyone that her focus is finding and capturing The Dark Cloud. The rest of the continent usually follows Akkron, so we should have cooperation from all the cities."

"So we don't need to be as secretive?" Ming Li asked.

Brake shook his head. "I wouldn't go advertising yourselves, but we should gain more support. Morale has gone up already in Akkron. People can see that Zera is already acting. Nobody enjoys living in the dark and Zera is giving them hope. She's also put up rewards for information on who is in the Dark Cloud."

"I've given Zera my list of known Dark Cloud members," Dovin told them. "She has issued arrest warrants for them. Hopefully, they are easy to find and can be arrested before they sense we are onto them."

"If we stop Zalliah, the rest of them might fall apart," Tal said.

Dovin rubbed his chin. "Gorbin won't give up. They are our two primary targets."

"How do we find them?"

"I'm not sure. I don't imagine Zalliah would stay on this continent. She's never been a fan of the dark. I wouldn't be surprised if she's spending time on the other continent or possibly on Earth."

Tal laughed. "She's never in the dark anymore."

Dovin raised an eyebrow. "What do you mean?"

"When she went into the cave at Meegore, the magic she got was to excrete glowing blue mucus in the dark."

"I've never heard of anything like that. It should make her easier to find. She's probably avoiding dark places, so she won't be discovered."

"Were you Zalliah's teacher?" Wren asked. "You said you taught her to teleport."

"I taught her to teleport. I taught her a lot of things. My family kept a lot of magical secrets that were only taught amongst us. We also experimented with them over the years. Teleporting used to be a lot more difficult until my uncle found an easier way. It was a mistake to not share our secrets with the world. If everyone has the power, it isn't as bad in one person's hands. It's my goal to educate the world. Put everyone on equal grounds."

"But if you hadn't taught Zalliah, she would be a lot less of a threat," Graham protested.

"She would also be less of a threat if everyone could do what she can."

"Why did you teach her?" Ming Li asked. "Just because you were her teacher? You didn't teach it to us."

"I wasn't just her teacher," Dovin said, looking around the room. "I'm also her father."

"I still can't believe Dovin is Zalliah's dad," Tal said, leaning against the kitchen counter. Everyone else had gone to bed, but Graham was hungry and Tal was in a talkative mood.

"It's pretty crazy. I can't believe Hamble never told us. He said he went to school with Zalliah." Graham said, going into the enormous pantry.

"Maybe he didn't know."

The pantry was full of food, just the way Graham liked it. He scanned the items. He opened a package of crackers and shoved one in his mouth. The door to the kitchen opened and closed.

"Tal, I've been looking for you," Dree said. Graham paused and wondered if he should pop out and let her know he was there.

"Oh?" Tal asked. "What do you need?"

"I've been pondering on things," Dree said. "We have no choice in this marriage arrangement. We need to try harder to get to know each other."

"Graham's in the–"

"Just let me talk," Dree cut in. "I don't need any answers from you right now. We started out wrong and we need to work to fix it." Graham held still and tried not to let the cracker package crinkle. "We haven't really gotten along, and I don't believe it's because we are incompatible. It's just because we've both been against this arrangement for so long. If we try, we might make it work."

"So, you want to go on dates or something?" Tal asked. Graham could almost picture him sweating.

"Something like that," Dree said.

"What are you doing?" Tal asked. Graham wasn't sure, but he thought Tal sounded panicked.

"Just go with it," Dree said, right before Graham heard a kissing sound. If he wasn't frozen before, he was now. He didn't even chew. "Think about it, okay?"

"Mm-hm," Tal mumbled. Graham heard Dree's departing footsteps and the door. He chewed his cracker and swallowed. He peeked around the corner. Tal was still leaning on the counter. "You can come out, just don't talk."

Graham smiled and strolled to the table. He stuffed another cracker into his mouth and tried not to let his eyes twinkle. "Want one?" he asked, holding out the bag.

"No, I don't want one," Tal said, running both hands through his hair. He slumped into a chair across from Graham and covered his face with his hands. "Uuuugh!" he said. "That was so weird."

"Good weird, or bad weird?"

"Bad weird. I can't believe she kissed me."

"I can't believe I had to hear it. Was it that bad?"

Tal leaned back. "It wasn't good."

"I'm thinking first kisses just suck."

Tal snorted. "What about second kisses?"

Graham raised an eyebrow. "I don't know about those."

"Oh, come on," Tal said. "I'm positive Wren kissed you when you were poisoned."

"Why do you think that?" Graham asked.

"Because Ming Li told her something about curing people with love's true kiss, and when we came into the room, she was as red as her hair."

"She was sunburned."

"Yeah, but she was obviously embarrassed. She totally kissed you."

"I wondered if she did. Even if she did, I was unconscious," he said, scratching his head. "Man, that makes me Sleeping Beauty."

"What?"

Graham sighed. "Nothing."

"Now I'm going to feel weird around Dree."

"Maybe you just need to try again. She caught you off guard."

"I really don't want to. I need to get out of this, not make it worse."

"I thought you decided to try," Graham said, eating another cracker.

"Dree is pretty, and she's nice, but I don't want to spend the rest of my life with her," Tal said, resting his elbows on the table. "I don't want to be like Drew. I don't want to regret not being with someone else."

Graham's eyes widened.

"Don't look like that," Tal said, sighing. "I'm not talking about Wren. I can honestly say I'm over Wren."

"Then who?"

"It doesn't have to be a certain person. I can't explain it. I just know it's not Dree."

"What are you gonna do?"

"No idea. I just hope she doesn't corner me again."

Wren was almost asleep when there was a knock on the door. She sat up and waved her hand, turning on the light. "Come in."

The door opened and Dree came in with Ming Li behind her.

"Is something wrong?" Wren asked.

Dree fiddled with her ring. "Yes. No. I just need someone to talk to."

"What is it?" Wren asked, forcing herself not to rub her tired eyes.

"I just kissed Tal," she said, sitting at the end of Wren's bed.

"Oh," Wren said, not knowing how to respond.

"Let's clarify," Ming Li said, frowning. "You kissed him, he kissed you, or you kissed each other?"

"I kissed him."

"Did he kiss you back?"

"I'm not sure. I was nervous."

"So, you just like, walked up and kissed him?" Ming Li asked, biting her lip.

"Kind of," Dree said, shaking her head. "I feel stupid now. I told him we should work things out between us."

"What did he say?" Wren asked.

"Nothing really. I didn't give him a chance."

"So, was it a good kiss?"

"What kind of question is that?" Ming Li muttered. "Of course it was."

“It wasn’t really,” Dree said, looking up at the ceiling. “I was so nervous. That might have been why. Now I don’t know how I’ll ever look at him again. He looked a bit terrified.”

“That’s not surprising,” Ming Li said, crossing her arms. “How would you feel if someone you despised your whole life came up and kissed you?”

“He didn’t despise her,” Wren said, when Dree’s frown got bigger. “He despised the arrangement.”

“I guess.”

“What should I do now?” Dree asked.

“I don’t know. I’m not good with this type of thing,” Wren said.

“Have you two ever kissed anyone before?”

“Sure,” Ming Li said as Wren shrugged.

“What was it like?”

They shared a look.

“Great,” Ming Li said. “It changed my mind about germs. It was Sen, though, and I’d never kiss him again.”

“You kissed Sen?” Dree asked with wide eyes.

“Yeah, it’s a long, stupid story.”

“What about you Wren?”

“Um ... I don’t know how to answer.”

Ming Li snorted. “She kissed someone. He was just unconscious at the time.”

Wren shot a dirty look at her friend. “It’s not as bad as it sounds.”

Dree raised her eyebrow and looked from Ming Li to Wren. “I kind of hoped you would have advice for me, but you sound about as inexperienced as I am.”

"If I were you, I would pretend it didn't happen," Wren said, ignoring the heat on her neck. "That's what I've been doing. Let him decide the next move. He already knows what you're thinking."

"So you kissed Graham, and you're waiting for him to make the next move?"

"I never said it was Graham," she said. Dree raised a brow. "Fine, it was Graham. He doesn't know I kissed him, and I actually did it to save him. I'm not a weirdo."

Chapter 9

"Last time we were hiding here, you knocked us out and tied us up," Tal said to Sen as they squatted behind a boulder in Boztoll. Graham rubbed his head at the memory.

Sen shrugged. "Yeah, well, this time you didn't jump out of a bright portal to announce your arrival."

"They've done a fast job adding street lights," Graham said, observing the lights lining the city. "Now that the entire continent is dark, do you suppose there are still Dark Cloud members here? They probably don't need to be."

"If Zalliah wasn't lying to Wren when she told her about her plan for Boztoll, then I bet there are still some here," Tal said.

"I'm in place," Ming Li's voice came into Graham's mind.

"Ming Li's ready."

"So are Wren and Austra." Tal said.

"Brake, Hamble, and Drew said they were ready a few minutes ago," Sen said, peering over the boulder. They had decided to have certain people talk to each other so that those who couldn't communicate easily wouldn't get headaches.

"We already know Hedder and Brog are ready," Graham said, trying to count the members in their group. "So we're only waiting on Hamble and Dovin?"

"Yes," Tal affirmed. "You know, this entire thing would be easier if Dovin would tell us how to block people's magic."

"I think he's right," Sen said. "The more people who can do it, the more dangerous it might be. I don't want to run into people who can block me."

"I bet he just wants to be the only person in the world who can do it."

Graham wasn't sure what he thought about it. "Let's just hope he really can block the entire city. I wish they had let us go to Earth to get some tasers. I don't get why they think that's a bad idea."

"If we bring weapons from a different world, we would bring more problems here," Sen said.

Graham nodded. "Brake and Dovin are ready."

"Now it's up to Li," Tal muttered. "I don't know if this is a good idea. Last time she blew away the clouds, she ended up in terrible condition and they weren't close to as bad as they are now. These clouds aren't letting any light in."

"Too late to change now," Graham said, keeping an eye on the road. "We just need to make sure we get her out before any Dark Cloud people come to see what's happening."

"I hope it really draws them out," Sen said. "They might just ignore it."

Tal ran a hand through his hair. "Dovin better know what he's doing."

"Just remember, as soon as she touches the ground, we won't be able to do magic," Graham said.

The plan was to draw the Dark Cloud out by blowing away as much of the cloud cover as Ming Li could. Tal would help levitate her until she disappeared into the clouds. As soon as she got back to the ground, Dovin would block all the magic in Boztoll. Tal, Graham, and Sen would make a beeline for Ming Li, and whoever got to her first would rush her out of the city and take her back to Flordillia. Everyone else would stay hidden and hope that the Dark Cloud members came out of hiding to try to put up more clouds. If they did, they wouldn't be expecting to have to fight without magic.

Graham still thought having tasers would be an advantage. Instead, he had a wooden club and a pouch full of ailam powder. He shook his head, looking down at the hunk of wood lying by his feet. The plan was to throw the powder on anyone that could be Dark Cloud, and the club he brought as backup. He thought about bringing the sword he took to the desert, but he felt more comfortable hitting a bad guy than stabbing them.

"There she is!" Sen said, pointing at Ming Li. She walked out onto the road and looked at the sky. Her black hair was braided tightly to avoid the tangles she got last time.

Everything she wore was black. She left her cape behind so she wouldn't have to worry about it snapping around her in the wind.

Graham watched her rise into the air. She kept her eyes focused above her.

"Don't look down, you've got this," Tal muttered, holding his hands up as he helped her. With luck, she wouldn't be as exhausted this time, with Tal helping her.

"I just saw someone spying on us from the forest," Sen said. "I've got it." He stayed low and disappeared into the darkness. Sen must have better eyes than Graham. Graham could barely make out a tree, let alone a person out here.

"She's on her own now," Tal said, lowering his arms. "I can't see her anymore."

"You keep your focus on Ming Li. I'm going to keep watching the woods," Graham said, squinting into the space where Sen disappeared. "I hope The Dark Cloud isn't spying on us, spying on them."

"Something's happening up there," Tal said. "I still can't see her, though."

"Should I go after Sen and make sure he's alright?"

"Nah. Sendo with a knife is scarier than anything that's out there."

"That's probably true."

"Li must be making some progress. I can see the clouds swirling around, so they must be thinner. I wonder how long she can take this."

Graham looked up at the sky. "That doesn't seem natural," he said, watching the clouds move.

"It's not," Tal said. "They shouldn't be swirling like that."

"What do we do?"

"I don't know."

Graham's eyebrows came together. "She needs to come down."

Tal nodded. "I tried to tell her. She didn't answer."

"It's getting faster. Is she making a tornado?" Graham asked, forgetting about Sen. The wind was picking up and their cloaks were flapping wildly. The entire sky looked alive. Dark blue and green lightning began flashing, and he felt a drop of rain.

"This isn't good," Tal said, running out from behind the boulder. He sprinted into the street and stared into the sky. "Li! Come down!" he yelled. Graham could barely make out what he was saying. Purple and blue swirled around the sky and the rain fell with a vengeance. Between the wind and rain, Graham could hardly see. He jogged over to Tal and tried to look up. Some doors opened and people peeked out before shutting them tight.

"Look!" Graham called, pointing up at a figure jerking back and forth in the air. She was coming down fast. Tal and Graham both put their hands into the air to catch her, but she was moving in such an unpredictable pattern that they couldn't stop her. Graham was panicking when suddenly she slowed down.

Brake came walking towards him, his hands in the air. His brows were knitted together in concentration. He lowered Ming Li's limp form.

Tal pointed. "She's going to hit that house!"

Brake narrowed his eyes and tried to move her closer, but the wind was too strong. "I'm going to have to put her on the top!" he yelled into the wind. "Go!" Graham and Tal sprinted to the house just as Brake lowered her to the roof.

"I'll go up. You stay here! I don't want to levitate. I'm gonna climb so I don't blow away!" Tal called. Graham wiped the rain out of his eyes and watched Tal climb a tree next to the house. Climbing didn't look much safer than levitating. The tree whipped back and forth, but Tal kept climbing. He disappeared over the roof and Graham waited.

"Graham! Are you there?" he called, leaning over the roof ledge. "She's unconscious. I'm going to lower her down to you!"

"Alright!" He yelled back. It was good the house wasn't very high. Brake appeared beside him. "I see her! Keep her coming." Tal lowered her unconscious body until he only had her by the wrists.

Brake raised his hands. "Let her go Tal!" he yelled. "I can levitate her the rest of the way." Tal let go and when Brake lowered her enough, Graham caught her. Tal swung his legs over the roof and jumped. When he landed, he took Ming Li from Graham.

"Li, are you alright?" he asked.

She looked up at him and smiled. "I'm not sure." Her head drooped and Tal frowned. "Did Dovin block the magic?" he asked.

"No," Brake said. "Get her out of here."

Tal nodded and teleported away.

"Now what?" Graham asked his dad.

"We need to find everyone and get out of here. We made things worse."

Graham tried to send a message to Wren, but he got no response. Next he tried Sen. Nothing. "I can't message anyone."

"The storm's too distracting. Where's Sen?"

"He chased someone into the woods," Graham said, pointing.

"Great. I'll go that way. You look for the others. If you find anyone, send them home."

"Alright!" Graham called, running in the direction he last saw Brog and Hedder.

The sky was still swirling with colors, and lightning was flashing violently overhead. This was worse than the regular bad weather in Boztoll, and this time it was their fault.

"What should we do?" Wren yelled to Austra. The wind and rain were slapping them in the face and they didn't know what the others were doing. She tried sending messages to her friends, but the wind was too loud.

"The sky is getting worse!" Austra called back. "Stay here and I'll go see what's happening!"

Austra rushed around the house they were hiding behind and Wren looked up at the sky. The lightning called to her, but she had no reason to do anything with it.

"Got ya!" a man hollered as he grabbed Wren's wrist.

"Let go!" she yelled, struggling to free herself.

He laughed as rain ran down his pale face. "You must be one of those Silver Eclipse people!"

He wasn't much taller than Wren, and he was scrawny. She stomped on his toe and he screamed, releasing her. Wren ran a safe distance and raised her hand to the sky. The man darted towards her. Wren drew lightning down from the sky and held her breath as it absorbed into her.

She let out a slow breath and smiled at the man. Holding her fisted hand in the air, her entire body crackled with lightning. She felt powerful. The man's eyes were as wide as they could go and he inched his way backwards. She took a step towards him and he turned and scampered away into the trees.

The reason they were here was to catch The Dark Cloud. Wren wasn't going to let this one get away. She took off after the man. With the lightning stirring inside of her, she didn't notice the rain or wind. The man zigzagged around trees, but Wren kept up.

"Stop or I throw it!" she yelled. The man stopped and turned slowly around, his hands raised in surrender. Wren held the crackling ball of light in her hand as she glared at the man. She couldn't show weakness, but what was she supposed to do now? "Go back to the city!" she commanded.

The man bit his lip and looked over his shoulder. The rain had plastered his dark hair to his forehead.

"If you run, I *will* throw it," Wren said, narrowing her eyes.

The man whipped his arms around and something crashed into Wren's middle. She fell to the ground, and he took off again. Wren jumped to her feet, rubbing her stomach as she ran. If nothing else came of this night, she was going to catch this guy.

She thought about throwing the lightning, but she wasn't ready to kill someone. Perhaps she could scare him, though. She clenched the lightning in her hand and flung the ball as hard as she could past him. It hit a tree in front of him with a loud crash. The tree immediately caught fire, and the man skidded to a stop. His eyes jumped around like he was trying to make a plan.

He looked frantic, but then his eyes became more focused and he charged at Wren. He plowed into her with his shoulder and she stumbled back, gasping for air. The man convulsed and fell to the ground. She must have had enough lightning left inside of her to shock him. He laid in the dirt panting. Wren stared at him as the rain beat down on her. The tree kept burning, but Wren didn't take her eyes off the man.

"Wren!" Graham called, jogging towards her. "I saw the fire. Are you okay?"

"Don't touch me!" she called out, backing away from him. "I caught that guy," she said, pointing at the man. "I can't touch him, or I might shock him again."

"Shock?" Graham asked, pulling the man to his feet. He glared at Graham, but didn't try to get away.

"I pulled the lightning into myself."

Graham raised his eyebrows. "Wow."

"Is the rain slowing down?"

"Valeena showed up. She's doing something that seems to help."

Wren peered up at the sky. It was still dark, but it wasn't swirling anymore. "What should we do about the fire?"

"I can't put it out and hold on to him."

"I can help," Brog said, lumbering towards them. He threw a handful of ailam powder into the man's face and caught him as he fell. He tossed him over his shoulder like it was nothing.

"I forgot about the ailam powder," Wren muttered.

Brog nodded at her. "I could use a portal. I told Brake and Dovin I would find you. When the fire is extinguished, meet them in Flordillia."

"What about Sen?" Graham asked as he shot water out of his hands and into the tree.

"Sen is accounted for. You were the last two."

Wren opened a portal and watched Brog disappear. When it closed, she sunk to the dirt and stared as Graham finished putting out the fire.

Graham poured one of his sour concoctions into Ming Li's mouth. She grimaced, but swallowed. Her head dropped back onto her pillow. "That should help with the headache."

"Why's it sour?" she complained, glaring up at him.

"I was experimenting. Better?"

"Yeah, the headache is. My body doesn't ache anymore either. Now I can probably sleep."

"Yell for me if you need anything else."

"Thanks, Graham," she said, pulling her blanket up to her chin. Graham left the room and flipped off the light.

Graham flew down the stairs and into the kitchen. He didn't want to miss anything. Everyone who had been at Boztoll was in the kitchen. They all looked exhausted, but nobody was hurt. Dree was even there, pouting at the table.

"Boztoll is going to hate us as much as they hate The Dark Cloud," Tal said. "We probably did something worse to the weather than they do."

"It was only a short amount of time. They know we're trying to help," Valeena said. "I was able to calm things fast enough. I talked to the governor and explained what happened."

"What did happen?" Tal asked, pacing across the floor. "Why did the sky react like that?"

"The clouds are different," Valeena said. "Different from even a few months ago. I'm not even sure they are clouds."

"Did we accomplish anything?" Sen asked.

"Wren captured a guy," Graham said, leaning against the counter.

"Yes, and we have decided to keep him here," Austra said, trying to smooth down her windblown hair. "It turns out we have a use for the basement, after all."

"Why keep him here?" Wren asked. "Shouldn't he go to prison?"

"He will," Austra said. "Right now, he is the only prisoner that we have that might know where Zalliah is."

"Sen, did you catch the person who was spying on us?" Graham asked.

Sen crossed his arms and frowned. "It was Dree." Everyone looked at the princess. She bit her lip and stared at her hands.

"Dree?" Brake asked. "How did you get there? You can't teleport."

"I grabbed hold of Wren's cloak when she teleported, then I hid in the trees."

"Why?" Wren asked. "And how did I not notice?"

Dree shrugged. "I'm tired of being the one that isn't helpful. I thought I could go be an extra set of eyes."

"That could have been dangerous," Dovin said, leaning back on a chair. "We need to know who is with us."

"Yeah, it was dangerous," she said, glaring at Sen. "Sen tackled me and had a knife to my throat. That's the second time."

"Why in the world would you think it was a good idea to hide in the dark and watch people who you know are looking for anything suspicious?" Tal asked. "You're lucky you didn't get hurt."

Dree stood and stomped out of the kitchen.

"Why, oh why, oh why?" Tal mumbled, resting his forehead on the table. "Why couldn't she just be ugly?"

"Give her a break," Sen said. "She really doesn't have a lot of helpful skills. We need to be patient with her."

"How's Ming Li?" Wren asked.

"She'll be fine," Graham reported. "She had a lot of aches and pains from being tossed around, but she'll be able to sleep most of it off."

"Who's going to interrogate the bad guy?" Tal asked.

"I wouldn't mind doing it," Wren said, rubbing her stomach. "He threw a rock or something at me, and he plowed into me with his bony shoulder."

"It should be someone scarier," Tal said. "I vote Austra."

Austra glared at Tal. "You believe I'm the scariest person here? Brog is a giant, for goodness' sake."

"Brog isn't scary though," Tal said. "I mean sure, he can fight, but he's not mean ... Not that you're mean," he backtracked. "How about Brake? I used to be scared of him."

Brake smiled. "I miss watching you all squirm."

"Yeah, you've definitely lost the intimidating presence," Graham said. "It's hard to be intimidated by someone who tells cow puns."

"I can still be intimidating," Brake said, frowning and raising his eyebrow.

"Nope," Graham grinned. "I've also seen you play basketball. It was pretty sad."

Brake's eyes sparkled. "Next time we play octaball. Then you won't be boasting. I'll talk to the man. If I can't get anywhere, we can send Austra."

"Perhaps I should be the one to go to begin with to save time," Austra said, glaring at everyone.

"Austra can do anything she sets her mind to," Drew said. "I vote to send her."

Graham wasn't sure, but it looked like Austra was pleased. He peeked over to Wren and she smiled slightly. Maybe she was getting used to the idea of her dad and Austra.

"Any information would be great," Dovin said. "If he doesn't know where Zalliah is, he must at least know who and where the other Dark Cloud members in Boztoll are. If Austra can't get answers, I will."

"You think you can do better than me?" Austra asked.

"I'm sure I could do better than all of you."

"So why don't you start?"

"Because my way might not be the best to begin with. I should only do it if other methods fail."

"What, are you going to torture him or something?" Tal asked with wide eyes.

"Something," Dovin said.

"Should we be talking to some of the Dark Cloud members that are in prison?" Graham asked, not wanting to think about what Dovin's methods might be.

"We've talked to them several times," Brake assured him. "We were able to get some helpful information, but the people we've captured have been pretty unimportant to The Dark Cloud. They know little."

"Is Karlof going to stay in prison forever?" Wren asked. Wren's uncle had tried to capture them and force Wren to take him to Meegore to get magic. Fortunately, they managed to overpower him.

Brake looked thoughtful. "Now that Zera has the law on our side, we should probably give them all official trials. They should be turned over to Akkron. Akkron has a secure prison."

"That we escaped from," Tal reminded him.

"Yes, but there are only a few people who know how to do that."

"And we might still be there if Dovin hadn't been there," Graham said, remembering the nasty prison bars. "Are you guys going to get in trouble for putting them in prison? I mean, where I'm from, you can't take the law into your own hands and lock people up."

"It needed to be done," Drew said. "I don't see why anyone would care. Well, anyone we didn't lock up."

"I'm surprised Zalliah hasn't tried to break her followers out," Tal said. "We have quite a few now. Shouldn't she need them or something?"

Dovin sighed deeply and looked at the ceiling. "There is something you all need to understand about people like Zalliah. She is in this for herself. No one else matters. That is one reason you never trust people like her. She will do what she needs to do to achieve *her* goals. Everyone else is expendable."

"She has to be loyal to some of her followers," Tal said, shifting his weight against the counter.

"To some degree," Dovin said, looking at him. "That doesn't mean she won't sacrifice her best friend if it helps her get what she wants. You all want to do what's right. Zalliah has never been that way. Even as a child, she was a bully. We worried about her, but nothing we tried seemed to help."

"It always surprises me when someone follows a bad guy," Drew said. "A good person is going to be loyal to their friends, and to other people. A bad person might have alliances, but they will break them to achieve their means."

"Exactly," Dovin agreed. "I believe you kids would sacrifice yourselves to save someone. Zalliah would not. I had hoped there was something that could be done to help her, but after Briggs ... I don't believe she can be redeemed. She's crossed lines, and she will cross them again. She needs to be found and tried for her crimes."

CHAPTER 10

Two days passed and Zera was sitting in a large chair in the parlor of the Flordillian house. Most of The Silver Eclipse were gathered, sitting on either of the two couches or on the floor. They didn't use the parlor much. For being in such a big, fancy house, the parlor was stiff and uncomfortable. Wren had only been in it two times. The only members missing were Brog and Hedder. Zera's long brown hair hung loose to her waist, and her eyes were sparkling.

"It is amazing how much I can accomplish now," she was telling them. "Working in the open is so refreshing after years of working in secret. I feel like I have so many things to tell you. I do not know where to begin."

"You can tell us about the tapestries in the Fleethouse," Hamble joked.

"Please don't," Tal muttered under his breath.

"There are people working day and night on Dovin's list. We have already arrested four people that all confessed to working for Zalliah. I believe we are making significant progress. None of them know where she is, unfortunately."

"How big is the list?" Wren asked.

"There were around fifteen people on it," Dovin said. "I only gave Zera the list of people I was one hundred percent sure about. I have speculations about others."

"It is a great start," Zera said. "Another exciting thing I think you already know. Austra is running for a fleet position." Everyone nodded. "Also, as of this morning, we officially reinstated Drew to his former position, with a full pardon."

Everyone clapped, and Drew stood and bowed. "Thank you, thank you." Wren smiled. She knew how much her dad loved being on the fleet. It had become a part of who he was. "Thank you Governor Zera," he said with a wink.

Dree grinned from the couch. "I love it when good people are in power."

"Governor Zera has an impressive ring to it," Tal said, smiling from his seat on the floor.

"It's exciting," Ming Li agreed. "I'm feeling renewed hope."

Wren studied her friend. She looked so much better. It had only taken one good night's sleep to get her back to herself. They had all agreed to never let her try to get rid of clouds again. It wasn't worth the risk.

"Now the next thing I have to say will be more exciting to some of you than others," Zera said with a twinkle in her eye. "The fleet and I have abolished the arranged marriage law for Akkron, and the other cities are following our example. The kings on the other continent were informed, and they have not protested thus far. Most people believe it was long overdue."

The room was silent as they all exchanged looks.

Tal's eyes were wide. "Wait ... like from here forward, or including the ones that were already arranged?"

"Anyone who is already in an agreement can choose to follow through with it, but they are no longer bound."

"YES!" Tal yelled, jumping to his feet. "YES! YES! YES!" He jumped up and down and hurried over to Zera and pulled her to her feet and wrapped her in a hug.

Wren laughed at the surprised expression on Zera's face. After she got over her surprise, she smiled and hugged him back. Valeena was grinning from her seat, but she didn't look surprised. The adults had probably already been told. The only person not smiling was Dree. She was sitting quietly on the couch with her hands folded in her lap.

"This is the best day ever!" Tal said, running his hands through his hair. "I feel like an enormous weight has been taken off of me!" He gazed quickly around the room and stopped when his eyes fell on Ming Li. He grabbed her by the hand and pulled her to her feet.

"What are you doing?" she asked, putting her hands on her waist. "You've gone crazy."

"I feel crazy," he said. He lifted Ming Li off the ground and spun her in a circle. She squealed as everyone else watched in confusion.

"He has gone crazy," Graham said, so only Wren could hear. She nodded in agreement.

Tal put her back on the floor and peered into her eyes. "Li, I'm sorry for every annoying thing I've ever said to you."

"Okay ..." she said, narrowing her eyes. "You're getting creepy."

Tal smiled and leaned down and kissed Ming Li on the lips. Wren's hands flew over mouth and she looked at Graham. She hadn't seen this coming. Hamble was snickering in the corner.

"Tal, really," Valeena scolded. "You're in a room full of people."

Tal pulled away and Ming Li was staring at him with eyes the size of octaballs. "She's right," he said. "You wanna go into the hallway?"

"I ... I ... um ...what?" Ming Li stuttered, putting her hands to her cheeks.

"Excuse me," Dree said, making her way across the room. She disappeared around the corner. Wren felt a pang of sadness for the princess.

"Are you coming?" Tal asked, holding his hand out to Ming Li.

She smiled. "Yes, I'm coming." She grabbed Tal's hand, and they both rushed out to the hallway.

Hamble chuckled. "I love hanging around with young people. It's so refreshing."

"You're really going to let them go out in the hallway together?" Drew asked Valeena.

"Sure, why not?"

"You know what they're going to be doing out there."

Hamble snorted. "Probably the same thing you would do if you were alone in the hallway with Austra."

"Hamble, I can take you down without even mussing my hair," Austra threatened.

"Give them a minute and then you better go talk to them," Drew insisted.

"Loosen up, Drew," Valeena said with a smile and a wink. "I'll give them two minutes. After that, I'll clear the hallway for you."

"Do you really believe this is a good idea?" Wren asked as they stood outside Jaaz's door. She was clasping her cloak around herself and frowning. The porch light made her hair glow a rosy copper.

"I think so," Graham said. "Jaaz is probably having an awful week. My mom said his parents were arrested, and now with arranged marriages being a thing of the past, there's probably no way he's ever going to win Solia." Jaaz wasn't really a friend, but Graham felt like he would need one.

"Alright. I'm sure it's going to be weird, though."

"Everything with Jaaz is weird." Graham knocked on the door. "It's people like him that keep life interesting."

The door opened, and Jaaz stood there in a bright blue tunic with green pants. At least his shoes were on the right feet.

"Hey guys!" Jaaz said. "Man, it's good to see people! Ever since it's been dark, nobody visits anymore. Well, nobody except Solia. Come in. She'll be glad to see you." He turned and bounced down a brightly lit hallway.

"Come on," Graham said when Wren hesitated.

"I don't want to see Solia," she whispered.

"I'll protect you," Graham said with a grin.

Wren grumbled, but followed him into the house.

"In here," Jaaz said, ushering them into a room. Solia sat on a chair, reading a book. Her pink tunic was perfect as usual, and a neat blonde ponytail hung down her back. "Look who's here."

"Hi Graham. Hey Wren," Solia said with what appeared to be a genuine smile. "We've been hearing good things about you guys."

Wren blinked twice and looked at Graham. He just smiled and sat on the couch. She sank down next to him.

"So, what brings you here?" Jaaz asked, sitting on the armrest of Solia's chair. Graham wasn't sure what to say. What if Jaaz didn't realize his arranged marriage no longer counted?

"We just came to see how you're doing," he said. "There have been a lot of changes now that my mom is the governor."

"Yeah, Governor Zera is pretty great," Solia said. "I bet she has the sun shining again anytime now."

"I doubt Zera can do that," Jaaz said. "But I'm sure The Silver Eclipse will work it out. You are all chosen, after all."

"Did you hear about arranged marriages?" Graham asked carefully.

"Oh yeah," Jaaz said. "That should make Tal happy. He seemed a bit annoyed by those."

"Tal had an arranged marriage?" Solia asked. "To Wren?" Graham was surprised she didn't appear annoyed. It wasn't that long ago she had been interested in Tal.

"No," Wren said quickly. "We've only been friends."

"What about that time he kissed you?" she asked, tilting her head.

Graham turned his head to study Wren. Red crept into her cheeks and she shook her head. "That was just on the cheek and he was just goofing around."

"I'm glad my parents never tried to arrange my marriage," Solia said, smiling up at Jaaz. He smiled back. Jaaz must not have told her that her parents had arranged her marriage, and to Jaaz. "Jaaz and I are dating," Solia said. "My parents never would've picked someone like him for me."

"You're dating?" Graham asked, smiling. Who would have thought? Graham and Tal had tried to help Jaaz catch Solia's attention, but they didn't really imagine she would fall for him. He must have stopped using his socks as tissues.

"Yep," Jaaz said. "And we aren't just secret friends anymore. Everyone at school knows we're dating."

"Jaaz is so great," Solia gushed. "He's helped me realize there is more to life than being beautiful and popular. My life is so much better now."

"Being popular is kind of fun," Jaaz said. "Apparently, anyone who dates Solia becomes cool."

Graham shook his head and grinned. "How are other things?"

"Well, my parents got arrested because they're evil and all. That was a bit of a bummer until Zera told me I'm technically old enough to live here by myself. She came here in person to tell me. That was good of her."

"Well, we just wanted to check in and make sure you were doing alright," Graham said, standing. "We can't stay. We have a lot going on."

"Let us know if we can help with anything," Solia said as they left the room.

Jaaz followed them to the door. "Isn't this great?" he said with his voice low. "She likes me without being forced to."

"I'm happy for you," Graham said, clapping him on the back.

Jaaz leaned in and whispered loudly into Graham's ear. "Did you ever tell Wren that her eyes were beautiful?"

"Ugh, Jaaz!" Graham said, rubbing his ear. He hated when people whispered so close.

"Well?"

Graham looked at Wren. She was looking at the floor with a small smile on her lips.

"I told her."

"Good, good. We're both doing well then. Next time, you should tell her that her hair is the color of a fox. A red fox. You have to be specific because there are white, tan, brown, and black. You don't want her to feel confused."

"Thanks, Jaaz," Graham said with a small grin.

Wren opened the door and bolted out. Graham followed, waving at Jaaz.

"That guy is so strange," she said. "He must be a miracle worker, though. That's the only time I've ever seen Solia act pleasant."

"I'm glad he's happy," Graham said as they walked down the dimly lit street. They were meeting his mom at the Fleethouse. "I know he betrayed us that first time, but I believe he's a good guy overall."

"So, are you going to find a girl for Hamble or Hedder now?" Wren joked.

"Why does everyone think I should be a matchmaker? I'm really not good at it. Tal's better. Well, he enjoys it at least. Speaking of Tal ... he kissed you?"

"On the cheek! He was just trying to make Solia jealous."

Graham smiled. It was too dark to see if she was blushing.

"Did it work?"

"She looked really mad, so I guess."

"What do you think about Tal and Ming Li?"

"That was totally unexpected," she said. "I had a suspicion she was starting to like him, and he seemed jealous of Sen, but I didn't see it coming. Did you?"

"I thought he liked her a while back, but then he told me she was like a little sister. It's going to make things weird for a while."

"Only if they keep kissing in front of everyone."

"I'm a little jealous," Graham said, looking sideways at Wren. She stumbled, and he steadied her as they continued down the street.

"Jealous that he kissed her?" she finally asked.

"Jealous that it happened when he was conscious."

Wren stared straight ahead. He knew. No. She would not be embarrassed. She was always the one getting embarrassed. She took his hand and looked up at his mischievous smile.

"You should be," she said. "Tal can go up and kiss a girl, while you have to fake being unconscious."

"Burn," he said with a laugh. Wren's heart fluttered in her chest. "Why did you kiss me, anyway? You probably only needed to touch me to make the ring work."

"I forgot about the ring," Wren admitted. "Ming Li told me I needed to kiss you because of some fairy tale she knows. It sounded ridiculous to me. Then Tal agreed it was worth a try. I wasn't going to, but I wouldn't have been able to live with myself if you died and I didn't try."

"Well, I appreciate being alive. Thank you. I'm glad Ming Li didn't try."

"According to her story, it wouldn't have worked for her."

"Why not?"

Wren dragged every ounce of courage she possessed to the surface. She stopped walking and when he turned to look at her, she reached for his other hand. "Because she said it had to be true love's kiss ... and Ming Li isn't in love with you."

Graham's eyes widened. She hoped he couldn't tell she was shaking. He gazed into her eyes and moved forward.

Wren couldn't take the suspense. Placing her arms around his neck, she went on to her toes and kissed him. He wrapped his arms around her and kissed her back.

Wren pulled away and looked up at Graham, keeping her arms around his neck. She had to make sure he wanted to kiss her.

He smiled down at her. "You know, your hair is the color of a fox." He leaned down and kissed her quickly. "A red fox."

"I can't believe you just said that," Wren said, pushing her face into Graham's shoulder.

Graham chuckled as he squeezed her. "Stuff like that works for Jaaz."

"You don't need Jaaz's lines."

"Well, I would have just said that you're foxy, but I don't know if that's a compliment here."

"What is going on?" Drew's voice boomed from behind her. Wren jumped back and spun around to see her dad storming towards them.

"Oh, man," Graham said, running a hand over his hair. "I can't take another one of these conversations."

"I'll handle it," Wren said, trying to sound confident. "Dad, what are you doing here?"

"What am I doing? What are you doing?" he asked, placing his hands at his waist. "Graham, I thought I told you no dating until she's seventeen."

Wren frowned. "You said sixteen."

"I changed my mind. I told Graham on your birthday."

"Yeah, well, we weren't dating."

"Then what were you doing?"

Wren bit her lip. "Not dating," she said defiantly. "Dating is agreeing to do activities together."

"It's also ... it's also ... what you were doing here in the street!" Drew said, throwing his arms into the air. "And you are always doing things together!"

"Yeah, but with the others as well." Wren rarely got into arguments with her dad, and she hated it.

"Just because Valeena is too lenient with Tal doesn't mean I'm going to follow her lead. I saw you hugging."

"Hugging? Right," Wren said, peeking at Graham. He shifted his weight from one leg to the other and frowned. Was the hug all her dad saw?

"Wait, did he kiss you? You both look far too guilty."

"Dad! Come on!" Wren protested, folding her arms. "What are you doing out here, anyway?"

"Right ..." he said, rubbing his chin. "Zera told me you would be coming from Jaaz's house. I tried to send you a message, but you were obviously not paying attention. Someone broke into our prison. A bunch of the prisoners escaped."

"Oh man," Graham muttered.

"Karlof was one of the people that got away. I'm afraid he might come after you again. I need to go with Zera and some others. You two need to get back to the house and stay with Brog."

"We can help," Graham offered.

Drew shook his head. "No. We need you all to stay safe. Go somewhere no one will see you before you teleport. Behind a house or something."

"Alright," Wren said. Drew turned and sprinted towards the Fleethouse.

"And no dating!" He called over his shoulder.

"Come on," Graham said, grabbing Wren's hand and jogging away from the streetlights. They ran between two houses and stopped. There were no windows on the sides of the houses, so this was as good of a place as any to teleport from. "And we are dating," Graham said. "Right?"

Wren felt heat creeping up her neck. "Right." Graham leaned down and kissed her again. Today was the best day ever. A wave of sleepiness came over her. Was Graham still kissing her? She might be falling. Why was she so confused?

Graham yawned and inhaled a mouth full of dirt. His eyes popped open, and he realized he was lying on his stomach on the ground. He spit the soil from his mouth and pushed himself onto his hands and knees, and peered into a grove of trees and purple crystals. Meegore.

"Are you alright?" Wren asked from behind him. He turned around to see Wren, sitting on the ground next to Karlof. He was holding a large knife. His brown, shaggy hair was even more unkempt than usual. The ugly scar running across his face made his mean smile even more intimidating.

Jumping to his feet, Graham tried to shoot a bolt of ice at the man. Nothing.

Karlof laughed. "You really think I'm going to let you do magic?"

"How did you get us here?" Graham asked. Wren's uncle had lost his magic years ago. There was no way he teleported them.

"I made some friends in prison," he said, getting lazily to his feet. "One of them owed me a favor. He got off pretty easy in my opinion. You two were a lot easier to catch than I thought you would be. I'm glad we came upon you while you were ... distracted."

"Why did you take Graham?" Wren asked, glaring at her uncle. "You don't need both of us to get into the cave."

"Yes, well, I'm not willing to hurt you," Karlof said, shrugging. "I don't mind hurting him. That will keep you obedient."

Graham rubbed his sticky arm. Rednax venom. That's why they couldn't do magic.

"I don't understand why you had to be this way," Wren said, getting to her feet. "You could have told me what happened to your magic and asked me to bring you to the cave."

"The rest of the group didn't want you taking anyone in, and I wasn't really a part of the group. They wouldn't have let you take me."

"Maybe not right away, but they would have eventually."

"We aren't doing 'what ifs.' That's a waste of time," he growled. "Now the three of us are going to go into the cave to get me some magic. After that, you can go on your way."

"Where's your friend that helped bring us here?" Graham asked, scanning the trees.

"He's around," Karlof said. "He'll stick around until I get what I came for. Now let's walk." He motioned them in front of him with the knife.

"What's keeping the giants from stopping you?" Wren asked as they walked.

"The giants are all on the other side of the island having some sort of party. They left only one giant guarding the cave."

"And what? We tell him you're here peacefully? I'm sure he'll believe that," Graham said, looking back at Karlof's knife.

"Yeah, I thought that might be a problem. That's why my friend knocked him out. I wouldn't have to result to this kind of violence if Brake handed out ailam powder to everyone, the way he does to you. I only had enough for the two of you, and it wasn't enough to keep you out for long."

"Ailam powder must be easy to get," Graham protested. "We usually have it."

"That's because everyone worries about you, so they give it to you to waste. Ailam powder is made by the giants, and they are particular about who gets any."

"Zalliah had some," Wren said. "Why would they give it to her?"

"Yes," Karlof said, rolling his eyes. "And I'm sure she came by it legally."

Graham took Wren's hand as they walked. She looked up at him with a half smile.

"And what does Drew think about this?" Karlof asked. "I can't imagine him allowing it. He doesn't like anyone to enjoy life."

Wren shot him a look over her shoulder and kept walking. "My dad's a good person. You just can't see it past your own problems."

"If he was such a good person, your mom would still be here."

"That isn't true," Wren protested. "Her death wasn't his fault. You just want someone to blame."

"If it wasn't for him, she never would have gotten mixed up with those people."

"If you want to blame someone, why not Fria? She's the one that pushed her off the cliff."

"I can blame more than one person," Karlof growled. "And I've already had my revenge on her."

Wren dropped Graham's hand and jerked to a stop. She spun to face her uncle. "What do you mean?"

"I mean, Fria was one of the others who escaped. Escaped for a few minutes, anyway. I'm not going into detail, but I made sure she won't be pushing anyone else off a cliff."

"You killed her?" Wren asked in alarm.

"Keep walking," Karlof commanded. Graham put an arm around Wren's shoulders and led her towards the cave. She sniffled and wiped at her eyes. Despite everything her uncle had done up to this point, Graham knew Wren still cared about him.

They passed the large crystal and two of the sides lit up to a magnificent purple. A giant was slumped to the side.

The rock slid away, revealing the opening in the cave. They all stopped and stared into the dark abyss.

"Are you crying?" Karlof asked.

Wren shook her head before resting it on Graham's shoulder. He held her closer.

"You should thank me, Wren. Fria deserved what she got. She killed Magnalee. I did the world a service."

Wren sniffed. "It wasn't your job to decide what she got. After we get out of here, I hope I never see you again. You are not the person I always believed you were, and it breaks my heart."

"Take some time to think this through, Wren. She deserved it. I am the person you have always known. I love you and I wouldn't ever hurt you."

"Are you serious right now?" Graham asked, facing the large man. "You don't drug someone you love and threaten them."

"I'm only doing what has to be done," he said, frowning.

"No. You are doing what you want to be done."

"Let's just go," Wren said, catching Graham's hand. "The sooner we get through, the sooner I never see him again." Graham pulled out his dragon scale, and it lit up the stairs. It had gone out before, but he boiled it again and started carrying it with him.

"Why do I keep ending up here?" Wren asked. "I hate this place."

"Slow down," Karlof commanded. "I can't see if your light gets too far ahead." Graham and Wren kept going at a steady pace.

“I’m sorry we ended up here,” Graham said. “We should’ve teleported immediately.”

“It’s not your fault.”

“I said slow down!” Karlof called.

“Do you suppose Padmire’s here?” Wren wondered as they ignored the man.

“Probably.”

They reached the bottom, and Graham opened the door that led to the slides. He didn’t see any reason to linger. Karlof reached the bottom, huffing and puffing. Months in prison must have him out of shape.

“When I tell you to slow down, you slow down!” he growled. “So these are the slides,” he said, coming near the opening. “From what you said before, I’m not looking forward to this. Now, do I make you go before me or after is the question. Maybe one before and one after.” He leaned over and looked down the slide. “That’s probably the best way. And I’ll take the scale with me.”

Wren took a couple of steps back. She narrowed her eyes. Graham shot her a questioning look, but she wasn’t watching. “Aaaaaaah!” she yelled as she charged forward and rammed into the back of her uncle. Karlof yelled out as he plunged headfirst into the opening. Graham reached forward and grabbed Wren before she could fall with him. They both landed on the cave floor and sat there as they listened to Karlof scream as he fell down the slide.

Wren looked at Graham and did a half smile. “I probably shouldn’t have done that.”

He got to his feet and offered her his hand. She grabbed it and he helped her to her feet. “I love you,” he said, smiling. Her eyes widened, and he motioned to the other slide. "Let's go. We don't have a lot of time."

Chapter 11

Graham and Wren raced through the cave in record time. They stopped when they came to the murky river. Wren kneeled down next to it and rubbed some of the ice cold water on her arms, trying to get the rednax venom off. Graham squatted beside her and did the same. They hadn't had time to talk because they were in such a hurry to get through and find Padmire before Karlof got to the end.

"What if I killed him?" Wren asked, focusing on her arm. "He fell head first, and that slide is not gentle."

Graham shrugged. "I doubt he's easy to kill. He already looks like people have tried."

"But what if I did?"

"Even if you did, he was the one who captured us. It's on him."

Wren pursed her lips. That didn't make her feel a lot better.

"Let's not worry about what might be, alright?" Graham said, drying his arms on his cape. He held out his hand and an orb of light appeared. He let it go out. Once a person got down the slide and asked for light, the cave would magically light up, but now he knew he could do magic again.

Wren stood and concentrated on warming her arms. She must have gotten all the venom off, because they dried quickly. Graham still hadn't learned how to heat himself.

"So, do you want to get on my back this time?" Wren asked with a smirk, trying not to reflect on Karlof.

Graham flashed his white teeth. "I don't see how it could turn out worse than last time."

"I didn't mean to dunk us," Wren said, remembering the time she had jerked back and knocked them both into the water.

"That was so cold," he said, scooping Wren up into his arms. "I'm not taking any chances." Wren wrapped her arms around Graham's neck and pulled his cape over his shoulder and onto her lap so it wouldn't get wet.

Graham stepped into the water and sank up to his knees. "This reminds me of the day we met. Except I wasn't walking through freezing water."

"I was so embarrassed," Wren admitted. "I couldn't believe you were carrying me."

"I didn't think it would be good to leave you in the woods overnight. Especially since I assumed you were crazy."

"It's really nice I can open a portal without getting exhausted like that now."

Graham's teeth were chattering. "A lot's happened in just a little over a year."

"It seems like a lot longer."

"Uh ... since we've been plenty awkward today, can I just get it all out of my system?"

Wren tilted her head and gazed up at him. "Um ... okay."

"Do you want me to ask you before I kiss you? I've heard some girls prefer that."

Wren's cheeks burned. "You don't need to ask. You can kiss me anytime ... unless my dad's watching. Or anyone else. I'm not into having an audience."

Graham smiled and leaned down and kissed her lightly.

"Why? Why? Why?" Padmire's shrill voice asked. Wren and Graham broke apart and looked up to see the small blue bungle hovering in the air. He was shaking his head. His enormous nose hung over his frown and his eyes were glowing. "Every time you kids come down here, you do or say things that are extremely painful to hear and watch!"

"When did you learn to fly?" Graham asked. "And how did you get your eyes to glow?" Padmire looked twice as big as usual. Two large, pointed ears grew out of his head and he was looking more like a goblin than a bungle.

Padmire landed on the ground in front of the water and sighed. "I can't fly. That was levitating. I've always been able to make my eyes glow. I was trying to scare you a bit, but it didn't have the effect I was going for." The pointy ears disappeared, and he shrank back to his usual size.

"You're wearing clothes," Wren said as Graham stepped up out of the water and put her on the ground. He pulled his cape back into place and held it close to himself.

"If I'm going to start seeing more people, I figured I should be more presentable," the bungle said, pulling on the small brown tunic. "It itches something terrible."

"I'll try to dry your legs," Wren said to Graham, kneeling and raising her hands. She concentrated on the heat. She still wasn't good at making the heat go past her own hands.

"I can feel it," Graham said. "You must be getting better. We probably shouldn't take time for this, though. Who knows what Karlof is doing?"

"Everything will be harder if you're cold. Even if Karlof tries to come fast, he doesn't know what he's up against. He's not fast on his best day and being in prison weakened him. He's going to struggle when he has to climb." She didn't add that he might be seriously hurt from her push down the slide.

Graham turned so she could dry the back. "I wish I could learn to do that."

"I'm not saying you should stop trying, but I bet you won't ever be able to do it. You can usually do everything so easily."

"You're probably right. It's dry enough."

Wren stood. "Now what do we do?"

Padmire looked at the ceiling and sighed. "There is an evil man in here. You shouldn't be wasting time. Follow me."

Wren was about to protest and say Karlof wasn't evil, but then she thought about Fria and changed her mind. Graham linked his fingers with hers and they followed Padmire into the last cavern.

"Is he close?" Graham asked.

"No. He's moving really slow," Padmire said. "He's pretty banged up from rolling down the slide. I'll actually be surprised if he ever gets up the wall. He's struggling."

Colorful bubbles floated around the room. Wren grabbed one, even though she knew they weren't important. There was still something fun about them.

"I can't believe I didn't scare you," Padmire said, kicking at the ground. "I've been practicing ways to scare anyone that might get in. Didn't you see the way my fingernails grew, and my ears? I imagined that would terrify anyone."

"We know you, so you didn't scare us," Wren said, trying to comfort him. "If I didn't, it would've scared me to death."

Padmire brightened. "Really? You aren't just saying that?"

"Really."

"So, what do we do?" Graham asked. "If Karlof can't get up the wall, he's trapped. There isn't food down here. He'll die."

"But he's evil," Padmire said, shrugging. "More than you both realize."

"He's still my uncle," Wren said, feeling conflicted. She remembered that Padmire could sense people's intentions. If he said Karlof was evil, it was probably true.

"He most likely killed Fria," Graham said.

"I know," Wren mumbled.

"I'm not saying we should let him starve to death or anything."

"Could you release each other, please?" Padmire asked, pointing at their hands. "The man is getting higher. He might make it."

"How do you know what he's doing?" Wren asked, letting go of Graham's hand to appease the bungle.

"There is a connection between me and the cave. I know everything that happens here. I only wish I could move around faster," he said, glaring at his webbed feet. "If my wings were a little longer, that would be nice. Aw, to fly. The only way I move fast is crawling along the ceiling. I can only levitate for a minute and that doesn't get me anywhere."

"If Karlof is going to make it, we should leave," Wren said. "He's going to be really mad about being pushed. We should get somewhere safe."

"Now he's going to possess magic," Padmire said. "That's not very comforting."

"But, since the reason he wanted us was to get magic, he might leave us alone now," Graham said, running a hand over his head. "He might go into hiding or something. He's got to realize people are after him since he escaped from prison."

"That's true," Wren said, biting her lip. "Karlof's always been lazy. I bet he disappears to the other continent and we never hear from him again."

Graham tilted his head. "Is that a good thing? Don't you think he should be punished? He's caused a lot of trouble for us."

"Uh, oh," Padmire squeaked. "I don't believe it's going to be an issue."

"What do you mean?" Wren asked.

"He fell."

"Fell?"

"He was almost on top," Padmire said. "I'm sorry Wren."

"Sorry?" Wren asked, a chill creeping up her spine. "He's dead?"

Padmire nodded. "Dead."

Wren took a deep breath. "Okay. What do we do?"

"Go back to Flordillia?" Graham asked. "Are you okay?"

Wren nodded, but a rebellious tear slid down her face. She shouldn't care. Karlof was not the person she had always imagined he was, but he had lived with her and her father all her life. It wouldn't be easy to change the way she felt. She let anger overtake the sorrow. He had made his choices, and they hadn't been good ones.

"You two go. I'll take care of your uncle," Padmire said. Wren nodded and walked to a raised platform. Graham came behind her and took her hand. They stepped up onto the platform and swirled back to the island.

"We need to check on the giant," Wren said, running to the front of the cave. She could hear Graham behind her. Brog was bending over the unconscious giant. He looked up when he heard her.

"Do you know what happened?" he asked.

Graham nodded. "Two of the escaped prisoners brought us here. They knocked him out."

"He is breathing," Brog said. "He will be alright. We caught a man hiding in the trees, so I came to check on Mot."

"Where's the man?" Wren asked. "He's part of The Dark Cloud."

"Tnarg is guarding him. You said there are two?"

"The other one fell in the cave," Graham said. Wren bit her lip and held back a sob.

"I will get the other one back to prison."

"Thanks Brog."

"So much has happened today," Tal said, yawning from the floor of Graham's room. "I can't believe Karlof is dead."

"Yeah, it was pretty crazy," Graham said, lying on his bed with his hands behind his head.

"I don't get how he snuck up on you two. Karlof didn't take me as the stealthy type."

"He had someone helping him. We didn't see who it was." Graham wasn't going to mention the other reason they had been easy to catch.

"Li and I should've come with you."

"Nah. It all worked out. Who can say what would have happened if there were more people with us? It might have been more violent."

"That's true."

"So ... did you talk to Dree?"

"Dree? No. Why?" Tal asked.

"You did a victory dance when you found out you didn't have to marry her. You made her feel bad."

"Why would she feel bad? She didn't like the arrangement anymore than I did."

"She did kiss you."

"Yeah, and that should've made her realize how bad it would be. It was a terrible kiss."

Graham looked at Tal. He didn't get it. "Even if she didn't want to be with you, you probably made her feel bad when you got so excited and kissed Ming Li. She left the room pretty fast. She grew up feeling rejected by her parents, so I'm sure you didn't help her self-esteem."

"I guess I didn't notice. I'll apologize tomorrow."

Graham nodded. "Good idea."

"There is one thing I can tell you," Tal said with a crooked smile. "Second kisses are way better than first kisses."

"So are third and forth kisses," Graham couldn't help adding.

"Yeah, how would you know?"

Graham smiled and stared up at the ceiling. "It's like you said. It's been a busy day."

"Wait ..." Tal grinned, leaning on his elbow. "Did you kiss Wren?"

"A few times," Graham admitted. "Although technically, she kissed me the first time."

"Man. It really has been a crazy day."

"Hamble would have enjoyed it. Drew caught us the first time, although he thought we were hugging."

Tal laughed. "I wish I had been there. I bet he was mad."

"Yeah, but he had to hurry away with my mom, so I probably got off easy. I'm not really looking forward to the next time I see him."

"I wonder how long it will take to round up all the escaped prisoners. It sounds like there weren't really that many. I think Brog said five."

"How did they escape?" Graham asked.

"From what I heard, it sounds like someone blew a hole in the side of the prison. It must have been a desperate attempt from someone. Brog assumes it's because they were planning on moving all the prisoners to Akkron tomorrow."

"Were they aiming to free certain prisoners?"

Tal shrugged. "They don't know. Brog believes they were trying to let everyone out to cause us more distractions."

"Did anyone else we've met escape? Like Melly and her cousin?" Melly was Austra's sister, who was trying to join The Dark Cloud when they captured her.

"No. I didn't know any of them. It doesn't sound like they were very dangerous. Your dad seems to believe Zalliah was trying to keep us away from something she's doing and this would give her time. Some of Akkron's guards are going after the prisoners. The adult members of The Silver Eclipse are keeping watch for Zalliah and anything strange.

"And they don't want our help?" Graham asked.

Tal shook his head. "Doubtful."

"Figures. Hopefully, someone comes and updates us tomorrow. We can do more than they give us credit for."

"I bet all they do is tell us to keep hiding."

"I can't believe Tal likes me," Ming Li said for the fourth time. She was sitting on Wren's bed painting her toenails purple. "He said he didn't realize it. It just crept up on him. I guess when he thought Sen liked me, it annoyed him, and the more he thought about it, the more he realized it was because he liked me. Then it made him mad because he knew he couldn't do anything about it."

"What does Sen think about it?" Wren asked, rubbing her sore foot from her seat on the floor. It had been a long day.

"I doubt he cares about it at all," Ming Li said. "He spent the rest of the day with Dree."

"Does he like her?"

"Not that I know of. He just feels like he should teach her some things, since she doesn't really know how to do anything. Sen can't take helpless people. He was teaching her to make pancakes yesterday. The day before, he showed her how to sweep the floor."

"Do you really like Tal, or is it like when Sen kissed you? Do you just like Tal because he kissed you?"

Ming Li looked up from her toes. "I'm not that shallow. You know, I've thought Tal was cute forever."

"Yeah, but you didn't like him the first few years you knew him."

"I kinda did."

"What do you mean?"

"I always found him funny, even when we didn't like him. It annoyed me that I thought he was funny, so I fought it. Then he liked you for so long, and that was really annoying. I imagined I was over it when Sen came along, but that was short-lived. I did my best to not think about him since we knew he had an arranged marriage and I was sure that if he didn't, he would go after you. The timing worked out pretty well, actually."

"You always say you don't have secrets."

"Well, this one was hard on me, so I was trying to keep it from myself."

"I just want you to be careful," Wren said. "This all happened really fast. I don't want you to get hurt or anything."

"I move fast, you move slow. You would assume as best friends we would even each other out."

"I don't move slow," Wren protested. "I just ponder things through longer than you do."

"You've had a crush on Graham for over a year. You're never going to let him in on it."

"He knows," Wren said, not wanting to go into detail.

"He might suspect, but until you say something, he doesn't. I'm surprised he never tried to kiss you again after that time in the cave."

"We're dating," Wren said, getting off the floor. "Well, we haven't been on a date, but we've decided."

"What?" Ming Li asked, knocking over her polish. She picked it up before it could spill. "What do you mean you're dating? When did you decide that?"

"After we talked to Jaaz. It's been an eventful day."

"So, how did it happen? Who started it? You aren't going to tell me enough. I can already tell. Man, I wish I'd been there."

"I doubt it would have happened if you'd been there."

"So tell me everything."

Wren shook her head as she rummaged through her drawer for pajamas. "No way. I don't want you slipping and telling everyone things at breakfast or something."

"Come on! What am I going to slip and say?" Ming Li asked, rolling her eyes. "I'm more likely to say something and embarrass Tal. He doesn't get embarrassed like you, though."

"My dad is mad enough as it is. I don't want you saying something in front of him."

"Why is he mad?"

Wren hesitated and looked at her friend. "He came looking for us and saw us hugging."

"He's sure against hugging. I don't get it. At least you weren't kissing."

"Yeah, he missed that part."

"Awwww! You two finally kissed?" Ming Li asked, bouncing on the bed clapping.

"Yes, and that's all I'm telling you. I don't want you talking about it to people."

"I'm not that bad. Plus, now I have my own stuff to talk about. You might not have noticed, but I like to talk about myself. I'm my favorite subject."

"I'm not looking forward to the next time I see my dad. He was in such a hurry because of the escaped prisoners.

He didn't get the time to properly lecture us. I keep hoping he'll be so preoccupied he'll forget."

Ming Li snorted. "Your dad? I seriously doubt it. He's probably running through different lectures in his head, trying to find the right one. I wouldn't be shocked if he was writing them down and practicing."

She was likely right. That sounded like her dad. Ben crawled out from under the bed and yawned. He tilted his head towards the door.

"He wants to go out," Wren said, opening the door. Ben ran down the hallway and started pawing at Graham's door. Wren stood halfway in the hall. "He loves this house. He didn't enjoy being cooped up in the old meeting house."

"He's the most spoiled dragon I've ever seen," Ming Li said. "Most people don't let them stay in the house whenever they want."

"He was out a lot more before all of this happened. It isn't really safe to let him run around Flordillia. We don't really understand the trolls or how they treat dragons."

"Trolls are nice from everything I read in my class about Flordillian. We studied a lot of their history and the language. History is boring, though, so I tuned most of it out."

"How can you find it boring? History is like an exciting story. Kings, knights, warriors. It's fun."

"Not my kind of fun, I guess."

"Ben, don't scratch the door," Wren commanded. Ben ignored her.

Graham's door opened, and he stuck his head out and looked down at Ben. "Hey Ben," he said, squatting down to pet the dragon. His relationship with Ben had changed since the maze. Graham didn't seek him out, but he didn't avoid him anymore.

"He likes you," she said.

"Are you sure you don't just like me, so you sent him to get my attention?" Graham asked, smiling as he came towards her.

"It was all him," Wren said, ignoring her warm cheeks. "Although that isn't a bad idea for the future."

"If you call, I'll come running," Graham said, kissing her lightly.

"Gag!" Ming Li yelled from the bedroom.

Graham laughed. "You two should be asleep. Tal went to bed thirty minutes ago. I have a feeling tomorrow might be another crazy day. If nothing else, I'm due for a lecture from your dad. I'm trying to figure out a way to avoid him."

"Me too. I'm hoping he'll be too busy to worry about us."

"I figured out the new magic I got from the cave."

"What is it?" Wren asked. Graham held his hand by Wren's face and she felt warmth.

"Padmire must have heard us talking about how I couldn't produce heat."

"That will be nice. I'm not great at it, but it's been useful so many times."

Ming Li stepped into the hallway. "I'm going to bed. My eyes are stinging. How can you two keep your eyes open? Your day was a lot crazier than mine." She hobbled down the hallway on her heels to avoid ruining her toenail polish.

Wren was tired. Tomorrow wouldn't be fun either. She was going to have to tell everyone about Karlof.

"What's wrong?" Graham asked.

"I'm going to have to tell my dad about Karlof. Someone is going to have to tell my grandparents as well."

"You have grandparents?"

"Yeah."

"I guess I shouldn't be surprised since people live to be over two hundred here."

"They live on an island. A lot of older people prefer islands. They have nice weather. They're far away, so we don't see them a lot."

"Like on the other side of the world?"

"No. There isn't anything on the other side. There's a legend about a third continent that is either invisible or under the ocean. They say that's why there aren't any islands over there."

"Has anyone looked for it?"

"Sure, but it's only a legend."

"You could probably visit your grandparents more now you can teleport."

"Yeah," Wren said, shrugging. "We don't have the best relationship. It's not bad, it's just not good. My mom's parents don't like my dad. My dad's parents are more fun, but we still don't see them much. I actually have great-great-great grandparents, but we only see them once every year or two."

Graham rubbed his chin. "I wonder if I've got grandparents."

"Probably. Your parents aren't that old. And doesn't Brake have a sister in Boztoll?"

"Yeah. I still haven't met her."

"Did you ever tell your dad that Coach Williams is his cousin?"

"Oh, yeah. I forgot I didn't tell you. My dad was really excited. He'd been sad when their family moved to Earth. I guess Coach William's real name is Magni or something like that. He's hoping to go visit him sometime now that he knows where he is."

Wren yawned. "It's neat he turned out to be your uncle. I can't keep my eyes open. I should probably go to bed. It sounds like we might have a busy day tomorrow."

CHAPTER 12

Breakfast the next morning was quiet. Graham looked around at Wren, Tal, Sen, Ming Li, and Dree. They appeared lost in thought as they ate their oatmeal. Brog believed that every day should start with oatmeal, and nobody had enough energy to argue with the giant. Graham wasn't sure if everyone was being quiet because they were tired or because they felt uncomfortable. Plenty of yesterday's activities could lead to anyone here feeling awkward.

"Would anyone like more?" Brog asked from his place by the stove.

A chorus of no thank you answered. Graham didn't hate oatmeal, but he could only take so much before the gag reflex kicked in. Tal put so much sugar in his there was no way it still counted as healthy.

The door opened and Valeena floated in. Her blond ringlets bounced as she made her way to the table. Her eyes darted around the group and then settled on Tal. "King Miadd has requested a meeting with you, Tal."

Tal choked on his oatmeal. "With me? Why?"

"I'm not sure," she said, glancing quickly at Dree. "I can only speculate."

"I can't imagine anything he wants from me to be good."

"I wouldn't go if I were you," Dree said. "He might be more of a danger to you than all the others wanting to go to Meegore."

"He probably just wants to tell you he still wants you to marry Dree," Ming Li said, frowning.

"I'm not sure he cares about that," Dree said, shaking her head. "I bet he has some plan to get you to take him to Meegore."

"Maybe he figures you're with us," Graham said to Dree.

"I doubt it. He's probably not even looking for me. When I ran away, I left a note and told him I was leaving. He should have no reason to suspect I would be with you."

Valeena narrowed her eyes. "It is strange he has had no one out looking for you. A missing princess seems like something to alert the world about. As far as we can see, the people in your kingdom don't even realize you're missing."

"I'm not valuable to him. Probably less now that he can't use me to make an alliance with this continent."

"It still seems strange. I assume they are keeping it a secret on purpose."

"It's possible," Dree said, dropping her spoon to the table. "My father is always scheming. I'm sure he's up to something."

"It is too bad people in power tend to use it poorly," Valeena said, smiling sadly at Dree. "I understand what money and power can do to a person. I let myself fall into the trap much too willingly. It's nice you were able to get yourself away from it."

Dree nodded. "That wasn't the life I wanted. My brother is a despicable person, but I'm glad I have him, so I won't ever have to take the throne."

"But if you took the throne, it would be different," Tal said. "I think you would be a compassionate ruler, especially after your father. The people would love you."

"Thanks," Dree said, looking at her hands.

"So what do I do?" Tal asked. "Do I meet with the king?"

Valeena stared at her son. "I'm not sure. He said you could bring one other person with you."

"What do the other adults think?"

"I haven't told them. They're all preoccupied, and I don't want to bother them."

"What should I do, guys?" Tal asked, looking around the table.

"You shouldn't go," Ming Li said. "We already have enough going on."

"It might be good to find out what he wants, though," Sen said. "I doubt he would really do anything to you when people know that's where you're going. He doesn't want to start a war between the continents."

"If I disappeared, it wouldn't start a war," Tal protested.

"You might be surprised," Valeena said. "You guys have been hiding away for so long, you don't realize how popular you've become."

Wren giggled. "Popular? Us?"

"You are all people are talking about. When they talk about The Silver Eclipse, they are talking about you five, not the rest of us. You opened the cave, you were chosen. Every time someone goes outside in the middle of the day in the dark, they think about you. You are their hope."

Graham took a deep breath. "So, no pressure? We only have the hope of the world on our shoulders."

"People believe in you. I believe in you. It's going to be fine."

"I suppose I should go see what King Miadd wants. Graham, will you go with me?"

"Sure," Graham said, even though it was one of the last things he wanted to do.

"Why Graham?" Ming Li asked. "I can be as helpful as he can."

Tal smiled at her. "Yeah, but you might distract me, Li. And I wouldn't be surprised if you blurt something out that would make the king angry."

Ming Li opened her mouth to protest, then shut it. "You're right. If anyone's going to say the wrong thing, it would be me."

"When does he want to see me?"

"He said as soon as possible," Valeena said. "Be careful. Don't make him angry. Take some ailam powder."

"We always have ailam powder." Graham said.

"We might as well go," Tal said, standing. "The longer we put it off, the more stressed I'm gonna get."

"Sounds good," Graham said, taking his bowl to the sink. He wasn't eager to see the king again, but he didn't want Tal to go alone.

"I hope you guys are careful," Wren said. "You don't want to end up in his prison again."

"There's little chance of that," Valeena said. "The king has to realize that it would cause a lot of trouble. Jump back at any sign of danger. I'm going to ask Dovin to go along and watch."

"You said I could only take one person."

"He can watch from a distance. I don't think the king will detain you, but I can't guarantee that. I would go, but I believe Dovin is better at talking people in or out of things."

"You brought us too close," Graham said as the guards outside the castle all jumped back in surprise. Tal had teleported them ten feet in front of the drawbridge.

"It's a good thing I recognized you," one guard grumbled. "You are lucky to be alive. The king is expecting you. He wants to meet you out here. Don't move."

Graham looked at Tal, and Tal shrugged. Outside might be safer than inside. At least it didn't confine them in a space where they could be easily captured. King Miadd appeared at the head of the bridge and walked towards them. He wasn't wearing armor like the first time they'd seen him. A golden crown sat on his head, and his red cape swayed behind him as he walked confidently towards them. A sword swung at his side.

He broke his way through the eight guards and motioned them away. "Good of you to meet with me," he said.

"We're kind of busy, so could we hurry?" Tal asked. Graham shook his head. That probably wasn't the best way to talk to a king.

King Miadd smiled, rubbing his brown goatee. "Young people are always in a hurry. Well, luckily for you, I'm in a hurry as well."

"I'm guessing you're going to try to get into Meegore? We don't need your water anymore."

"Yes, I know," the king smiled. "I'm not as daft as my daughter seems to think I am. She took water from the well. Some of us can put two and two together. She's with you, or she was. I imagine she bribed you to do something."

"If you don't want to get in the cave, what do you want?" Graham asked.

"I didn't say I didn't want to get into the cave," he said, flashing his white teeth. "But there is so much more to it than that. I want unlimited access to the cave."

Tal laughed. "Oh? Is that all?"

"Anytime I want, you take me there."

"No chance," Tal said.

"If you don't agree to my terms, I'm afraid I'm going to side with her," the king said, pointing behind them. Graham turned his head, even though he knew who he was going to see.

Zalliah stood twenty feet from them. She smiled and waved. Her brown hair fell around her shoulders and she was wearing an impractical light yellow dress with a blue cloak.

"I thought you were smarter than that," Tal said. "If you side with her, she's going to overthrow you, eventually."

"She isn't interested in this continent," the king explained. "Now, do we have an understanding?"

"Not at all," Graham said. "Why would we have an understanding?"

"You are trying to fix your continent. How much harder will it be if The Dark Cloud messes this one up as well? Do you want that on your conscience?"

"That would be on yours, not ours," Graham said.

"You really want to ruin your kingdom just to get more magic?" Tal asked. "Did Zalliah tell you about the magic she got when she was at Meegore?"

The king looked sharply at Zalliah. "What magic did you get at Meegore?"

Zalliah strolled over to them as if she didn't have a care in the world. She stood next to the king. "That is neither here nor now. Are they agreed?"

"Why in the world would we agree?" Graham asked, throwing his arms into the air. "So, you're saying if we don't give you access, you're going to let Zalliah ruin your continent and let everyone die? How does that make sense? If your continent is covered in clouds, then nobody can grow food and there's no hope for anyone."

"Yes, so I guess you better agree."

"You're insane," Tal said. "We don't agree."

"It's amazing how stubborn you can be," Zalliah said, not looking troubled. "You've little choice. You let us in, and we will put the next phase of my plan into action."

"And that would be?"

"I'm sure Wren told you. I didn't mean to let her escape when I told her my plan. It's time to clear out the mess in Boztoll and make all the people indebted to me."

"Why would they feel indebted to you? It's your fault it happened in the first place," Graham said.

"Yes, and they've been in the dark long enough. They will still appreciate it. Your mother may be the governor now, but it won't last. I have plans."

"What are your plans with this continent?"

"King Miadd will rule it, of course. With help from Meegore, he can rule the entire thing."

"There really should only be one ruler on each continent," the king said.

"You really think she's going to let you have it?" Tal asked. "You don't know her. She'll want it all."

"Don't be silly, Talon," Zalliah replied. "One person can't rule the entire world. You don't understand me as well as you think you do."

"He might not, but I do," Dovin said, coming out of the trees.

"Dovin, nice to see you," Zalliah cooed. "To what do we owe this pleasure?"

"Miadd, you cannot side with her. You will regret it."

"Do I know you?" the king asked.

"No," Dovin said. "But I can promise you, if you side with her, she will turn on you."

Miadd put his hand on his sword. "I don't believe I invited you to this meeting."

"I have this," Dovin said, pulling a small vial from his pocket.

The king raised an eyebrow and studied the vial. "What is it?"

"A truth serum. Ask Zalliah to take it and then ask her if she's being honest with you. Whoever drinks it has to answer any questions honestly."

"I'm not taking one of your serums," Zalliah said, tossing her hair over her shoulder.

"If you took it, it would relieve my mind," the king said, tilting his head as he watched Zalliah.

"It might be poison," Zalliah said. "I don't trust him."

"You know I wouldn't poison you," Dovin said, uncorking the vial. "I'll take some first." He took a swallow from the bottle. "See? Not poison."

Zalliah grinned from ear to ear. "Your idea's about to backfire on you. You just drank a truth serum! It's too perfect. What are your plans?"

"I came here to save King Miadd from your scheme. I wish I could convince you to turn from this ridiculous plan you've concocted."

"What is the biggest secret you are keeping from me?"

"No," Tal said, grabbing the vial from Dovin. "It's your turn."

"I'm not taking it."

"Then how can the king trust you?"

"He knows he can trust me."

"Actually, I don't," the king said. "Take the serum and then we will continue with the alliance."

"I'm not taking it. I don't trust it."

"Then I don't trust you."

"Don't be as stupid as your reputation says you are," Zalliah scoffed. "You're letting them get in your head."

The king's eyes narrowed. "I have my answer," he said, pulling his sword from its sheath and stabbing it through Zalliah's middle.

Graham sucked in a breath. Zalliah sank to her knees as the king replaced his sword. The king nodded at them and turned and strode away. Dovin dropped to Zalliah's side and pulled off his cape. He pushed it into her stomach to stop the bleeding.

"That's not going to do anything," Zalliah said with labored breath. "Stop touching me," she said, falling backwards.

"Fix this," she sputtered, looking at Graham. "I'm sure you can." Her head fell backwards as she passed out.

Graham looked from Dovin to Tal. They both looked as lost as he felt.

"I've never fixed something like this," he said, searching through his bag.

"Why are you always so stubborn?" Dovin asked glaring at Zalliah, still holding his cape in place.

Graham took out a bottle that should stop the bleeding. "Do I try?" he asked.

Tal shrugged and Dovin looked pale. He moved Dovin's hands and cape and poured some of the liquid onto the wound and the bleeding dried up. The wound didn't close.

"This is so gross," Tal muttered, looking away.

"We'll take her with us," Dovin said, picking her up. "I understand she's evil, but she's still my daughter."

"You can't take her to our place," Tal protested.

"I'll take her to my house," he said.

"No," Graham said. "She's in bad shape, but she can't be free to escape."

"Then I'll take her to the prison in Akkron. I'm sure Zera will allow her a good bed until she's recovered."

"Should we be letting her recover?" Tal asked. "She is the most dangerous person in the world right now."

"We can't just let her die," Graham said. "If she's in prison, that should be good for now. Maybe The Dark Cloud will fall apart without her. We can let it be known that she was captured."

"Then the rest of them might go into hiding."

"We can discuss it all later," Dovin said. "If we get her locked up, she won't be a threat."

Tal sighed. "Okay, but I vote Drew has to fix the cell she's in so that there's no way to escape into the sewer."

"How long do you suppose they're going to take?" Ming Li asked as she and Wren sat on the stairs in the Flordillia house.

"No clue," Wren said. "I'm not going to start panicking for at least another hour," she lied. She was already stressed. King Miadd didn't seem trustworthy.

"We need to do something to take my mind off it."

"Do you want to play a game?"

"A board game, so I lose, or a sport, so you lose?"

Wren shrugged. "Either."

Hedder appeared in the entryway in front of them.

"Ugh," Mind Li muttered. "We need to figure out a way to make teleporting make a noise or something. Like a doorbell. I'm tired of getting scared every time someone pops in."

"You might be happy I popped in," said the former history teacher. "Look what I found." He held up a worn leather book.

"Yay, a book," Ming Li said sarcastically.

"It has a chapter dedicated to the silver eclipse," he said, squashing his way between the two.

"You could say excuse me," Ming Li grumbled, scooting over.

Hedder flipped through the book and held it open. "Here's the list of tasks we already had from the first book," he said, pointing. "It's word for word the same."

"So, it's not helpful," Ming Li said.

Hedder shook his head. "If you look on the page before, it says that the tasks listed here are only suggestions."

"What do you mean by suggestions?" Ming Li asked, snatching the book from Hedder.

"Careful, some pages are loose. It says the tasks aren't as important as the journey of those seeking to create the silver eclipse. From what I understand, it wants to make sure you are worthy."

"So we could've done easier tasks?" Wren asked. "Or tasks that were easier to figure out?"

"Why didn't the first book say that?" Ming Li asked. "We could've figured something out a lot faster."

"The tasks were meant to challenge you," Hedder explained. "The list of tasks was just a suggestion. I don't see why you're upset. You completed the tasks. It says that you need something from each task and you have those items."

"It's still irritating," Ming Li complained.

"I don't know," Wren said. "It might have been more difficult to come up with things on our own. How would we decide what is counted as a worthy task?"

"I guess that's true. It's still annoying, though."

Hedder took the book back and flipped a few pages. "Look at these pictures."

Wren and Ming Li leaned over the book and looked at a sketch of a man pointing his hands at the ground where a bunch of vines were wrapped around themselves. Another man was throwing a ball of fire at the vines. The next page showed the vines on fire.

Hedder turned the page. It had a drawing of three people standing around the fire, holding their hands in the air. Something dripped from their hands and some type of pot was steaming on the fire. A mass of something that resembled scribbles was hovering above the pot.

"I knew it," Ming Li said. "We have to mix the items in a cauldron and cackle."

"It says nothing about imitating chickens," Hedder said, looking confused.

"What's on their hands?" Wren wondered. "Do we melt all the things together and stick our hands in it? That doesn't sound pleasant."

"There are other pictures," Hedder said, turning the page. This picture had a man shooting lightning from his hands into the pot. Across from him, another man was shooting something else in.

"What's that guy doing?" Ming Li asked. "Is it ice?"

"It might be," Wren said, looking closer.

"Then there's this," Hedder said, flipping the page. A picture of a woman with wild hair blowing in the wind was raising her hands high and more scribbles looked like they might be rising with the wind the woman was producing.

Wren giggled. "I get it. Some pictures are out of order."

"I'm glad someone gets it," Ming Li said, leaning back and resting her elbows on the stair above her.

"Isn't it obvious?" Wren asked her friend. "Tal is going to need to bring in some vines and Sen throws a fireball at them. We put some kind of pot full of the items on the fire. I send in lightning and Graham sends in ice. Maybe the lightning and ice do something to the items that bind them together or something. Then we all levitate whatever is in the pot into the air and you blow it up to the sky."

"Hm. It doesn't make sense to me. Why is the pot on fire if it needs lightning and ice?" Ming Li asked, raising her eyebrow. "And how am I supposed to blow it clear up to the moon? I can make a decent wind, but nothing like that. Do you realize how high up the moon is?"

"I'll leave you two to work it out," Hedder said, jumping to his feet. "And you are welcome."

"Thanks," Wren said as he headed for the kitchen.

"Seriously," Ming Li said. "There's no way."

"It's magic. It's possible you only need to get it started and it will go the rest of the way. Or perhaps it's only symbolic, and it doesn't really have to go all the way to the moon. Maybe it only needs to block it."

"What if we do it wrong and ruin all the stuff we collected?"

Wren paused. "No, this is it. I think it's going to work."

"Now's the part where you say we need to read the rest of the book to see if there's anything else that might be useful."

"I'll look through it. Hedder said there was a chapter dedicated to it, so I'm guessing that's all we need."

"So now all we need to do is find Zalliah and the rest of her cronies and then we can actually do it," Ming Li said, shaking her head at the ceiling.

"You don't need to sound so pessimistic," Wren said, smiling at her friend. "This means we finally have hope and some guidance."

"Have you ever made a fire?"

"Sure."

"I mean, besides with lightning."

"No."

"You can't make a good fire with vines like that, and even if you could, they would be gone really fast," Ming Li said.

"You will not discourage me," Wren said.

"I'm not trying to. I'm being realistic."

"I'm sticking with my theory. It's all magic, so it's going to work out somehow."

"I hope you're right."

"Me too."

Chapter 13

Graham watched the healer examine the wound on Zalliah. He had failed. He'd clotted the bleeding, but that was all he could do. She probably needed to be healed from the inside out, and he'd only healed some of the outside. He might have made it harder for the healer to fix anything.

"Don't look so guilty," Tal said, looking around the prison. Zera didn't want to take any chances with Zalliah. They brought a bed and a healer and placed Zalliah in a cell. "None of this is your fault."

"I should be able to fix it. I haven't learned enough."

"Tal's right," Dovin said. "Zalliah brought it on herself. It's all on her and King Miadd."

"But if I knew more–"

"You said it takes years to be a healer or whatever in your world," Tal interrupted. "You've only been learning things for a little over a year and you don't have anyone to teach you. You've done some great things. Don't stress out over situations you can't control."

Graham had already tried putting his hand over the wound to heal it. It hadn't done anything. Why did it work for some things and not others?

"I think she had it coming," Tal admitted. "She stabbed my dad. It seems like it all turned out even."

"When your life settles down, I wouldn't mind taking you on as an apprentice," the gray haired-healer said, glancing up at Graham. "I've heard great things about you. As for this woman, I might be able to help her."

Graham turned to the sound of keys jingling. A guard was letting Nalisha and Tnarg into the cell. "Does anyone want to leave?" the guard asked.

"In a few minutes," Dovin said. The man nodded and left.

"Good to see you're alright," Tal said to Nalisha.

"Ailam powder can't get me down for long," Nalisha said, smiling. "I'm just glad I get the chance to guard the witch now."

"You're going to guard her?" Tal asked.

"Yes. Me and Tnarg," she said, grinning at the tall giant. He patted his sword and nodded. "They want to be extra careful with her," Tnarg said. "Nalisha volunteered us."

"I can't imagine it being very fun," Graham said. "It's cold in here."

"Anything is better than being underground all the time," Nalisha said. "And anywhere is wonderful if Tnarg is there."

Tnarg coughed and looked away.

"You two should go," Dovin said to Graham and Tal. "There isn't any reason for you to stay."

"The fewer people here when I operate, the better," the healer said.

"But I might be able to learn something," Graham protested.

"Now isn't the time," Dovin said.

"The girls are probably wondering what happened with the king," Tal reasoned. "Let's go."

"Alright," Graham said reluctantly. They passed the guard and left the prison. Magic couldn't be used inside, so they had to wait to teleport until they were a few feet away from the building.

When they arrived at the house in Flordillia, Brog was sitting by the fountain in the entryway.

"I have been waiting for you," he said, standing.

"Is something wrong?" Graham asked. "Where are Wren and Mind Li?"

"Nothing is wrong," Brog said, glancing in the direction of the kitchen. "I just wanted to talk to you." Graham and Tal waited. Brog didn't say anything.

"Brog?" Tal asked. "What did you want to talk about?"

"Oh," the giant said, looking around. "Um ... Both groups of giants are thinking about mixing our groups. We will split up and one group will live on Meegore and one will live under the desert. Every six months we will switch places."

"That sounds like a good idea," Graham said, sharing a confused look with Tal.

"Yes. Vronika has lots of good ideas."

"I still can't believe you got married and made us lose the bet with Nalisha," Tal said. "I never would have thought you would meet someone and marry them in a day."

"Vronika is very persuasive."

"That's what Nalisha said."

"Did you give her the medicine I sent?" Graham asked.

"Yes."

"Well, I'm gonna find the girls and get something to eat. I'm starving," Tal said.

"The food is not very good in the kitchen," Brog said, shifting nervously. "Perhaps you should go and eat somewhere else."

"What are you talking about?" Tal asked. "The food in the kitchen is great, and where else would we go?"

"Do you know the lifespan of the average rednax? They live about fifteen years in the wild. We do not know how long they live in captivity, because no one wants to keep them as pets."

"Brog? Are you alright?" Graham asked.

Brog wiped sweat from his forehead. "Of course. Rednax can come in different colors. It depends on the region they are from. We use their venom when we want to block someone from doing magic. Calling it venom is an odd choice. There is not anything venomous about it. You can drink it and it is safe."

"Brog–"

"Have you ever heard that moon frogs can regrow their toes? It does not seem like something that would be useful very often, but they are rather clumsy."

"I'm not–"

"Vronika likes animals," he continued, staring up at the ceiling. "She likes them as much as I do, although she has never seen many of the ones we are familiar with. She knows mostly about lizards and snakes. She really likes seeing new ones."

"Brog!" Tal said loudly. Brog stopped and swallowed hard. "Tell me something, Brog. Did someone come in and switch your body with Jaaz?"

Brog's eyebrows came together. "No. Why would you ask that?"

"Because you're being really weird."

"I do not believe bodies can be switched."

Tal snorted. "So what's up? Why are you babbling and acting nervous?"

Brog's laugh boomed out and echoed across the entryway. "Nervous? I am not nervous. I am just, just ..." he rubbed his head. He leaned towards them and whispered. "The girls are making cookies and they told me to distract you if you came in before they were done."

Tal and Graham shared a glance and then burst into laughter.

Graham wiped the tears from his eyes. "All your sweat and twitching was because of cookies?"

"Distracting a friend is a part of deceiving, and it is not in my nature. It gives me stress."

They laughed again, and Brog sat down on the fountain and wiped his head again.

"Hey," Ming Li said, poking her head around the corner. "Come see what we made for you."

Graham and Tal left Brog to recover and joined Wren and Ming Li in the kitchen.

"Tada!" Ming Li said as they entered. "We made cookies!"

Graham smiled at the large assortment of cookies on the table. Some of them were burned, some were doughy, some were flat, and some looked just about right.

"The middle ones are pretty good," Wren said, smiling at Graham. She had flour all over her green tunic and some on her forehead. Ming Li wasn't any cleaner.

"How long did it take you?" Tal asked, looking around the kitchen. It was a disaster. They were not clean bakers.

"Forever," Ming Li said. "We needed to do something, so we weren't just worried about you two. We thought it would be fast, but it turns out baking isn't something you can just inherit from your mom."

"Yeah," Wren giggled. "We cook more like Brake. The middle ones are really good, though."

"Did you make poor Brog stay out there waiting the whole time?" Graham asked.

Ming Li rolled her eyes. "No. He just kept giving us too much advice, so we finally kicked him out."

"We thought it would be nice to eat cookies while we tell you about the awesome stuff we figured out today about the silver eclipse." Ming Li said. "And you can tell us what happened with King Miadd. I bet it can't beat what we have to say, though."

"I wouldn't bet on it," Tal said, sitting down and stuffing a cookie in his mouth. "Not bad."

"You didn't even eat one of the good ones," Ming Li said, handing him another one. "That's the batch that had egg shells in it. Not my fault. That was all Wren."

Graham looked suspiciously at the cookies and took one from the middle. He took a small bite, hoping to avoid any shells.

"Those are safe," Wren said, grinning.

"Who gets to clean up?"

"We'll get to it."

"It seems like you would have to try to make this big of a mess," he said, looking at the goop on the bottom of his shoe. "Is this egg?"

"That was Ming Li," Wren said. "It turns out we aren't very good at stirring."

"I'm just glad my mom can't see me," Ming Li said, sitting beside Tal. "She never taught me Chinese, or how to cook."

"They're good," Graham admitted, taking another bite. They weren't anywhere near as good as Mali's, but they were better than not having a cookie.

"Wren's weird," Ming Li said. "She keeps eating the burned ones."

"They aren't that burned," Wren protested. "I can't stand doughy cookies. They make me want to gag."

"So, you two missed us so much you had to distract yourselves?" Tal asked, grinning at Ming Li.

"We were just worried you might make the king mad and end up in the dungeon," Ming Li said. "Then we would have to go rescue you, and we have better things to do."

"Come on Li. Just admit you missed us."

"It's not like you were gone for days or something," she said, rolling her eyes. "I think Ben missed you. He had an accident on your bed."

"What?"

"Sorry," Wren said. "He got shut in your room and couldn't get out. I cleaned it up, though."

"That's so gross," Tal moaned. "I guess it's my fault. I closed the door."

"You have so much flour on you," Graham said, grinning at Wren. "Haven't you heard of an apron?"

"Yeah, but we looked and couldn't find any." She smiled mischievously as she walked up to Graham and hugged him. "Now you're covered in flour too," she said, looking at his messy blue tunic. He just smiled and tried to brush off his shirt.

"What's burning?" Brake asked, entering the kitchen with Drew in tow. "What happened here?"

"Don't worry, we're gonna clean it up," Ming Li said. "We made cookies. Don't eat the ones on the left."

"Don't tell us," Drew said. "It's *batter* than it looks."

Brake nodded. "I'm sure it is. Everything happens for a *raisin*."

"Not again," Ming Li whined. "And there are no raisins here. A raisin is the saddest thing to happen to a cookie."

Drew smiled. "That's a pretty *crummy* attitude."

"Don't get us wrong," Brake said. "We understand you kids are *baking* this world a *butter* place." Brake and Drew laughed and everyone else shook their heads.

"Have they caught any of the criminals?" Graham asked, trying to change the subject.

"We have all of them," Drew said. "It's not surprising, considering they were the ones that were easy to catch the first time around. I'm sorry about Karlof. I understand that must be hard," he said, putting a hand to Wren's shoulder.

Wren shrugged. "I'm alright. It's heartbreaking, but it was harder back when I realized he was trying to use me."

Drew frowned and looked from Wren to Graham. "Did Graham help with the cookies?"

"No."

"Then why is he covered in flour?"

Ming Li grinned and Tal jumped up from his chair. He pulled Ming Li to her feet. "Let's go somewhere that's not here," he said with a crooked smile. She nodded, and they sped out of the room.

"Look at this place," Brake said. "Everyone here is going to be covered in something."

Drew crossed his arms and narrowed his eyes at Graham. "It's about time we had that conversation we didn't have time for the other night."

"I would really rather not," Graham said, taking a step farther from Drew.

"What conversation?" Brake asked.

"After these two went to check on Jaaz, I found them hugging each other in the street."

"Oh?"

"Isn't that enough?"

Brake laughed and sat in the chair Tal had vacated. "I'll just watch."

"Look at them," Drew said. "I'm sure he hugged her again. You should talk to him. He is your son."

Brake's eyes sparkled, and he looked at Graham. "Did you hug Wren?"

"No, she hugged me," Graham said with a smile.

"You're going to turn this on her?" Drew asked. Graham shrugged.

"It's true," Wren said. "He was making fun of all the flour, so I was making sure it got on him too."

"See?" Brake said. "All innocent."

Drew shook his head. "What about the other night? In the middle of the street?"

"I think that was me too," Wren said, tilting her head and gazing at Graham. "It's hard to remember. It's been a crazy week."

"Graham, I'm going to ask you a question I asked you once before, and I want an honest answer."

Graham's stomach dropped. Why was this conversation happening?

"Come on Dad," Wren begged. "Can't you just drop it? We've figured out how to summon the silver eclipse."

Brake and Drew's eyes widened. Graham's might have as well.

"No, we can talk about that later," Drew said, refusing to be distracted. "Graham. Have you kissed Wren?"

"Dad! Seriously! Why are you doing this?" Wren's face was a nice shade of pink.

"Let it go, Drew," Brake said, still looking amused.

"I haven't heard anyone say no," Drew muttered.

"A lot's happened today," Graham said. "We need to go meet and talk about the silver eclipse, and Tal and I need to update everyone on Zalliah."

"What about Zalliah?" Brake asked.

"We caught her."

"What!" Wren exclaimed. "Why didn't you tell us?"

"We were distracted by cookies. We didn't actually catch her. King Miadd wounded her pretty badly. She's in the prison in Akkron."

"Does Zera know?" Brake asked.

"Yes. She made the arrangements."

"Let's call everyone together," Brake said. "Everyone can share information."

"I obviously can't get the information I want," Drew grumbled.

Wren crossed her arms. "I kissed him first. Now you can leave Graham alone. Are you happy?"

"Not at all. If you kissed him first, that means he kissed you second."

"Drew," Brake said, clapping his friend on the shoulder. "Can't you hear how ridiculous you sound?"

"Don't stress Dad. It only lasted a few seconds. It was nothing like you and Austra."

"It better not have been," Drew said, raising his eyebrow.

"I don't know why we're having this conversation in front of people. How about this? You let me date Graham, and I give you my blessing with Austra?"

Graham looked at Drew. He could see the conflicting emotions on his face.

"I'll think about it."

"Alright," Brake said, winking at Graham. "Let's gather everyone and make sure we're all up to date on everything."

Graham nodded. Anything would be better than this conversation.

Wren scrubbed the last of the cookie mess off of the table and sighed.

"What are you thinking?" Graham asked, leaning on the broom.

"So many things I can't keep them straight," Wren admitted, washing out the rag. "I can't believe Zalliah was captured on the same day we figured out how to do the silver eclipse. We've been working towards those things for so long. It just seems strange both happen at once. And I'm thinking about my dad. Sorry about that."

"It's alright," Graham said, sweeping a pile of dirt into a dustpan. "It's part of a dad's job."

"I wish he would talk to me and not do it in front of everyone else. In some ways, he's like Ming Li." Wren inspected the kitchen. It was as clean as when they started the cookies.

"I'm surprised he isn't here watching us," Graham said.

"I wouldn't be shocked if Brog were sitting outside the door spying for him."

Graham dumped the dustpan and leaned the broom against the wall. "What did you think about the meeting?"

"That it was a waste of time," Wren said, thinking back to all the disagreeing that had gone on. Some people wanted to make the silver eclipse now while others thought they should wait until more of The Dark Cloud were caught.

"Yeah, nothing productive happened," Graham said, grabbing a cookie off a plate and sitting at the table.

"I bet Ming Li used the meeting so she could pretend she forgot about cleaning the kitchen. I wonder where she went. Thanks for helping me. It would have taken forever by myself."

Graham winked at her. "Anytime." Wren's stomach fluttered.

"Do you think the other Dark Cloud members will give up now that Zalliah's been captured?" she asked, sitting next to him.

"I hope so, but I doubt it. I bet Gorbin will try to take over as soon as he hears she's in prison."

"The clouds are so unnatural. How many people actually have the ability to do something like that?"

"Probably not a lot. I bet the whole thing was done by one or two people. Dovin said Zalliah was always trying to figure out really hard magic that nobody else could do. I bet she's the one who does most of it," he said, biting into the cookie.

"Maybe she's the only one who does it. I wonder if without her here to maintain them, the clouds will eventually clear up."

"I bet at least one other person can do it," Graham said, leaning back in his chair. "Before there were clouds everywhere, they were only over Boztoll. Zalliah was in Akkron most of the time, so it doesn't seem likely that she would be the one to do it."

"But she can teleport, so she could have come every day for a few minutes and nobody would notice she was missing."

"I guess that's true. I still bet she would teach it to at least one other person. And now the whole continent is dark; I doubt that's being done by one person."

"I feel like these clouds are different from the last ones," Wren said, leaning towards him. "Ming Li couldn't blow them away at all. And earlier, when the clouds were over Boztoll, it was dark, but not the kind of dark we have now. I wonder if they discovered a way to make a different type of cloud."

"I wouldn't doubt it. Even on cloudy days, you can see outside with the sun blocked. Whatever's going on here isn't natural. That's why we are going to have to do the silver eclipse, even if it's all Zalliah. I bet she's figured out a way to make the clouds stay without bringing new clouds in everyday."

"What if it doesn't work?" Wren said, her eyes widening. That was something she hadn't thought about. "What if the magic or the silver eclipse only works on regular weather?"

"It will work," Graham said, taking her hand. "I'm sure it will."

"Gut feeling?"

"Yep."

The door creaked and Ming Li peeked in. "Oh darn. Someone already cleaned the kitchen."

"Already?" Wren asked, raising her eyebrow. "It took forever."

"Well, you can't say I didn't come back to help. Goodnight." The door closed, and she disappeared.

"Is it already time for bed?" Wren asked.

Graham yawned. "Already? This day has been so long. This week has felt like a month at least."

"A lot has happened."

"There's something I've been thinking about," Graham said, dropping her hand. "I keep thinking that once we fix things, we'll go back home and life will go back to some type of normal."

"It will be weird to go back to school."

"The more I think about it, the more I wonder if it's possible."

"Why?"

"We're still the only ones who can open the cave. Will it ever be safe to try to live normally?"

"What do you mean?" Wren asked, resting her arms on the table.

"Even if we capture all The Dark Cloud, there will always be people like Karlof out there who want to go into the cave and get magic. Or get more magic."

Wren frowned. "I never thought about that. Maybe we can offer to take people every once in a while."

"Do you really want to spend your life going through the cave with people?" Graham asked, raising an eyebrow.

"No," Wren admitted. "I hate the cave. Does that mean we have to hide forever? That doesn't sound like a fun life."

"We could go live on Earth," Graham said. "I don't really want to leave my parents, though."

"Maybe once it's all over, Padmire can make it so we can't open it anymore. He's the one who blocked it in the first place, from what I understand."

"I never thought about that," Graham said, smiling. "I bet he can do something. We'll have to ask him about it next time we see him."

"If he can't, we could always blow the cave up," Wren said. "That way, it wouldn't ever be a problem again."

"But it wouldn't ever be helpful again, either. And it's big. I doubt we could do a good job of destroying it."

"What are we destroying?" Drew asked, entering the kitchen.

"Nothing," Wren said. "I was just joking about destroying the cave at Meegore so people wouldn't be able to get in anymore."

"That would be quite the feat," Drew said. "A lot of people tried to break into the cave over the years and no one could figure a way in. I don't see that changing now."

"I guess."

"I just came to say goodnight."

"Goodnight," Wren said.

"I'll walk you to your room," he said, crossing his arms and looking sideways at Graham.

Wren grinned. Her dad was so predictable. "Goodnight Graham," she said, standing. "I guess it's past my bedtime."

Chapter 14

"So, Zalliah's going to live?" Graham asked his mom two days later.

"It appears so," Zera said as she mixed berries for a pie. Being governor was stressful and Zera needed a few hours to do something that made her feel normal. She asked Graham to meet her at Brake's house so they could catch up. Well, he guessed it was all of their house now.

"It's strange the way things happen," Graham said, leaning against the counter. "I thought we would end up in some kind of standoff with her, and King Miadd took her down with no effort."

"I am thankful for that," Zera said, glancing up at him. "There are still dangerous things ahead, but I am happy to have Zalliah out of the picture."

"Has she said anything?"

"She is claiming amnesia."

Graham frowned. "She was stabbed in the stomach. It doesn't seem like that would cause amnesia. I guess it could happen after losing too much blood. There's still so much I don't know."

"Lying is not out of her comfort zone. Dovin does not believe her. He thinks she is trying to get us to underestimate her so she can escape."

"She can't escape, can she?"

"No," Zera said, dumping the berry mixture into a crust. "Drew made her cell more secure. Even if she knew about his little hidden way to escape, it would not work there."

"Is she claiming she doesn't know who she is?"

"No. She is claiming she remembers nothing after she turned sixteen."

"That's convenient. Isn't that just before she came up with her Dark Cloud idea?"

"Perhaps. I am not sure when she started it all."

"Is she completely recovered?" Graham asked, grabbing a handful of berries and popping one into his mouth.

"No. She cannot get out of bed. She lost a lot of blood. The healer did his best."

"I felt helpless. The first thing I'm going to do when this whole mess is over is learn more about healing."

"Even if Zalliah had died, it would not have been on you."

"I know. And I get that she's bad. I got overconfident about my abilities. I've healed some things so easily. With Briggs, I didn't get a chance to try. He died before I could even think of where to start."

"Learning is like that quite often," Zera said, rolling out the crust.

"The healer at the prison said someday I could be his apprentice. Do you think that's something I could do?" he asked, wiping berry juice from his hands.

"That would be a good idea if it is something you would like. You can do things no one has done in hundreds, if not thousands, of years. It would probably be helpful to have a mentor, even if he cannot do the same things you can."

"Should some of us go talk to Zalliah?"

"No. I cannot see any benefit to it. I made an announcement in Akkron that we have captured her. Your attention needs to be on whatever is going to happen next."

"I wonder what that will be."

"My guess is that the rest of The Dark Cloud members are going to go into hiding, or someone else will step up."

"I bet Gorbin will," Graham said, watching his mom expertly weave pieces of crust into a neat lattice pattern.

"You are probably right. Gorbin has a big ego, and he was Zalliah's number one man. I do not see the organization dying out, so you all need to be on your guard."

"I wish we could just summon the silver eclipse and be done with it."

"Zalliah has been locked up for two days. The clouds are not changing in any noticeable way. Either the magic she used is very powerful, or there are others keeping it up. You do not want to risk acting too soon and having everything repeat."

"I guess I'm just being impatient. Did the man Wren captured in Boztoll give any information?"

She let out a heavy breath, and pushed a lock of hair from her eyes. "Not at all. Dovin talked to him for hours and either he does not know anything, or he is really good at playing dumb. We moved him to Akkron."

"It seems like he would have to know something."

"We do not know how much Zalliah lets each follower know. I did hear something interesting. Your father told me you are dating Wren," his mom said, looking up with a twinkle in her eyes.

"Unless Drew kills me."

"He told me about that as well. Drew is a good man. He just needs time to get used to it."

"So, you're okay with it?" Graham asked.

Zera smiled. "Wren is a nice girl. She has a strong spirit and a good soul. She has my vote."

Graham felt a lump in his throat. All of his life, he had had little to love. He loved Kaylee, and in his own way, Aunt Temperance. It was so different now. Even though his life had been chaotic since he came here, he was still so much happier. Having parents that cared about him and Wren ...

"Are you alright?" Zera asked.

"Yeah, fine," he said, swallowing hard. "I was talking to Wren yesterday. We're a little nervous about what will happen after this is all over."

"I am sure you two will be fine."

"Not with us. With the cave."

Zera placed her neat crust over the pie filling and tilted her head as she studied him.

"If the cave still opens for us, people are still going to want us to take them in. There might be a lot of Karlofs out there," he explained.

"That is true. What do you want to do about it?"

"We thought about asking Padmire if he can make it so we can't go in anymore. We don't really know how much control he has over the cave."

"That is a good idea. He could probably do it now. Do you really need to go in again?"

"I hope not. It is nice I can finally warm myself up. I doubt I could have ever done it without going inside. There are benefits, but we don't want to become like the people who were getting too powerful and greedy."

"That is smart. Now we should spend more time talking about Wren," Zera said, with a sly grin.

"Should we go talk to Zalliah?" Tal asked, sitting near a stream on the other continent. Wren loved teleporting. It was nice to pop into a place that had sunshine whenever they wanted.

Ming Li flung a rock into the water. "There's no doubt she's lying. It's just too convenient to suddenly get amnesia once you get caught."

"Even if she isn't lying, she needs to stay in prison," Tal said. "She isn't the type of person we can let escape."

Wren twirled a wildflower, or possibly a weed, between her fingers. "It sounds like Zalliah made plans to take over when she was fairly young. Even if she thinks she's only sixteen, she might still have similar thoughts. You don't just wake up one day and decide to make an elaborate plan to take over the world."

"She's patient too," Graham said, sitting next to Wren. "The Dark Cloud's been around for a long time."

"Talking to her isn't going to help us," Sen said, tossing his boots and stepping into the stream. "Zalliah isn't going to spill anything new. She's going to be more guarded than ever."

"She seemed eager to tell me her plan when we were at Meegore," Wren said. "She enjoyed talking about it."

Graham shook his head. "Yeah, but she was planning on taking you with her and forcing you to help her. She wouldn't have told you if she thought you would get away."

"Or she lied about it," Tal said. "And if she didn't lie, she might have changed her plan now that she told it to you. Watch where you step, Sen. There's a crayfish hiding behind that rock near your foot."

"Where?" Ming Li asked, leaning towards the water as Sen moved in the other direction.

"I didn't see it. I just sense it's there. Behind the reddish rock."

"Do they bite?" Ming Li asked, crawling to the edge of the bank.

"They pinch."

"Oh," she said, almost falling backwards as she retreated.

Tal laughed. "It's not a terrible pinch, but still should probably be avoided."

"I've never heard of a fish that pinches. We don't have those on Earth."

"They aren't really fish. They're crustaceans. More like a lobster. Do you have lobsters?"

"Yes."

"We have crayfish on Earth," Graham said. Ming Li looked at him with one brow raised. "Some people call them crawdads."

"Oh, I have heard of those. It's strange there are so many of the same animals here and on Earth, but then so many different ones. I wish I could show you guys a kangaroo. Talon would love that."

"I still want to see a giraffe," Tal said. "Those things sound epic."

"Maybe when this is all over, we can go to Earth and show you a zoo," Graham said.

Wren's head jerked up. She heard something like a low growl. "Did anyone hear that?"

Everyone paused and listened.

"I don't hear anything," Graham said.

"It's a dragon," Tal said, standing and staring into the trees behind them. "She's coming fast."

Everyone that was sitting jumped to their feet and followed Tal's gaze. Sen stepped out of the water and squinted, trying to see.

"Are we talking a Ben sized dragon?" Graham asked, taking a step backwards.

"Nope," Tal said. "We're talking about a huge, only seen-on-this-continent sized dragon. It feels familiar."

A golden dragon popped out of the trees. It was at least twenty feet tall. Graham took another step back and fell into the stream. Wren glanced away from the majestic creature and turned to him. The water wasn't deep, but he was soaked. The water must be warm because he just sat there staring at the dragon.

"They don't eat people, you know," Wren said, smiling. "They don't even blow fire unless they feel threatened."

"It's huge!" Graham said. Tal put his hand out for the dragon to smell.

"She's beautiful," Wren said. "I've never seen a dragon this big. And look at how she sparkles in the sun!"

"She's the dragon from the desert," Tal said, rubbing her head. "The one Zalliah was riding. I wonder why she found us. She's happy."

"I guess that's a good thing," Graham muttered.

"Do you think she'll let me touch her?" Sen asked, stepping next to Tal.

"Sure," Tal said. "Just stick out your hand first so she can smell you. Are you smiling, Sen?"

Sen chuckled as he held out his hand. "It happens occasionally."

Wren grinned at Graham. He was still sitting in the water, looking nervous. "Are you going to sit there all day?"

"I might."

Wren offered him her hand. "Come on. I won't let the big dragon hurt you."

Graham shook his head and took Wren's hand. She should have paid more attention to the mischief that popped into his eyes. Graham yanked on her hand, and

Wren found herself on her hands and knees in the water with him.

"I can't believe you did that!" Wren said, sitting back on her legs. She pushed her hair out of her face and glared at him. "I thought you were way too mature for something like that."

Graham laughed and got to his feet. He pulled her up. "Now we're even."

"Even?"

"For when you dunked me at Meegore."

"That was an accident."

"And freezing. At least this water is warm," he said, taking Wren's hand. "And it's not deep."

"Stop flirting and come pet the dragon," Ming Li said.

"Come on," Wren said, pulling him out of the stream. Graham sighed as they walked closer to the dragon. Wren squeezed his hand. "They really are friendly."

"Maybe, but look at those teeth!"

"They're big, but at least they aren't gross like Padmire's."

Ming Li scratched the dragon's chin, and it leaned towards her. "I've been meaning to talk to Padmire about that. He's ancient, so he needs to take care of his teeth."

"Put your hand out," Tal commanded Graham. Wren smiled as he nervously obeyed. The dragon smelled him. Graham closed his eyes as the dragon licked his hand.

"Breathe," she reminded him. "We don't need you passing out."

Graham took a deep breath and stepped away. "Okay, I'm done."

Wren held her hand out to the dragon and giggled as he licked her. "I wonder if my dad would let me keep her."

"I wouldn't count on it," Dovin said, walking up from the side of them. "From what I see, your collection of animals is running free on Meegore. You don't need any more."

"They love it there," Tal said. "And they love Brog. We don't have a lot of time to take care of animals right now."

"Well, this is Magma," Dovin said, patting the dragon. "I've had her since she hatched."

"So, that's why Zalliah had her," Tal said. "She didn't seem to like her."

"No. She's never liked Zalliah. I have several dragons and none of them like her. She snuck in and took them that day Briggs died in the desert."

"I didn't know anyone in Akkron had big dragons."

"I keep them on this continent. I have a house here with a lot of land. Since I can teleport, I didn't have to live in Akkron to teach school."

"Did you bring her here?" Wren asked.

"Yes."

"For a reason?"

"Gorbin and some others were spotted at the goblin mountain." Dovin said, frowning. "There is nothing good that can come from Gorbin and the goblins making a deal."

Graham ran a hand over his hair. "What do you think he's doing?"

"Who knows? He could be bribing them. Goblins have no moral compass and neither does The Dark Cloud. We need to stop whatever it is they are doing."

"Why do we need a dragon?" Sen asked. "We could teleport."

Magma rubbed her head against Dovin affectionately. "You can teleport to the base of the mountain, but then you are at the goblin's mercy. Will they let you up? Maybe. Gorbin and his followers are climbing the mountain, which means they don't know how to summon the goblins. That's good news, because it means he doesn't already have a relationship with them. If you take Magma, you can go to the top."

"Do we need to go now?" Wren asked. "We aren't prepared."

"I have what you need," Dovin said, snapping his fingers. A pile of supplies fell at his feet. "Brake said you left without capes."

"We weren't expecting to need them," Graham said, pulling his cape out of the pile. "Knives and crossbows?" he asked, picking up a small blade.

"I have dragon scales for all of you as well. Keep them in your pockets in case you need light. You never know when you won't be able to use magic," Dovin explained. "That's why so much magic was lost a long time ago. People were getting lazy. They relied on it too much. It became unpopular to use magic. It was looked on as a lazy person's solution to life. People prided themselves on doing things for themselves. That's why abilities like teleporting were lost."

"I don't get that," Ming Li said. "I would rather teleport. It's so fast."

"Yes, but they had a point. If you rely on magic, you lose other skills. What happens if you use magic for everything and you end up losing your magic? Magic can be a crutch. It's amazing, but you shouldn't rely on it. How many times have you been in a situation where you couldn't use magic?"

"More than we would like," Tal said.

"I don't know how magic works at the top of the mountain. I'm assuming it only works for the goblins since you can't teleport up there."

"I have my own knife," Sen said, a blade appearing from nowhere.

"Are you coming with us?" Wren asked Dovin.

"I will."

"Can we all fit on the dragon?"

"Yes, that won't be a problem. It would be best to teleport to the bottom of the mountain and then have her fly us up. We don't want to waste time. We'll leave as soon as we eat lunch."

"Won't that give Gorbin too much time?"

"No, it's going to take them a long time to get up the mountain. Hedder's going to meet us at the base."

"Hedder?" Ming Li whined. "If Hedder is our backup, that doesn't give me a lot of hope."

"Seriously," Graham agreed. "Can he fight?"

"From the stories I've been told, your own fighting methods are unconventional to say the least," Dovin said, raising his eyebrow. "It will be fine. He's the only one that was available, and he's good with a sword."

"All the others know about this?" Tal asked. "I'm kind of surprised what people let us do."

"You are chosen," Dovin said. "That gives people a confidence in you they probably shouldn't have."

"Well, chosen should count for something, right?" Tal asked.

Dovin nodded. "It does ... but that doesn't mean you should rely on being chosen to save you. There have been many people chosen for different tasks over time, but that doesn't mean they survived."

"That's reassuring," Ming Li said, her mouth curving down. "So you're saying we might die?"

"Anything could happen," Dovin said. "I'm not trying to scare you. I'm trying to help you understand you aren't invincible. Don't trust in being chosen to save you. I could tell you countless stories from history about people who died while fulfilling their destiny."

"Lovely," Ming Li mumbled.

"I'm not saying it's going to happen to you."

"Can't you see auras?" Tal asked.

"Yes, but they tell me very little. They don't predict the future, they only show me shadows."

"What if you interpret them wrong?" Wren wondered.

"I'm sure I have before. That's why I take nothing as a constant."

"Do you ever regret the way you've interpreted them?" Graham asked.

"I do."

"For instance?"

"Zalliah is my biggest regret. Her aura was always so strong. I thought it meant she was destined to do wonderful things. I taught her from a young age to make sure she was ready for her future. That's one reason I feel responsible for everything that's happened."

"You didn't teach her everything," Wren said, trying to be comforting. "At least you didn't teach her to block magic."

"Yes, and I'm very grateful I held that back. I should have taught you five more at a younger age. I saw the auras, and unlike Zalliah's, I could tell you were meant to save the world. It was very clear."

"How many times are there people that need to save the world?" Ming Li asked.

"As long as there is evil, there will need to be good people to fight it. Evil has always been here, and I assume always will be."

"So, are we fighting a hopeless fight?" Wren asked.

Dovin looked surprised. "Of course not. Never give up hope. Don't let it all be on your shoulders. Your fight is now with The Dark Cloud. Later, it will be someone else's fight. Be the person who inspires the next group of heroes. It's easy to sit by and do nothing. That's what most people do. Be the person who can fight for right even when it's not popular. Especially when it's not popular. I believe in you. I believe in all of you."

Wren nodded. They could do this. She wouldn't think about the part about maybe dying in the process. They would be the people who would do the right thing, even when it was difficult. She glanced around at her friends, and they all nodded at each other. They were ready.

CHAPTER 15

Graham stood at the bottom of the goblin mountain and shared a look with his friends. Snow and wind assaulted their faces, and it was hard to see through the storm. Magma was the only one that didn't seem concerned with the weather. She walked around, nuzzling the snow into piles. Dovin sent a message to Hedder, and he appeared beside them. He had a sword at his side.

"No use waiting," Dovin called over the storm. "Down Magma." The dragon pressed her stomach to the ground. "Everyone climb on. I made this harness that will keep us from falling off. At least that's my hope. It would still be good to hold on."

Tal didn't hesitate as he carefully climbed up the dragon. He hooked himself to Dovin's makeshift harness and then looked at the others. "Come on. What are you all waiting for?"

Graham sighed. He turned to help Wren, but she was already halfway up. He climbed, willing his arms to stop shaking. This was worse than riding an alicorn. The scales were smoother than he imagined, and his foot slipped twice. When he got behind Wren, he sat and fiddled with the harness.

"Has anyone ridden a dragon before?" Dovin called out. They all shook their heads. "Take off is fast. It's like nothing you've experienced. They take off faster than any alicorn or pegasus I've ever seen. Hold on tight and try not to throw up."

"Lovely," Graham muttered as he held on tight and closed his eyes.

"Up Magma!" Dovin called.

Graham tried not to yell as they shot like a rocket into the air. Ming Li's scream pierced his ears and even Wren let a small yelp escape. Graham had never ridden the slingshot ride at the amusement park, but he assumed this was probably what it felt like. He was almost positive his stomach was still on the ground. He kept expecting it to even out like when they rode alicorns, but they kept flying upwards at a terrible speed.

As quickly as it started, it stopped. Everyone jerked around as they landed and probably would've fallen off without the harness. Graham unhooked himself and slid to his knees on the snow covered ground. He took a few deep breaths and hoped his stomach settled soon. He could hear someone throwing up nearby.

Dovin chuckled. “Dragon riding takes some getting used to. That’s why most people prefer other methods of travel.”

“I’m sticking to alicorns,” Wren said, getting to her feet. Her legs were quivering.

“Why am I always the one who throws up?” Tal asked, wobbling over to them.

“That was the worst experience of my life!” Ming Li said, sinking down into the snow. “Climbing would’ve been preferable.”

“I thought it was fun,” Sen said, studying the mountain top.

“As did I,” Hedder agreed. Graham just shook his head.

“Now what?” Wren asked. “Do we summon the goblins or something?”

“No need,” said a wiry, gray goblin as he appeared near Magma. “The shrieking carried across the world, I’m sure. I hope you never need to sneak up on someone.” He rubbed his bald head and glared at them.

“Good to see you again, Vork,” Tal said, still looking a little pale.

“I assume you want to go back to the maze? I just let some others in. Nasty group. I’m pretty sure you don’t want to be inside with them.”

Graham pulled his cape tighter. “I thought you didn’t like to let people in?”

“I don’t. I only let them in because they were threatening.”

“Why did they want to go in?”

Vork snorted. "Same reason as everyone else. To get a golden tear. That group won't get one. I've never seen a group like them succeed."

Graham glanced into the maze. "What do you think they need the tear for?"

Vork shrugged. "Who cares? It is gold. It's also supposed to possess special powers. We don't know what they are, so don't ask. I assume you are here to stop them?"

"Yes."

"Then I'll take you there at once."

Wren cuddled up to Graham, and he put his arm around her. Vork waved his hand, and the ground shook. Everything became dark, and when it was light again, Graham had to squint. It was really bright and their eyes needed to adjust. They stood in a calm grassy area in front of the fifteen foot hedge.

"We thought we would need to beg or something," Ming Li said.

"I'm exhausted from dealing with that last group. The goblins were planning on ways to defeat them if they made it out, but we would prefer to let someone else deal with it. If you fail, we will be out here, waiting for them."

Hedder walked towards the maze. "This is incredible," he said. "I can't believe I'm seeing the legendary goblin maze."

"Why didn't you bring the crazy woman?" Vork asked. "She fights like nothing I've seen before."

"What crazy woman?" Dovin asked.

"He means Austra," Ming Li said. "She beat him up."

Vork growled. "I wasn't trying. I wouldn't want to hurt a woman." Ming Li chuckled. "Yeah, keep telling yourself that."

"The maze changes," Graham told Dovin and Hedder. "If you look away, a hedge grows up and blocks you. It separated us all really fast last time."

"I remember the story," Hedder said. "So we need to stay together and keep our eyes ahead."

"And don't follow the fairies," Ming Li said. "They're little punks."

"And there's a scary little boy in there," Wren added. "Do we follow the lion if he appears again? I mean, we don't need a tear this time."

"The question is, will Gorbin follow the lion?" Sen asked.

"Even if he does, I don't believe he'll get a tear," Graham said. "He doesn't take me as the compassionate type. He won't pass the test."

"Everyone has their weapons?" Dovin asked. They all nodded. "Then let's go."

"Don't lose me," Wren said, linking her arm with Graham's as they walked through the maze.

"No chance," he said, smiling at her.

"Be prepared for anything," Dovin said, keeping his eyes forward. "We don't know what Gorbin knows about this place. I hope that he's fairly ignorant and won't know he can't use magic here. If they don't have weapons, we hold the advantage."

"Zalliah seems to believe that Gorbin isn't very smart," Wren said. "She implied that he can't do anything without her."

"Don't underestimate Gorbin," Hedder said. "If nothing else, he's strong."

"He's not as dependent as Zalliah might have wanted you to imagine," Dovin agreed. "I've spent a lot of time observing him when he was on Earth. He runs a smooth company. It's well respected, and he's considered a wonderful businessman. He's very successful, and he did that without Zalliah."

"Shouldn't we make a plan?" Hedder asked. "If the pathways change, I'm assuming we won't all make it through. Should we only make right turns?"

"We tried that last time," Graham said. "It didn't really work."

"When we wandered in random directions, we seemed to make more progress," Tal agreed.

"I kinda think you only make progress if the maze lets you," Wren said.

"That is smart of you," said a voice from behind. They all spun around to see the creepy boy. He was wearing the same faded brown tunic as before and stared at them with the same blank expression. "I'm surprised to see you here again."

"So are we," Ming Li muttered.

"Are you connected to the others that came in earlier?"

"No," Wren said, shaking her head. "We are looking for them, though."

"Doesn't that make you connected?"

"They aren't good people. We are here to stop them."

"I suppose that is good," he said, still not reacting. "We dislike their type here. We used to see it all the time. For a long time, it was quiet. We hope the chaos does not start up again."

"Chaos?"

"Many self-serving people used to come here. It interrupted the peace in the maze."

"Can you tell us where to find them?" Dovin asked.

"I could," the boy said with a smile that didn't reach his eyes. "But that is not how things work around here. I will tell you where they are if you give me one of your weapons."

"No deals," Graham said.

"But it might make it faster," Hedder protested.

"No, we can't trust him," Wren said. "He's not really a boy. He can turn into smoke."

"That does not make me any less real," he said.

"The path we were on is gone," Tal said. "He distracted us."

"We will meet again, if you wish," the boy said. He faded into smoke and blew away into the breeze.

"That dude totally gives me the chills," Graham said. They all started walking back the way they had come. There wasn't another way.

"There's a little opening here," Wren said, pointing at the hedge. "I'm not sure it's supposed to be here." It was thin, and the hedge looked like it had been broken. Sharp twigs poked out in odd directions.

"Might as well try," Tal said. "It's possible Gorbin broke his way through."

"It had to be someone strong," Ming Li said. "We tried last time, and we couldn't get through."

Wren slipped through the opening, cringing as a branch scratched her arm. She came out on another path and Graham quickly joined her. Hedder was next. Wren watched in horror as the hedge fixed itself and closed before anyone else made it through. "No!"

Graham cupped his hands and yelled through them. "Can you hear us?" No response.

"We were even watching!" Wren yelled at the maze. "That wasn't fair!"

"Perhaps we can climb over," Hedder said.

"They won't be there," Graham told him. "This place is crazy that way. We might as well keep going."

"Why do you suppose they came here?" Wren wondered.

"It seems obvious to me," Hedder said. "It's not just this place. Zalliah was in the desert. Now The Dark Cloud is here. They are copying you. I would almost bet on it."

Graham's brows came together. "Copying us?"

"Yes. My guess is they lost control of the weather, or they don't know how to fix it without the silver eclipse."

"So they're trying to create one themselves?" Graham asked.

"I believe so. It would go well with the plan Zalliah told Wren previously. If she can create a silver eclipse before you do, she will look like a hero and perhaps trick people into trusting her."

"She did pocket a handful of sand when we were in the desert," Graham remembered.

They walked for a few minutes in silence. Hedder's explanation made sense. Wren made sure she kept her eyes ahead. Who would've thought she would be walking through a maze with Graham and her history teacher one day? Professor Hedder made it feel awkward.

"I just saw something," Hedder said, looking at the ground. Wren kept her eyes focused and didn't look at whatever Hedder saw. "Perhaps a mouse."

"I thought I saw a mouse last time we were here," Wren said, stepping over a five-inch stream of water. The stream crossed several places in the maze. Between the stream and the berries that grow on hedges, people in the maze wouldn't starve.

"I hate mice," Hedder said, watching the ground.

"We should get more berries," Wren told Graham. "They really improved the taste of your medicine."

"Maybe someday I can ask the goblins if I can buy berries from them," Graham said. "It really does help. I wonder what the berries are called."

Hedder sniffed. "Back to everything needing a name?"

"I don't think that's weird when you're talking about a berry," Wren said, defending Graham. "I've never heard of a berry without a name."

"Yes, but look what happens when Graham feels the need to name everything. We end up with a world called Basura."

"There's nothing wrong with Basura," Wren said. "The fact that it means garbage in a world most people don't even know about doesn't make it garbage here."

"I didn't name it anyway," Graham said. "That was Sen's dad."

Hedder shook his head. "And it caught on so fast it's too late to change it. The recent addition of the school history book even refers to it as Basura, and it's only been a few months."

"I don't understand why you don't see the advantages of naming things," Graham said, stepping over a puddle. "When you teach history, don't you think it would be easier to say, 'There was a fight between the trolls and the goblins at the Tyson river,' than to say, 'There was a fight between the trolls and the goblins at the river where a knight once died when he ran out of water?' Names make things nice."

"But if you explain what happened at the river, it lets people know exactly what happened, so they don't have to wonder which river it is. A name is just a name and they might all get confused." Hedder said.

"But sometimes that isn't important. If someone wants to go to a river, they don't need to understand its history."

"I disagree."

"There are names for cities and islands. Are you opposed to that?"

"No. It's normal for cities to possess names."

Wren smiled. "Give up Graham. You aren't going to win."

"What if you name the rivers after a person who did something there? Wouldn't that be as good and easier to say? You still get a historical reference in there."

"Perhaps," Hedder said, still checking the ground for rodents as they walked. "You will never convince me of the benefit of having two names, though. That is just making everything more difficult."

Graham just smiled and kept walking. "Look, a fairy."

Wren glanced up to where he was pointing. A dainty fairy with black hair and a long blue dress was flying in zigzags above them.

"Wow," Hedder said in awe. "I've never seen one this close before."

"Last time we followed a fairy, she took us back to the beginning," Wren said. "We should probably ignore her."

"Ignore?" the fairy said, flying into Wren's face. Wren jumped back to avoid getting hit. "No one ignores a fairy. People bask in our glorious presence."

"We're busy. We don't have time for that," Wren said.

"Yes, well, I can be of help to you."

"No, thank you."

"You haven't heard my proposition."

"It isn't wise to trust anything in this maze."

The fairy landed on Graham's shoulder and tilted her head as she studied Wren. Graham looked like he wanted to flick her away, but he was too polite.

"I admit, we have caused mischief in this maze for thousands of years," she said, shrugging. "But that doesn't mean we can't be helpful when the occasion calls for it, and it is calling loud and clear."

"What do you mean?" Graham asked.

"The others who are in this maze are not welcome. They are destroying the beautiful hedge and ruining this beautiful place with their garbage and their foul language. We do not appreciate their kind."

"We need to find them so we can try to capture them," Wren said.

"Yes," the fairy said with a deep sigh. "And yet, we are not comforted in this. Their group looks threatening, and they are here in their own self-interest. You are a few scattered groups of children."

"I'm not a child," Hedder protested.

The fairy studied him and then shrugged as if she didn't believe him. "We want them out."

"Then why don't you tell us where they are?" Graham asked.

"We may be mischievous," the fairy said, "but that doesn't mean we are cruel. We do not want your deaths on our heads, and we all fear you cannot control the other group."

"From what we've been told, there are lots of people that never made it out of the maze. What happened to them?"

"It's true. We can trap people in here. When people come in for malicious purposes, they cannot pass the test of Borzo because they have no compassion. No kindness. When you entered last time, you passed the test because you were willing to sacrifice what you wanted to save a person who had wronged you. Only people like you can navigate the maze, find what they want, and leave."

"So if we just leave them here, they're trapped?" Wren asked.

"Yes, but we do not want them here. It's exhausting for all of us when we have people like that trapped in here."

"What's Borzo?" Graham asked. "The lion?"

"Yes."

"What about the stone dragon that chased us last time?" Wren asked. "Could he help us?"

The fairy laughed. "He will help if he wishes. He is not controlled by anyone. That creature does only what he wants. He has no conscience the way the rest of us do. If he sees a visitor, he will attack whether or not they are enemies."

Wren shuddered. "So we need to hope he finds them before he finds us?"

"Exactly."

"What about Borzo? Can he help?"

"Borzo is not violent," the fairy said, her wings rubbing against Graham's face. He looked uncomfortable. "He can hypnotize a person into a deep sleep, but they have to stare into his eyes first. Most humans avoid making eye contact with a lion."

Hedder narrowed his eyes. "When others were stuck in the maze, what happened to them in the end?"

"Eventually, they died. Some went mad, and many of them fought amongst themselves. Of course, the stone dragon finished some of them. Then there is Fiend. He only tolerates things for so long before he takes action. It is not pleasant for any of us to share the maze with them. We prefer when we are left alone. There was a long time with no disturbances, and then you all entered. We were relieved you were compassionate, so we did not need to trap you."

"Who is Fiend?" Graham asked.

"The boy in the maze. He can be more terrifying than the stone dragon."

"I believe it. He gives me the creeps."

"I'm surprised the goblins never come in," Wren said.

The fairy grimaced. "We do not deal with goblins. They never have good intentions. We have done our best to make them terrified of what they might find here."

"Can't fairies do any helpful magic?" Hedder asked.

"Of course we can!" she said, stamping her foot on Graham's shoulder. "But we are bound by certain rules here. If we were not, none of this would be a problem."

"So, what do we do?" Wren asked.

"Those you seek have been separated from one another. They are in small groups."

"It would've been nice if we hadn't been separated," Wren said. "Why did you do that?"

"That is the hedges doing, not ours."

"Can you lead us to our friends?"

"Perhaps, but two of those you seek are going to come around the corner at any moment. You must deal with them first." The fairy flew up and over the hedge.

"Was any of that helpful?" Graham asked, yanking the crossbow that was draped over his shoulder into his hands.

"At least we had a warning," Wren said, grabbing her own crossbow and pointing it at the corner the fairy had warned them about.

"Are you really going to shoot them?" Hedder asked. "I seriously can't imagine either of you pulling the trigger." He pulled his sword out of its sheath.

"We can aim at their legs or something," Wren said.

"Your aim is that good?"

"I've never shot one before," she admitted.

"The safety is on," Graham told her, reaching over and clicking something into place. "Sen taught me a little."

Two cloaked men rounded the corner and stopped short when they saw the three of them. They weren't wearing masks, but Wren didn't recognize them. One was tall and lanky and the other was short, with a brown beard.

"Stop right there," Wren said with a confidence she didn't feel. She hoped they couldn't sense it.

They looked at each other and laughed. "Gorbin's going to be happy with us," the tall one said.

"You've got two crossbows pointed at you," Graham said. "I wouldn't be laughing."

"Yeah, well, Zalliah told us about you, and we don't think you've got it in you to actually shoot us." He took a step forward.

"Why don't we have any ailam powder," Wren said under her breath.

"Because we used it all," Graham said.

"There's a person behind us," Hedder said. "You two go after them. I've got these two idiots." He spun his sword expertly.

Wren looked behind her. It was Gorbin. Hedder wouldn't have sent them after him if he'd known. Gorbin stood with an enormous smile on his face.

Wren sprinted towards Gorbin, her crossbow ready, and let out her best battle cry. "Aaaaah!" His eyes widened, and he disappeared around a corner. She had hoped she would catch him off guard. She darted around the corner, not turning to see if Graham followed. Gorbin ran down a long pathway, his dark cloak flying behind him.

For having so much mass, Gorbin was fast. A lot faster than Wren. The Dark Cloud must not have realized they couldn't use magic here, or he'd be carrying some type of weapon. Wren wished she had practiced with the crossbow. She aimed low, but didn't dare to shoot. Instead of hitting him in the leg, she would probably shoot the ground and waste the advantage of having a weapon.

Graham should've passed her by now. She couldn't hear anything behind her. Something must have happened. With her luck, the hedge probably grew up behind her before he rounded the corner. Gorbin's lead was growing and Wren's legs burned.

Gorbin stopped and turned to face her. She kept the crossbow aimed at him as she got closer. Something was strange about the path ahead. As she got closer, she realized the ground broke away and there was an enormous gaping hole. It was at least ten feet across to the other side. Wren slowed to a walk and kept her weapon pointed at him. She made the angriest face she could manage and hoped her bluff would make Gorbin think she would pull the trigger.

"I don't have time for you!" Gorbin growled. "Turn around and walk away and I won't hurt you."

"You won't hurt me?" Wren asked, gesturing at the crossbow with her head.

"I've got things to do here. Just go."

"I don't think so."

"I am not obsessed with you kids the way Zalliah is. I've no qualms about killing you."

"And I have none about killing you," Wren lied.

Gorbin took several quick steps towards Wren and she stopped and sucked in a breath. If he charged her, she was going to be forced to act. Before Wren could decide what to do, Gorbin turned and ran a few feet towards the pit and jumped. His jump was too short, and he fell. Wren ran to the side and looked down. Gorbin was fifteen feet down, holding his ankle and groaning in pain.

Pointing the crossbow into the hole, she glared down at the man. "Give up now. It's your only option."

"I've got plenty of options," he said, glaring up at her. "I only ran from you because I'm on a schedule. There is no time to waste on silly little girls." He stood and limped towards the other side of the pit and disappeared. There must be a tunnel under where she was standing.

Wren secured her crossbow on her back and looked behind her, hoping that by some miracle Graham would reappear. Nothing. Could she jump ten feet? If she could get to that side, she would be able to see where he went. She would need a good running start. Wren walked backwards until she had enough room, and she ran as fast as she could. When she reached the hole, she sprang forward with all her might. She hit her stomach against the other side and started sliding. She dug at the earth with her fingers, but there was nothing to catch onto. A wave of panic washed over her as she slid into the pit.

Wren's legs hit the ground and buckled, causing her to sit hard on the dirt floor, but she was alright. There must have been enough of an incline in the dirt wall to allow her to fall slowly. She looked to the spot where Gorbin disappeared. There was a dark tunnel, and he was nowhere to be seen. Wren got to her feet and dusted herself off. Should she really charge into a dark tunnel by herself? She looked up. There was no way she was getting back up. The tunnel was the only option.

Chapter 16

Graham rounded a corner in time to see Wren jump and disappear. He raced to the spot and stopped before he could fall into an enormous hole. "Wren!" he called as he looked into the pit.

The ground rumbled and knocked him backwards. When he got back to his feet, the hole was gone. "Wren!" he yelled, kneeling on the ground. He tried to dig his fingers into the hard packed dirt. "Let her out!" he yelled. He didn't know who he was yelling at. The fairy, the lion, perhaps the maze itself.

"Graham! What are you doing?" Tal asked, running up beside him.

"Wren's down there!" he said, still trying to pry away the dirt.

"Under the ground?"

"Yes! There was a pit here, but it covered itself before I could get to her."

"I don't think you're going to get to her like that."

"Gorbin's down there too."

The corners of Tal's mouth turned down. "That's still not going to help. This place makes little sense. She's probably somewhere else."

Graham got to his feet. Tal was right. All he was doing was wasting time. "You lost everyone else?"

"Yeah. The maze separated us pretty fast this time. Then an annoying fairy came and told me a bunch of stuff that wasn't helpful and flew off."

"If all the creatures here want Gorbin and his people out of here, they could be more helpful."

"I agree."

"I can take you to your friend," the creepy little boy said, coming up behind them.

"We aren't giving you anything," Graham said.

"It will be enough if you rid us of those other people. Your friend is with the worst of them all."

"Where is she?"

"Follow me." He turned and walked away. Graham and Tal shared a look and then followed. Graham didn't trust Fiend or whatever his name was, but what choice did they have?

"The maze was not wise to separate you this time," Fiend said. "You are not faring well apart."

"Don't you have some control over the maze?" Tal asked.

"The maze controls itself."

"But you know where all our friends are?"

"Yes."

"Are they alright?" Graham asked.

"It depends on which ones you mean. Most of them are fine. One is not."

"Which one?"

Fiend kept his head forward. "The one with the sword."

"Hedder?"

"Yes."

"What's wrong with him?"

"He killed one of the cloaked figures, but now he is no more."

Graham and Tal looked at each other in alarm.

"You mean he's dead?" Tal asked.

"Yes."

Graham's heart beat faster. "What happened?"

"He lost his sword, and he fought with the other man, and he did not win."

Graham didn't know what to say. They shouldn't have left Hedder by himself.

"Stand here," Fiend said, pointing to a spot on the ground. It didn't appear any different from any other spot in the maze. They stood where he told them. "Do not worry. I am ready to bend the rules. The man must be stopped."

The ground rumbled, and the dirt beneath them gave way. Graham screamed as he fell. He landed hard and covered his head as dirt cascaded down onto him. It seemed to rain down for a solid minute. When it stopped, Graham shook his head and brushed the dirt from his hair. Tal sat next to him, doing the same.

“Where are we?” Graham asked, inspecting the green meadow they sat in.

“Not in a tunnel,” Tal said as they got to their feet. Dirt poured from off of their clothes. Graham tried to brush off his arms. They were both completely covered.

“Are we still in the maze?” Graham tried to make a light. “I still can’t do magic. How are we in a meadow?”

Tal shrugged. “It’s a magic maze. Why not have a magical meadow underneath?”

“But it doesn’t make sense.”

“Magic doesn’t have to make sense. There!” Tal said, pointing.

Graham turned to see Gorbin standing in a patch of wildflowers with Wren ten feet away, holding her crossbow on him. He wasn’t running anymore.

“Let’s go,” Graham said, taking off in Wren’s direction. Tal was close behind him. The weeds and flowers were thick, making it hard to run. Wren turned to look at them and Gorbin rushed her, knocking her to the ground.

“We distracted her!” Tal called as they quickened their pace. When Gorbin got up, he had Wren in a headlock. The crossbow was nowhere in sight. He turned towards them, with Wren’s knife pressed against her throat.

“Stop!” Gorbin commanded as they drew nearer. They skidded to a halt.

“Let her go!” Graham growled.

“I don’t think so,” Gorbin hissed. “I’ve had enough of all of you.” Sweat ran down his cheek, and he wiped his face in Wren’s hair.

Wren's eyes were full of fire. She didn't appear scared, only angry.

"Now, here's what we're going to do," Gorbin said right before Wren stomped on his toe. He cried out and released her. She bolted over to Graham and Tal.

"His leg is hurt from falling," she said.

"You are going to pay for that," Gorbin said, limping a few steps towards them.

"No, you are not welcome here," Fiend said, appearing from out of nowhere. "I do not follow the rules of the maze as my friends do." His eyes glowed red. Graham grabbed Wren's arm and took a step back.

Smoke swirled around Fiend, and there were now three of him. More smoke and three more. In less than a minute there were enough Fiends to surround Gorbin. They all had glowing eyes and the same blank expression.

"Get away from me!" Gorbin yelled as they closed in on him.

One Fiend turned around and looked at them. "Run."

They didn't need to be told twice. The three of them turned and raced across the meadow. They could hear Gorbin's screams echoing in their ears. Graham tried to block them out and put as much distance between himself and the terrifying scene as possible.

"This way," Wren yelled, turning slightly left. There was a small mound of dirt up ahead. "There's a hole in the backside of that mound. It will take us back to the tunnel and into the Maze!"

"It changed," Graham said as they rushed forward. "The hole you fell in disappeared."

The meadow seemed endless as they ran, with weeds brushing their legs. Graham didn't dare glance back, the memory of the multiple Fiends with their eerie expressions causing a chill to run over his back. He didn't even try to comprehend Fiend's powers or what was transpiring.

They curved around the mound and bent down to fit into the opening in the back. After a few steps, they were able to stand at full height inside a tunnel.

"The tunnel isn't long," Wren said, catching her breath. "I was glad Dovin gave us the dragon scales. I don't know if I would have dared follow Gorbin into the dark." She pulled out her scale, and it flooded the tunnel with light. Graham and Tal followed her example.

Graham inspected the tunnel. It was just a small path that had been dug out of the earth. "You probably shouldn't have gone after him by yourself."

"Probably not," Wren shrugged, "But that's why we're here, right? Come on," she said, moving down the tunnel.

"Now what?" Tal asked. "I'm guessing we won't be seeing Gorbin again. Do we try to find everyone and leave? We don't know how many Dark Cloud members came into the maze."

"I'm having a hard time thinking," Graham admitted with a shiver. "That was pretty creepy back there. I hope we don't run into Fiend again."

"At least he's kind of on our side," Tal said. "We should focus on finding everyone and then we'll decide what to do."

“We’re going to have to figure out how to get up to the maze,” Graham said. “The pit was covered, and the dirt was packed tight.”

They turned a corner and walked into the bright maze. “No pit,” Tal said.

“That’s one time I’m glad the maze changed,” Wren said with a sigh of relief.

When Graham looked over his shoulder, the tunnel was gone, and the maze stretched on as far as he could see. “I hope we’re done with this place after this.”

“Help!” a voice called out.

“That sounded like Li,” Tal said, sprinting forward. Graham and Wren followed. “Li! Li! Can you hear me?”

“Yes!” she called back. They rushed around a corner and found Ming Li with her leg stuck in the hedge about two feet off the ground.

“What happened?” Tal asked, dropping to his knees. He examined the hedge and her leg.

“It won’t let go of me,” she complained, trying to yank herself free.

“Were you trying to climb?” Graham asked, raising his eyebrow. She was stuck from her knee down.

“No,” she said, turning pink. “I was getting frustrated, and I kicked it.”

Tal looked up at her with a lopsided grin. “Let’s try not to take our anger out on the hedge, alright?” He pulled at the branches encircling her leg and she pushed against the hedge. Nothing.

“I can’t stand on one leg for long.”

“You should apologize.”

"To the leaves?" Ming Li asked, rolling her eyes.

"Yes," Tal said, tilting his head as he watched her. "It's a living thing. More so than some plants. It wasn't really nice to kick it."

"I'm not apologizing to a bush."

Tal grinned. "Do you wanna live here?"

"No," she huffed.

"Come on. It's worth a try."

"Fine. I'm sorry I kicked you," she said, crossing her arms.

"Now try to mean it."

Ming Li shot him a look. "I'm really sorry I kicked you. I won't do it again."

Tal nodded. "Keep going."

"Will you please let me go?"

Graham forced his smile to stay hidden.

"Nothing's happening," she said, throwing her arms in the air.

Tal ran his hand over the hedge. "We've had a hard day," he said to the plant. "Li is hot and tired and she let her anger get the best of her. Will you please let her go?" The hedge shook and Ming Li pulled her leg out, falling backwards. Graham caught her before she could go all the way down.

"Thanks," she mumbled as he stabilized her.

"Are you alright?" Tal asked, holding out his hand.

"Fine," she said, taking it. "It feels stupid talking to plants."

"I do it all the time."

"Yeah, but you're a little crazy."

He winked. "True."

"We better hurry and find the others," Wren said. "Is it just Sen, Hedder, and Dovin? I hope they're all together."

"Not Hedder," Graham said reverently. "He didn't make it."

"What do you mean?" Ming Li squealed. "He died?"

"Yeah."

Wren wrapped her arm around Graham's and tears came to her eyes. "Let's go," she said. "The sooner we get out of here, the better."

"I was with Sen and Dovin until about fifteen minutes ago," Ming Li sniffled. "Dang it. Why are my eyes leaking? It's not like I was close to Hedder."

"But he did do a lot for us," Graham said. "He deserves people to care."

Ming Li nodded and wiped her eyes. "Dovin captured two people. We couldn't decide what to do with them, so Dovin and Sen tied them up, and we had to leave them. No sign of Gorbin though."

"Gorbin might be dead," Wren said, holding tighter to Graham as they walked.

"What do you mean?" Ming Li asked.

"Fiend got him," Graham said.

"Who's Fiend?"

"The smoke boy. Turns out he can multiply."

Tal grinned. "Most eight year old kids can multiply."

Ming Li rolled her eyes. "Not funny, Talon. One of that kid is scary enough. What did he do?"

"Can we talk about something else?" Wren asked. "I know I'm going to have nightmares about it."

"You're holding my hand," Ming Li said to Tal.

He chuckled. "Is that surprising?"

"Kinda."

"Why?"

"Well, we aren't like Wren and Graham. Ever since they decided they were dating, they've been holding hands all the time and stuff. You just kissed me a few times and then went back to normal."

"I was going to hold your hand earlier, but I was all sweaty and I didn't want to gross you out."

"Well, you're covered in dirt and you stink now and I'm still holding your hand."

Tal laughed. "That's true."

"So, are we, like, together or what?"

"I hope so."

"Good. Me too."

Wren leaned closer to Graham. "I really want to walk faster, so I don't have to listen to this, but I don't want to get separated."

Graham just smiled. If Ming Li wasn't focused on him, he found her hilarious.

"Fairy," Wren said, pointing at the fairy they had talked to earlier.

"It's time for you to leave," she said, fluttering in front of them.

"What about our friends?" Graham asked.

"They are waiting for you outside the maze."

"What about the rest of the bad guys?" Ming Li asked.

"Their leader is no more. We will deal with the remaining people. They will never leave."

Graham looked at Wren and saw the worry in her eyes. They followed the fairy, and she pointed to an opening. They exited and found Dovin, Sen, and Vork waiting for them.

"I believe they have kicked us out," Dovin said.

Graham nodded. "What's going to happen now? Do you suppose The Dark Cloud will fall apart without Zalliah and Gorbin?"

"I wouldn't be sure Gorbin won't find his way out."

Graham gazed up at the sky. "I'm pretty sure he's dead."

Dovin's eyes widened. "Oh. Well, alright. I suppose we can leave as soon as Hedder comes out."

"Also dead."

Dovin stared into the maze for a few moments with an unidentifiable expression on his face. "Then I guess it's time."

"Did we accomplish anything?" Tal asked, clenching his fists. "What was the point of us going in there? Everything that happened would have happened anyway. All we did was get Hedder killed."

"We didn't know what would happen," Dovin said, gazing up at the sky. Graham wondered if Dovin was feeling guilty.

"I will take you to your dragon," Vork said. Everything went dark, and then they were standing on top of the goblin mountain in the snow. Magma lumbered over to them. She didn't seem bothered by the weather.

Graham took a deep breath. Down was probably worse than up. He looked at his friends. Tal was pale.

"Can you take some of us to the bottom?" he asked Vork.

"I suppose," he growled.

"Who wants to go on the dragon?" Dovin asked, climbing up. They all stared at him. "No one? Where's your sense of adventure?"

"I've had enough adventure today," Tal said, and the others nodded in agreement.

"Alright. I'll meet you at the bottom."

Wren watched everyone as they sat in the parlor in Flordillia. No one was speaking. Graham had just explained to everyone what had happened in the maze. There had been questions at first, but now it was just quiet.

"I will make an announcement to Akkron," Zera finally said. "I will let it be known that Gorbin is dead. We will also have a memorial for Hedder."

"What's next?" Hamble asked.

"A shower for some people," Brake said, studying Graham. They were all dirty, but Graham and Tal looked like a gigantic pile of dirt had been dumped on their heads.

"I hope The Dark Cloud falls apart after this," Austra said. "Zalliah and Gorbin are the only two that have stood out as leaders. With them out of the picture, things should improve." Drew squeezed Austra's hand and winked at Wren. She didn't have enough energy to interpret that right now.

“I still want to talk to Zalliah,” Tal said. “I know she’ll deny knowing anything, but it will make me feel better to see it for myself.”

“We should talk to Padmire as well,” Wren said through a yawn. “I want to ask him if he can block our access to the cave after this is all over.”

“That would be a good idea,” Drew agreed. “You wouldn’t be targets for power seekers anymore.”

“What happens to me when this is all over?” Dree asked.

“I guess you can choose,” Hamble said. “You can stay here, go home, or we can help you establish yourself somewhere.”

“I get to choose?”

“Of course.”

“I’m not very good at making decisions.”

“We’ll help you,” Sen said. “Don’t worry. We won’t leave you helpless.”

“Thank you.”

“We can decide what we are doing tomorrow,” Zera said. “Right now, it would be best for everyone to shower and go to bed.”

“And dinner,” Tal said. “I’m not skipping that.” Wren nodded. Her stomach had been growling for over an hour.

“Where’s Brog?” Wren asked as everyone disbursed.

“He’s been busy now that the giants are trying to merge their groups,” Drew said as they made their way to the kitchen. “I assume being married takes some of his time as well. I met his wife, and I’m pretty sure she keeps him in line.”

"Keeps Brog in line?" Wren laughed. "Brog is always in line."

"True, but she's making the decisions in that relationship."

"Can we eat on my balcony?" Wren asked. "I want to talk to you. Austra can come too."

Austra's eyes widened, but she nodded. The three of them grabbed some sandwiches and took them up to Wren's balcony. It wasn't what Wren would call bright, but the trolls had done a good job of putting lights all over the city. She sat on the balcony and took a bite of her sandwich. She didn't know what it was, but it tasted great.

Drew and Austra sat and quietly ate. An uncomfortable silence fell over them, but Wren didn't want to talk until she wasn't hungry. She saw Austra send her dad a questioning look, and he just shrugged.

Wren shoved the last bite of sandwich into her mouth and chewed quickly. "I don't know how to ask this without being awkward," she said. Drew's eyebrow lifted. She wasn't sure, but she thought he was hiding a smile. "I'm just going to come out and ask. What are you two's intentions?"

Austra sat up straighter and tossed her black hair over her shoulder. "Intentions?"

"Yes. Your intentions towards each other." Wren could feel heat creeping up her neck.

"We haven't talked about it," Drew said. He coughed. "Nothing's happened since that one time in Meegore."

"Nothing?"

"Nothing. We didn't even talk to each other about it."

“My goodness,” Austra said, fanning her face with her hand. “Why are we being interrogated like this?”

“I’ve thought a lot about it,” Wren said. “I just want you both to know that if you decide to date or get married, you have my blessing.” She jumped to her feet. “That’s all I have to say. Now I’m going to leave and you can talk, or whatever, and we never have to talk about this conversation again.” She turned and raced off the balcony and through her room. She wasn’t sure, but she thought she heard her dad laughing.

CHAPTER 17

"Down, Walter!" Graham said, laughing as the curly labradoodle jumped up and down in excitement. "Did you miss me?" He patted the dog's head. Walter wagged his tail and licked Graham's hand.

Ming Li was petting Zebra. "It's good to see you aren't scared of your own dog."

"I'm not scared of animals," Graham said. "They just make me nervous."

"That means you're scared."

"We got Walter as a puppy, so I'm used to him. My aunt didn't like to deal with his moods, so I ended up taking care of most things. Kaylee liked to play with him, but she didn't like to help with any of the day-to-day chores. She fed him once. Possibly twice."

Graham looked around Meegore. Aside from the Naverbs singing in the trees, it was quiet. Wren hadn't wanted to come to the cave, so she went to the prison to see Zalliah with Tal and Sen.

Ming Li ran her hand over Zebra's back. "I wonder what Tal will do with Zebra once this is all over."

"He has a stable full of alicorns and pegasuses. Pegasi? Whatever they're called. She would probably be fine there."

"I bet she would like to stay here. She gets to run around free, and Brog spoils her."

"That's true. I bet Walter would choose to stay with Brog over me any day."

"That is a bet you would win," Brog said, coming up behind them. Vronika was with him. Her hair was in three tight braids and she still wore armor. Walter sprang away from Graham and started jumping on Brog. Brog picked him up and held him like a baby. Walter licked his face.

"Brog has a fascinating talent with animals," Vronika said, pride shining in her eyes. "I've seen nothing like it. I am trying to convince him to make an animal sanctuary on the island."

"I am not sure Haltina would approve," Brog said. "We have changed so much already. I worry about upsetting her."

"We haven't seen Haltina in a while," Graham said. "Is something wrong?"

"Haltina is very old," Brog said. "She will not be around much longer. She spends her days resting. Now, why have you come?"

"We need to talk to Padmire," Graham said.

"Brake told us of your adventure yesterday. We hope that means everything will soon come to a happy close."

"So do we. It's good The Dark Cloud left the islands alone. It's nice to come somewhere and feel the sun."

"Yeah, it is." Ming Li agreed. "Walking around in the dark is depressing."

"We're hoping this will be fast," Graham said. "We're counting on Padmire coming to the cave entrance to talk to us, so we don't have to go through."

"Now that the cave has been opened, he comes out now and then."

Vronika rolled her eyes. "He's a grumpy little thing. You would assume some sun would help his moods."

"He just looks grumpy no matter what," Ming Li said. "I prefer that look to his smile. That just makes him appear downright scary."

Graham laughed. "You think Padmire's scary?"

"No, but he looks scary."

"Well, we should probably get started. If we have to go through the cave, it will take time."

Brog and Vronika left with Walter and Zebra, while Graham and Ming Li wandered to the cave. Two sides of the crystal lit up, and the rock slid away from the entrance. They looked down into the dark abyss.

"Hey Padmire!" Ming Li yelled. "Can you come up and talk to us?"

"I wonder how long we should wait."

"No clue," she said, sitting on the grassy ground. "He always claims we do things too fast for him, so I'm guessing it might take a while."

Graham joined her on the grass. "I hope the silver eclipse goes smoothly. The closer we get, the more nervous I am."

"It will. I'm not going to worry about it. If it doesn't work, there really isn't anything we can do. Austra said that if we can do it within the next week, there will be time for this year's crops to be planted and harvested."

"That's what she said?" Graham asked, a large weight settling in his stomach. "One week isn't very long. What if The Dark Cloud are still functioning without Zalliah and Gorbin?"

"We still have to do it. We can't go through another year without crops. Who knows if the other continent will even help us again? Our relationship with Kind Miadd has gone downhill."

"That's true. It was his fault, though."

"You called?" Padmire asked from the top of the cave. He crawled down the wall and jumped to the ground. "It was good of you to wait here for me. You are the most impatient group."

"We've been wondering what will happen with the cave once the weather is fixed and The Dark Cloud isn't a threat," Graham told him. "Will we still be chosen?"

"And will we still be able to open the cave?" Ming Li added.

"Well, those are complicated questions," Padmire said, scratching his blue head. "The cave opening and closing is up to me."

"We're worried that we won't ever get to live normal lives if people are constantly trying to get us to bring them here."

"That is a valid concern. I can restrict your access if you wish. As for whether you will still be chosen, that has nothing to do with me. I have no answer for you."

"If you restrict our access, will you be stuck in here again?" Ming Li asked.

"I wasn't stuck before. I could've opened the cave at any time and left."

"You chose to stay here all those years?"

"Well, stay is a funny word. It's all relative. I might have come out a time or two when no one was looking."

Graham grinned at the hammer nosed bungle. "So you weren't in the cave for hundreds of years?"

"No one can prove anything."

"If you block us, is there any way we could ever contact you?"

"I can hear things outside the cave. If you come and beg at the entrance, there is a slight chance I would have pity on you and let you in. Is blocking the cave what you want?"

Graham nodded. "It would be best. Otherwise, we can't live normal lives."

"Then I should block you now. It sounds like your quest is almost complete."

"I guess so," Graham agreed.

"Go in one last time," Padmire said. "Take some of the yellow dust."

"We already have some for the silver eclipse," Ming Li said.

"Take some more, and guard it well. The dust is more than it seems."

"Oh?" Graham asked.

"The dust is a large part of the magic of Meegore. Without the dust, there is no magic."

"I don't understand."

Padmire looked at the sky and shook his head. "I have to explain everything," he muttered. "If you were to fly through the cave, you would leave without getting any new magic. If you avoid the dust, you avoid the magic."

"What do we do with it?"

Padmire sighed. "Whatever you want! I'm giving it to you as a parting gift. You can sprinkle it on someone who doesn't possess magic and it will give them magic."

"Really?" Ming Li asked, her eyes lighting up. "My mom wouldn't come to the cave, but she might let me put dust on her."

"Don't tell anyone you have it, or people will try to steal it. Of course, take some for your other friends."

"Thanks Padmire," Ming Li said. "We're going to miss you." She patted him on the head and he sighed.

Wren and Tal stood in the walkway that ran in front of Zalliah's cell. Sen sat on the floor, leaning against the wall, already looking bored. Zalliah was propped up in a bed. Her long brown hair was in a loose braid over her shoulder. She looked at them with questions in her eyes.

"I'm assuming you are like all the others," she said. "You've come to question me about things I don't know?"

"I'm hoping to question you about things you do know," Tal said, holding onto the prison bars.

"All I remember is that one day I was going to school with all my friends, and the next I woke up here with my father telling me I'm not sixteen, I'm forty-five, and I tried to take over the world."

"That must be a lot to take in."

"It was. I didn't believe it at first, but then I looked in a mirror. It was quite the shock. I am pleased I aged so well. I don't look a day over thirty, in my opinion."

"It all sounds too convenient," Wren said. "You are the most wanted person in this world and suddenly you don't remember any of your crimes?"

"I really don't, and I don't see why no one believes me. I'm no liar."

"You actually are," Sen said from the floor.

"You're stalling so you won't get sentenced," Tal said. "It won't matter. No one's going to let you out and no one is coming to break you out."

"I don't remember ever having followers."

"Well, they aren't coming. It only took Gorbin five seconds after you were captured to take over."

"Gorbin?" Zalliah laughed. "Why would I do anything with Gorbin? That kid is a goof. I doubt he'll ever amount to anything."

"Well, he managed to take over The Dark Cloud," Wren said.

"People keep saying 'The Dark Cloud' like I should know what that is."

"You should. It's your group. Or it was."

"Not much of a name ... If I turned evil, I doubt I would involve Gorbin. I mean, he has always had a thing for me, but that wouldn't make me choose him as an ally."

Tal snorted. "Gorbin had a thing for you?"

"Yeah. It's pretty annoying."

"He must've gotten over it, because he was off on a mission with your followers before you even had time to recover."

"What happened to me, anyway? I mean, they said I was stabbed, but who would want to stab me?"

Sen raised his hand.

"It was King Miadd," Wren told her.

"A king stabbed me?" she asked, leaning against her pile of pillows. "I must have gotten a lot of attention if a king would take the time to stab me."

"You seem proud of that," Tal said.

She shrugged. "You have to admit, that's impressive."

"Even if you don't remember anything, you don't seem to care that you were evil."

"I'm not going to dwell on a past I can't remember. It seems like such a waste of time. I'm curious about how I allowed Gorbin to work with me. It annoys me to know he took over something that was mine."

Tal studied her with disgust in his eyes. "Well, he doesn't have it anymore. He's dead."

Wren wasn't sure, but it looked like Zalliah might have flinched.

"Oh? How did that happen?" she asked, smoothing out her blanket.

"That's not important," he said. "Why don't you just give us a list of all your followers and perhaps your punishment won't be as bad as you deserve."

Zalliah threw her head back and laughed. "Even if I remembered, why would I tell you?"

"Because you are getting punished and they are all going to run free," Wren said. "You told me most of them were dispensable to you. Why let them off and take all the punishment yourself? I don't see you sacrificing like that."

Zalliah locked eyes with Wren and her jaw moved from side to side. "I remember nothing."

"No one is going to come for you. At best, you live here for life," Tal said.

"I can't say it will help after all these years," Zalliah said. "When I was in school, I might have had some plans to take over someday. I kept a list of people I thought might help me. Perhaps I still keep records. If so, I would have hidden it in the oak tree. My father knows the one."

"I'll send Dovin a message as soon as we get outside," Sen volunteered.

"Anything else you want to tell us?" Wren asked.

"No Wren, I don't believe there is," she said, flashing her white teeth.

They filed out of the prison and walked away from the building.

"I still think she's faking," Tal said.

"I know she's faking," Wren agreed. "She called me by name. We didn't tell her our names."

Graham and Ming Li entered Mali's Bakery through the front doors. Ming Li said her mom didn't like people teleporting in because it scared her. An Asian woman who looked a lot like an older version of Ming Li came from around the counter and smiled.

"Ming Li! You visit me!" she said in a heavy accent. She wrapped her arms around her daughter. "You stayed away long."

"I know. I'm sorry. Mom, this is Graham."

"Nice to meet you," Graham said, shaking her hand.

"Good to finally meet you. Brake talks about you."

"Mom, you said you don't want magic–"

Mali shook her head. "I hate caves."

"What if you didn't need to go in?" Ming Li pulled out a pouch of yellow dust and showed it to her mom. "All you need to do is sprinkle some of this dust on you."

She looked skeptically down into the pouch. "Maybe a small bit."

Ming Li took a pinch of the powder and sprinkled it on her mom's head.

Mali narrowed her eyes. "Am I supposed to feel different?"

Ming Li laughed. "You just spoke in Akkronese! And your accent was perfect!"

Her eyebrows rose. "Really? I don't care about magic, but it would be nice to communicate with my customers better." She laughed and gave Ming Li another squeeze.

"Trying to speak strange English or whatever they speak here is such a headache. I feel liberated!"

"We can't stay. I just wanted to make sure you were taken care of. Don't try any magic while I'm gone. I don't want you hurting yourself."

Mali rolled her eyes. "I'm not planning on learning any magic. It seems lazy to me."

"It comes in handy."

"Just be careful. I know Brake keeps things from me, so I won't worry."

"Don't worry. We're almost always careful."

"That sounds like my girl." Mali hugged her again. "Customers come in talking about you all the time. You're all giving people hope."

"We're getting so close to fixing everything. I bet we're all back home in a week."

"Good," Mali said, grabbing a bag and filling it with cookies. "Here, take this."

"Thanks, Mom." Ming Li grabbed the cookies, and they teleported back to Flordillia. They went straight to the kitchen because that seemed to be the place people liked to congregate.

Wren, Tal, and Sen were sitting at the table with Brake and Drew.

"How did it go?" Wren asked. Graham quickly filled them in on events at Meegore, and then Tal told them about their visit to Zalliah.

Dovin teleported into the room and Graham jumped. Ming Li was probably right, and they should figure out a way to get teleporting to make a sound.

He smiled at them and held up a small blue book. "I can't believe I never checked Zalliah's tree. She was always hiding things in it when she was younger. Since she never comes around anymore, I didn't even think about it."

"What's inside?" Graham asked.

"Everything we need. She has the names and dates that people joined The Dark Cloud. Once I give this to Zera, it should be a quick cleanup."

"Zalliah's lying about having amnesia," Wren said. "She knew my name. She said it on purpose. She wants us to know she's lying."

"I wouldn't doubt it," Dovin said, frowning.

"Can't you just give her some of your truth serum?" Graham asked.

"There's no such thing as truth serum," Dovin said. "Zalliah knows there are some things I kept from her. I had hoped if I bluffed and said I had truth serum, she would give up her lie, which she did."

"I wondered about that," Tal said. "I'd never heard of truth serum before."

"We might be ready," Brake said. "After we talk to Zera, we should set the day for the silver eclipse. Where should it be performed?"

"Boztoll," Graham said with confidence. "That's where the clouds started, so that's where it should happen."

"I agree," Wren said. "Those people deserve to see the sun again."

"It will fix the entire world at once," Brake said, rubbing his smooth chin. "I think you're right. It would be nice for them to get to be the place where something special happened after all they've gone through."

"We need to let everyone know what's going on," Graham said. "Can we call a meeting?"

"Zera won't be able to come," Brake said. "I'll go talk to her. Tal, your mom's been busy getting all of your father's things in order. Will you go tell her?"

Tal got up from the table. "Sure."

"Who does that leave?"

"Hamble and Austra," Wren said.

"Hamble's upstairs."

"I'll go," Ming Li said, leaving the kitchen.

"Austra is campaigning," Drew said. "I can go tell her."

"Should we tell Brog?" Wren asked. "It might be nice to have some giants patrolling around when we summon the silver eclipse."

"That's a good idea," Brake said. "If Zera agrees, we should talk to the governor of Boztoll and clean out The Dark Cloud members there first. It would still be good to have the giants around in case there is someone we miss or we don't know about."

"I really don't feel they will be a problem anymore," Dovin said. "Without a leader, they should be running scared. We can't trust that, of course. We should be watchful."

"It's suspicious to me that Zalliah would give us a list of her followers," Tal said.

"It's typical Zalliah," Dovin said. "If she's going down, she's going to want to take everyone with her. She is only loyal to herself."

"But shouldn't she hope she escapes someday?"

"She's probably planning on it, but if she's going to be miserable, she's going to make everyone else join her."

"I thought she would care a little that Gorbin died," Wren said. "I mean, she flinched, but that was it."

"She cares," Dovin said, smiling sadly. "She is self-serving and unpredictable, but she cared about Gorbin."

"She never seemed to."

"They dated in school. I suspect they did after as well, but if they did, they kept it quiet. The way she always ridiculed him was just a cover. That's not important right now. It's time to get things in order."

Graham's stomach was a mess of nerves. They had been working towards the silver eclipse for so long, and now it was actually going to happen.

Wren looked at the items for the silver eclipse that were gathered in a large pot in the middle of Boztoll. They didn't take up much space in the pot. How was this going to work? If Wren grabbed a bolt of lightning from the sky and sent it into the pot, could anything control it? The more she thought about it, the more dangerous it sounded. Even if Graham was shooting ice in at the same time, what was to keep the lightning from exploding the pot and everything else nearby?

Fog billowed around her as she scanned the streets. They were deserted. Where were her friends? Didn't they know she couldn't do this without them? Wren walked cautiously forward. Where were all the people? They couldn't just disappear.

The ground rumbled and Wren steadied herself before she could fall. A crack in the street started near her feet and began to spread. "No, no, no!" she squealed, backing up. Wren sprinted down the street, trying to get away from the crack. She could see something up ahead. Was it lava? It was headed straight for her.

Wren made a sharp right and passed between two houses. A squawking sound above her had her searching the sky. It was the stone dragon from the maze! He shrieked and dove at her. She tried to scream, but nothing came out. Before it could get her, someone knocked her to the ground.

"That was a little careless of you," said Governor Briggs. "You're making me miss an important meeting."

Wren looked up at him with narrowed eyes. "You're dead."

"That's a rude thing to point out. Just because I'm dead doesn't mean I don't have places to be."

"None of this makes sense."

"That's the way of dreams."

"I'm dreaming," Wren said, letting out a relieved sigh. "Of course I'm dreaming. None of this is real."

Briggs shrugged. "You can't get hurt, if that's what you mean."

"I just need to wake up."

"It isn't time for that. I came here to give you some advice."

"Advice? From you? I don't see any reason you would be sent to give me advice."

"Dream advice is a funny thing. You can only get it from someone you know, and it has to be someone who is dead."

Wren got to her feet. "Then why wouldn't my mom come? Or even Hedder?"

"Hedder's too new to the whole being dead thing. As for your mom ..." he glanced around. "Magnalee!" he called. "She's nervous."

"She's here?" Wren asked, looking around.

"I'm here," a woman said, stepping out from behind a house. Her long blonde hair blew in the breeze.

Briggs rubbed his goatee. "I told her we would waste less time if she came by herself. I'm sure you don't want to talk to me."

Wren couldn't take her eyes off the woman in front of her. She looked just like the painting in her grandparent's home. Magnalee opened her arms and Wren hurried to her. She threw her arms around her and sighed.

"I have little time," Magnalee said, stroking Wren's hair. "You must perform the silver eclipse correctly. You must have realized that sending a bolt of lightning into anything is not a good idea."

"I was just pondering about that," Wren said, looking at her mom. "But what can we do?"

"It is not lightning from the sky that you must summon. It is lightning from inside you."

"I can do that?"

Magnalee nodded. "It is not the same as the lightning you had before. It was a gift from the cave. The last time you entered."

Wren took a step away from her mom and held out her hand. "I can't do anything."

"You don't want to do magic in a dream. Especially the kind that might start a fire."

"That's all we've time for," Briggs said.

"You're dead," Wren said. "What could you possibly need to do?"

Magnalee laughed softly. "We keep busy. I must leave you now. Be careful. I'm proud of you." She smiled and faded into nothing.

"Wait!" Wren protested. She had so many questions. She turned to the place Briggs had been, but he was gone as well. "Come back!" she yelled into the fog. "Come back!"

"Wren, wake up!" Ming Li's voice filled her head. Wren sat up with a start. She was in her bed and Ming Li and Graham were standing in their pajamas, staring at her.

Tal peeked into the room. "What's with the yelling?"

Wren pushed a strand of hair behind her ear. "I was talking to Briggs and my mom."

"What do you mean?" Graham asked. "You were having a dream."

"Yes, but they were really there. My mom said I can bring out some kind of lightning from inside myself." Wren threw her legs over the side of the bed and got to her feet. She held out her hand and tried to decide what to do. She frowned as she willed something to happen.

"It was just a dream," Tal said, with a yawn. "Why would my dad come talk to you? I don't see him as the helpful type of angel."

Ming Li snorted, and Wren smiled at the image of Briggs with a halo and wings that popped into her head. Briggs was no angel.

"He came because my mom was nervous," she explained.

Tal shifted. "My dad wasn't really the supportive type."

"Well, I don't know why, but he was there." Wren took a deep breath and closed her eyes. She could feel something in the pit of her stomach. She focused on the feeling and pulled at it. Her entire body felt warm and something ran down her arm. She opened her eyes and a crackling ball of lightning sat on her hand. It was warm, but it wasn't burning her.

"Wow," Graham said, staring at it.

"This is the type of lightning that goes into the silver eclipse. There's something more stable about it. When I throw it in with Graham's ice, it won't blow everything up."

"Are you sure?" Ming Li asked. "It doesn't look stable."

Wren smiled. "It's fine. It's going to work. I do want to try a few things to see how it reacts."

"I've figured out how to grow vines that burn, but don't burn up," Tal said.

"How did you manage that?" Graham asked.

"Research. It's a slow growing vine that most people don't bother with because of how slow it grows. It's not a concern for us because I can get it to grow fast. I already tried it a few times."

"You can just make it pop out of the ground?" Wren asked.

"Nah. I have seeds. Brog actually got them for me. I was going to tell you guys about it earlier, but every time I think about it we're talking about something unrelated."

"Does this mean we're ready?" Wren asked.

"We might want to experiment a little," Graham said. "Like put Wren's lightning and my ice together and see what happens. We don't want to blow up the items after all the effort it took to get them."

Wren looked at her dark balcony window. "Is it morning? I can't tell."

"It's early, but yes." Ming Li said. "I'm usually the only one awake at this time."

"So do we experiment today?" Tal asked.

Graham nodded. "How about experiment today, rest tomorrow, then the silver eclipse the next day?"

Tal smirked. "We should probably let Sen in on everything. His room is too far away to hear Wren's screams."

CHAPTER 18

Graham slumped down to his knees in a clump of weeds and rubbed his eyes. It was a good thing they decided to experiment because it wasn't going well. They had been in a deserted field on the other continent for hours, trying to create a scenario that would be similar to the silver eclipse. The field was now covered in scorch marks.

"I'm so sorry," Wren said, putting a hand on his shoulder. "Are you alright?"

He tried to smile, but it felt more like a grimace. "I'll live."

"That's like the third time it's hit you."

"Fourth, but who's counting?"

"Did it burn you?"

"Not this time."

Tal sat in the dirt. "This was just supposed to be a quick run through."

Ming Li frowned. "I'm glad we decided to practice, and we didn't just show up and cause a scene in Boztoll. I'm already exhausted, and all I've done is sit here and watch."

Graham couldn't figure out what they were doing wrong. Tal would grow the vines, Sen would throw a fireball and start them on fire, and then they would put a large fireproof pot on top. Graham would shoot ice at the same time Wren threw a handful of lightning into the pot. As soon as the lightning and ice hit, it sounded like an explosion and the pot flew into the air, usually hitting Graham. The other times it moved the vines and caught the weeds on fire. Graham was getting tired from putting out all the fires.

"Whatever the problem is comes from what Graham and Wren are doing," Sen said. "We should stop our parts and only have the two of them try."

"That's a good idea," Tal said. "If we keep this up, I'm gonna run out of seeds."

"We might need to add an extra day of practice," Wren said.

Graham shook his head. "We've taken too long as it is."

"You seem so tired."

"And you've got burn marks on your arm," Ming Li added.

"I've got something I can put on it," he said, pointing to his bag. Wren grabbed his bag and started fishing around in it.

"What am I looking for?"

"It's a vial that looks like it has gray lotion in it."

"This?" she asked, holding up the vial.

"Yes."

Wren opened it and poured some on her hand. She grabbed Graham's arm and carefully rubbed the lotion into the burn. It was better almost immediately.

"I can do it," he said.

Wren smiled. "Nope. You're always rubbing something weird on us. It's your turn to be uncomfortable."

"Too bad you don't need to rub any onto his face," Tal said, grinning. "Then you could stare into his eyes and see if his pupils are dilated."

"Haha," Graham said, getting to his feet. Tal would never let him live down that moment in the cave.

Wren went on her toes and kissed his cheek. "Just ignore him. He's just jealous he didn't think of it."

Graham smiled and put his arm around her. "Should we try again?"

Ming Li giggled. "The silver eclipse or staring into each other's eyes?"

Tal raised an eyebrow. "They could stare into each other's eyes and summon the silver eclipse. Perhaps that's what they're missing."

"Maybe we will," Graham said. He still occasionally wondered how he got so lucky to have Wren's attention.

"You couldn't pay me enough to hang out with you guys if I was dating someone," Sen said, shaking his head.

Graham smiled. He couldn't imagine Sen with a girlfriend. That would mean he would have to talk to someone regularly.

"They can take it," Tal said. "See, Wren's only a slight shade of pink. Last year, she would have been three shades of red."

"I find it interesting that you are the one doing the teasing," Sen said. "I mean, I had to kiss your girlfriend for you."

"Ah, man," Tal said, looking up at the sky. "I should've known that would come up, eventually."

"Seriously," Ming Li said, giving Tal a playful shove. "Next time I have a last request, I hope you jump in."

"You know I will. Things were different back then."

"I bet you two can't even look into each other's eyes," Wren challenged.

"We can too," Ming Li said, turning to Tal. "Look in my eyes."

"Fine." Tal shook his head and looked down into Ming Li's eyes. His mouth twitched.

"I hope you aren't about to laugh," Ming Li scolded.

Tal grinned. "Sorry, you can't force moments."

"Hey guys!" came a voice from behind Graham. He jumped and turned to see Jaaz walking towards them with Brake. Brake was carrying a basket.

"What are you doing here?" Ming Li asked Jaaz.

"My house burned down, so Brake said I could come watch you guys."

"Your house burned down?" Graham asked. Jaaz didn't appear phased.

"Yeah. Governor Zera thinks it was someone who was angry about my parents belonging to The Dark Cloud."

"I brought you some lunch," Brake said, handing the basket to Tal. "We thought you would all be back by now."

"It hasn't been going as smoothly as we hoped," Ming Li said, peering into the basket. "Did you make this?"

Brake laughed. "No, it was Hamble."

"Oh good," she said, pulling out a sandwich. "No offense Uncle Brake."

"None taken. What have you been doing? It looks like you've been working on burning down the place."

"Don't worry," Graham said. "We'll figure it out."

"You look exhausted, Son."

"Yeah, but I'm fine."

"Well, I need to get back. Can you all drop Jaaz off at Zera's old place when you're done?"

"Sure."

Brake nodded and teleported away.

"They almost trust me," Jaaz said. "Not enough to go to your hideout, but enough to let me hangout with you."

Graham sighed. They really didn't need Jaaz distracting them. "Okay, let's eat and then try again."

Wren flew backwards and hit the ground. "Oof!" She struggled to catch her breath.

"Are you alright?" Ming Li asked, running up to her. Tal was right behind.

She took a few deep breaths. "I'll be fine," she said, sitting up. Graham was getting up from about twenty feet away. He ran over to her.

"Are you okay?"

"Yep."

"That was crazy!" He held out his hand and pulled her up. "I don't know if we're going to survive this."

"I have an observation," Jaaz said, coming near them. "You keep hitting the ice and the lightning together at the same time. That seems to result in a minor explosion. This last time, the ice was faster than the lightning and when the lightning hit, it made an even bigger explosion. You need to do it the opposite way."

"I have no idea what you're talking about," Graham said.

"Shoot the lightning first, and then have the ice hit it."

"I don't see why that would make any difference."

"Couldn't hurt to try, could it?"

"It actually could," Wren mumbled, rubbing her sore wrist. She had a feeling it wouldn't be the only thing sore tomorrow.

"Should we try?" Graham asked her.

"I guess."

"Okay, we need to time this exactly right. You shoot the lightning down towards that rock, and as soon as it leaves your hand, I'll try to hit it."

"Alright. Everyone stand back in case it bounces." Wren waited for everyone to back up.

"Ready?" Graham asked.

"Ready. Here I go in three, two, one." Wren shot a ball of lightning at the rock. Ice blasted the ball, and it all seemed to freeze in place. The ball and the ice became one solid mass of ... something. It was clear and resembled a crystal. It hovered a few inches above the rock.

Wren released a slow breath. "It worked!"

"Guys, come here!" Graham called. Tal, Ming Li, Sen, and Jaaz came running over. "We did it!"

"Alright, now we need to levitate it into the air," Tal said. Graham, Wren, Tal, and Sen all aimed their hands at the floating mass and raised it higher into the air. When it was above their heads, Ming Li raised her palms and shot a blast of wind at the object. It flew fifty feet into the air in record time. Wren focused on keeping it steady.

"In theory it will go higher when we actually do the other steps," Graham said. "Let's lower it." Ming Li dropped her arms and the other four slowly lowered the item to the ground.

"Yes!" Ming Li yelled, jumping up and down. "It's going to work!"

"I knew I would be useful to you guys some day," Jaaz said, with a grin that stretched across his face.

"Thanks Jaaz," Graham said. "Who knows how long it would have taken us to figure it out?"

"I'm a pretty useful person when I put my mind to it."

"I guess we can go back," Wren said.

"Do we have to?" Jaaz asked. "It's been forever since I was out in the light." He spread out his arms and closed his eyes, holding his face up to the sun. "It feels so nice."

"If everything goes as planned, things should be back to normal in a few days," Graham said. "I'll take Jaaz back and meet the rest of you after."

Wren grabbed all the leftovers from lunch and shoved them back into the basket and then teleported back to Flordillia. The others weren't far behind her.

"Did you figure it out?" Brake asked, coming down the stairs in the entryway.

"Yes," Ming Li said. "Well, Jaaz did anyway. Who would have thought?"

"Everything should be ready then," Brake said. "I talked to Zera this morning. She met with the governors from the surrounding areas yesterday and gave them the names of Dark Cloud members in their cities. They all agreed to round them up immediately and at the same time, so no one could be warned."

"When will they do that?" Tal asked.

"It's done, actually."

"Already?"

"They all struck at once. They did it this morning."

"What if Zalliah's list wasn't correct?" Wren wondered, setting the basket near her feet. "What if she made it as a decoy?"

"We talked about that. Everyone who was taken into custody will be treated innocently until we prove things one way or another."

"Except they can't leave," Hamble said, entering the room with Valeena.

"We are pretty sure most, if not all, of them are guilty," Valeena said, giving Tal a quick hug. "The lists didn't surprise any of the governors. Most of the names were former criminals or people that were already suspected."

"So they captured all the Dark Cloud?" Wren sighed with relief. Graham teleported into the room.

"I doubt it," Brake said. "I would bet we have most of them. There are some on the list who are still on Earth. They probably worked for Gorbin. We can deal with them later. They aren't bothering with anything here, so they shouldn't have anything to do with the weather."

"It's going to be weird to go back to school," Ming Li said.

"And awkward," Wren added. "Everyone's going to be talking about us. I hate that."

"The talk will all die down and go back to normal sooner than you think," Brake reassured her.

"It's going to be different with Hedder gone," Wren said. "He's been my teacher every year." Hedder hadn't been her favorite teacher, but she hadn't minded him like some people did. "I wish we hadn't left him in the maze to go after Gorbin. If we'd stayed, maybe he would've survived."

"Let's not focus on what might have been," Hamble said. "Hedder was more capable than you all knew, and he told you to go. We'll always appreciate what he did and I suspect he would've been happy knowing he went out as a hero. He's going to make the history books for sure."

Tal frowned. "The irritating thing about the maze is, we didn't even need to go there. Fiend would have taken care of it."

"Hamble is right, though," Brake said, with a stern glance around the room. "Dwelling on what should have happened won't help. If it makes you feel any better, Hedder was the one who pushed to go to the maze. We were all undecided, and he felt like you should go."

The room was silent for a moment as they all thought about Hedder.

"What will you do, Tal?" Mining Li asked. "Your life will be pretty different."

Tal scratched his neck. "I don't know. Will we stay at our house?" he asked Valeena.

"Do you want to?" she asked. "We could stay, or we could sell it and live somewhere else. Whatever we do, we'll be together. No more traveling for me."

Tal looked relieved. "I don't care where we live. We can talk about it after it's all over."

Valeena nodded. "What are you going to do, Sen?"

He shrugged. "I guess I'll go find my family on Earth."

"What if you don't like it there?" Graham asked.

"I'll find a way back."

"Maybe Dovin can teach you to teleport between worlds," Wren said.

"When it's over, Graham and I can start a matchmaking business," Tal said, grinning. "There has to be money in it."

Graham groaned. "That sounds awful. I barely survived Jaaz."

"But think of all the Jaaz's out there. They need us. Plus, we have a perfect record."

"One person."

"Two. Jaaz and Solia. Come on. It could be fun."

Hamble laughed. "I might go back to teaching just to watch."

"We could help Hamble next," Tal said. "He seems to enjoy watching relationships unfold. He deserves one of his own."

"No, no, no," Hamble said, waving his arms in a nixing motion. "I like to observe, not be a part of it. I like to laugh on the sidelines."

Tal raised an eyebrow. "Just imagine what you're missing."

"I am fine going through life alone. I'm not missing anything."

"That's too bad," Valeena said, flashing him a smile. "I was hoping you were going to ask me to the victory ball Zera is planning."

Hamble's entire head turned red, and he started coughing. Valeena's eyes sparkled as she smacked him on the back.

Tal smiled. "Mom, don't tease Hamble like that. You might kill him."

"Who says I'm teasing?" she asked.

"Breathe Hamble. She's joking."

"I know," Hamble said, catching his breath. "I just swallowed funny."

"You know, it's not a bad idea," Tal said, looking thoughtful. "I'm not opposed to having Hamble as my stepfather."

"Not funny," Hamble growled.

"Nope. I've decided. Are you in Graham? We're going to get Hamble and my mom together."

Wren grinned. The thought of Hamble and Valeena as a couple was funny. She was always so composed and perfectly put together. Hamble wasn't exactly a Jaaz, but he took little time on appearance.

"I don't think so," Valeena said, shaking her blonde ringlets.

"Thank you," Hamble muttered.

"I don't need their help," she said, linking her arm with Hamble's. He let out a yelp.

"I just remembered something," he said, dashing off towards the kitchen.

Valeena laughed, and everyone else joined in.

Brake tilted his head and tried to give her a stern look. "That was mean, Valeena. He's going to go into hiding now."

She smiled. "He'll live. He needs more excitement in his life."

"But you shouldn't tease him."

"Who said I'm teasing?"

"I can't wait to see my brothers again," Sen said. "They are so much easier to be around than you people."

The next day dragged on. Graham was regretting their decision to take a day to rest. It would have been better to get it all over with. He watched Wren. She was sitting on the uncomfortable parlor couch trying to read a book. Maybe rest would be good. Wren was moving slowly today. He suspected she had gotten hurt more than she had admitted yesterday. He saw the way she rubbed her back when she thought nobody was watching.

"Are you alright?" he asked, sitting next to her.

"Fine," she said, glancing up.

"I can heal you."

"No, I'm good. I'm a bit sore, but I should be fine tomorrow."

"Do you want me to look at your wrist?"

"It's fine," she said, holding out her arm and moving her wrist.

"Let me see," he said, taking her hand. "It's a little swollen."

"It's fine," she said, putting her book on her lap. "I don't want you to heal me. It will just make you tired and you need all your energy tomorrow."

"So do you. And you need your hand. It's not a hard fix."

"I wish we would have done the silver eclipse this morning," she said, changing the subject. "Today seems like it's going on forever."

"I was thinking the same thing." Graham smiled and kissed Wren's wrist. His stomach turned, because he healed it without using medicine. That never went well.

"Hey!" Wren protested. "Why did you do that? Now you're sick."

"It'll pass," he said, trying not to wither on the floor. So much for a romantic gesture.

"I'll go get you some water," she said, jumping up. She raced out of the room and was back in less than a minute. She handed him a cold glass, and he sipped the water.

"Thanks."

"Don't do things like that. I would have been fine." She twisted her wrist around a few times. "It feels much better, though. Thank you."

The door creaked open and Padmire came in. "I came to tell you goodbye," he said. "I was going to close the cave to you the other day, but I decided to wait until I'm sure you are successful tomorrow. I just talked to the others, and they told me your plan."

"Does that mean you care about us?" Graham asked.

Padmire rubbed his blue head and frowned. "I care about the world. If you don't succeed, then I have to help you more."

"You've already helped us a lot," Wren said. "We appreciate it."

"If you are successful tomorrow, more things will be fixed than just the weather. Things are going to change for some people more than others."

"What do you mean?" Graham asked.

"It's something you will have to experience for yourselves. I don't want to explain in case I'm wrong. I have a feeling the entire world is about to change. Whether it's for the better, I'm not sure. Change is rarely easy, but often necessary."

"Now, you're making me nervous," Wren said.

"No reason to be," the bungle said. "I'm sure it will all end up the way it's supposed to."

"What if there isn't a way it's supposed to? It seems like most things are up to chance," Graham said.

Padmire sniffed. "Chance? A lot of things are up to chance, but think of all the things that aren't. Was it just a chance that Wren made a portal that just happened to be where you were? That's preposterous to even think about. You're both chosen. The chances of her going to that world and finding you would be slim. And Ming Li? She found Brake. You were all brought together in ways that wouldn't have happened by chance."

"So, fate?"

"Something like that. You were all pulled together to do what you needed to. Now it's your job to not mess anything up."

"No pressure," Wren said.

"We're ready," Graham assured her.

"I know. I can't help being nervous."

"I'm going now," Padmire said. "This is probably the last time I'll see you. I will wait and watch tomorrow, and then I will go back to the cave."

"Will it ever open again?" Graham asked.

"I'm sure it will. There are always bad people, so there will always be a need for heroes. It's happened many times in history, and it will continue to happen."

"So people will go back to touching the crystal to see if they're chosen for anything?"

"No. I've had the crystal moved back inside the cave. It will make it more peaceful for the giants."

"If people need the cave again, how will you know?"

"I can't tell you all my secrets," Padmire said, putting his hands on his hips. "You don't need to worry. I'll always know."

"Thanks for all the help you've given us," Wren said. "There's no way we would have gotten this far without your help."

"That's true," he said, puffing out his chest. "And that makes it worth it to me. I like to be useful."

Graham smiled. "I'm sure Zalliah won't forget you, either. She'll think about you every time the light turns out."

Padmire grinned, his sharp yellow teeth showing. "I am proud of that."

CHAPTER 19

Wren was sweating. Her nerves were really getting to her. She shed her cloak and tossed it in a sparsely lit yard in Boztoll. They were going to summon the silver eclipse in the middle of the street, but then they realized they needed dirt for Tal to grow the vines. One citizen of Boztoll volunteered his yard. This was it. It was the moment they had been working towards for so long.

She looked around the city. Aside from the wind, it was quiet. Brake, Drew, Austra, Hamble, Dovin, and Valeena had convinced all the people to wait outside the city until everything was done. They didn't need any distractions. The adults, along with the giants, were patrolling the borders to make sure they weren't interrupted.

"Aren't you cold?" Ming Li asked, pulling her cloak tighter. "I'm freezing."

"I don't know what I am," Wren admitted. "I'm sweating, but now my arms are cold."

"Nervous?"

"Completely. What if it doesn't work? All the people out there are counting on us."

"It'll work."

Wren tilted her head and looked at her friend. "How can you be sure?"

She shrugged. "It just has to."

Graham, Tal, and Sen came around the corner dragging a huge cast iron tub with them. They decided they needed something bigger than a pot, and Dovin had hunted this down. It was three feet across and two feet high, and from the way the boys were struggling, heavy. They had all ditched their cloaks.

"Are we ready?" Ming Li asked.

"We need a quick breather," Tal said, putting his hands to his knees.

"Am I the only one that's nervous?" Wren asked.

Graham stretched his back. "I'm a little nervous. I'm more excited though. It will be nice to be done with it all."

"Everything changes after this," Ming Li said. "Even going back to school is going to seem really weird. Last time we were at school, we didn't even like Talon."

"You can stop pretending you didn't like me back then," Tal said, standing.

"Thinking you were hot and liking you are two different things."

"Let's not go there," Sen said. "Can we do this?"

Tal nodded. He pulled a seed from his pocket and took a resolved breath. Kneeling on the ground, he pulled out the grass until he made a small bald spot on the lawn. He dug away at the dirt, trying to make a hole big enough for the seed. They learned the other day that if he didn't plant it deep enough, it would pull out of the ground when the vine grew big enough to be useful.

"There are so many little roots in the way," he complained. "Let me try something." He studied the ground and wiggled his fingers. The little roots left from the grass all sunk deeper into the ground and disappeared. "There we go." He pulled away more dirt and placed the seed into the ground and covered it.

"My heart feels like it's trying to escape from my chest," Wren said as Tal stood.

"Here it goes." Tal raised his hands, and vines shot out of the ground. He moved his hands in fast circles and the vines wrapped around each other until they were in a tight wad.

"It still seems weird that the vines don't burn up," Ming Li said.

"People used to use them in their fireplaces because they have a nicer smell than coal and they don't put out a lot of smoke. You're up Sen."

Sen pulled up his sleeves and walked towards the vines. A ball of fire appeared in his hand and he threw it on top of them. Purple flames roared to life, and Wren took a step back. It had surprised them when they were practicing the other day when the flames burned purple.

"Everyone's going to need to help lift the tub," Graham said. "It's really heavy." They all grabbed a spot and carefully lifted it over the fire.

"I hope it doesn't put the fire out," Tal said as they lowered it into the flames. They were unaffected. The fire burned brighter. A sweet smell filled Wren's nose.

Ming Li jumped back. "I don't get how this works. It defies everything I know about fires. It should catch the grass on fire or something."

"Magic doesn't need to make sense," Tal said. "That's why it's magic."

"Throw the stuff in quick," Graham commanded. Wren dumped in the water from the well of Truth. Tal tossed in a handful of yellow powder from Meegore. Sen dropped the stone heart. The sound of it hitting the bottom startled Wren. She needed to get a hold of herself. Graham deposited the golden tear and the small amber earring.

"Where's the hair?" Wren asked.

"Here," Tal said, holding up a few strands of Fria's hair. He dropped them into the tub, and Ming Li tossed in the sand.

"Ready?" Graham asked Wren. She bit her lip and nodded. Tal, Ming Li, and Sen took a few steps back.

Wren took a deep breath. "Now!" she yelled as she shot a small ball of lightning at the items in the tub. Graham was only a fraction of a second behind her, blasting her lightning with ice. A bright flash caused them all to cover their eyes, and Wren felt herself flying through the air. She hit the ground and rolled.

Jumping up, she looked at her friends. They were all scurrying to their feet.

Wren panicked. "Did we mess up?"

Tal jogged over to the tub and looked inside. "No, come look!" They all hurried over and gazed inside. The items had all become a solid golden object. It had a slight glow.

"Should it be gold?" Ming Li asked, her eyebrows scrunched together. "I thought it would be silver."

"We don't have time to worry about that," Tal said. "Let's levitate it."

Graham, Wren, Sen, and Tal raised their arms and lifted the golden object into the air. Ming Li planted her feet against the ground and aimed her palms as it got higher. Wind burst from her and pushed it higher. It shot up with such great speed, Wren had trouble keeping it steady.

The golden mass disappeared into the clouds and they all slowly lowered their hands, keeping their gazes fixed on the clouds above. Wren could hear her heart pounding in her head, and a chill ran up her spine. She willed her breathing to stay steady.

"Is it getting lighter?" Ming Li whispered.

"The clouds are moving," Graham said.

He was right. The place where the item had disappeared was slowly opening up from its cloud cover. A full moon appeared in the open space. The silhouette of something crossed in front of the moon, and then a blinding flash followed by the loudest boom Wren had ever heard. It was so loud it drowned out any other ambient sound.

A streak of silver shot across the heavens, leaving a shimmering trail that seemed to go on forever. Wren watched in awe as it seemed to mix with the stars. There wasn't a cloud in sight. The event had occurred so quickly, Wren couldn't help wondering what they had just witnessed.

As they gazed at the now calm sky, something wet hit Wren's cheek and ran down her face. She wiped at it. It was silver. Silver droplets fell like rain. They glittered in the moonlight.

"We did it!" Tal yelled, punching his fist into the air. "We did it!"

Wren and Ming Li hugged each other and jumped up and down.

Graham held out his hand and captured some drops. "No one ever mentioned silver rain."

"That was the neatest thing I've ever seen," Sen said, staring up at the moon.

"What's that sound?" Wren asked, peering into the distance.

"It's people." Graham said. A rush of cheering Boztolneans came bursting into the streets. Before Wren could think, she was being hugged and patted on the back from all directions. People were laughing or crying and yelling out praise.

Music sprung up from somewhere and people started dancing in the street. Wren saw a few giants joining in.

Drew broke through the crowd and kissed Wren on the head. "You did it! My ears are still ringing, but you did it!"

Wren laughed. "It worked! I've been so worried!"

"I need to find Austra," Drew said, disappearing into the crowd.

Graham grabbed Wren around the waist and spun her around. She squealed as he placed her on her feet. "I'm glad that was you. I wasn't a hundred percent because I'm still seeing spots from that flash."

"You know I love you, right?" Wren said, grinning.

"And I love you," he said, leaning down and kissing her.

"Come on, you two," Ming Li said, watching them break apart. "Are you trying to be your dad and Austra?"

"I don't even want to imagine that," Wren said.

"Well, just a warning. I heard him propose."

Wren nodded. It was okay. Her dad would be happy, and that would make her happy.

"Come on, let's dance like all these crazy people!" Tal said, pulling Ming Li away.

"Do you want to dance?" Graham asked Wren. "I don't know how, but it looks like anything goes." Wren looked around at all the funny dances going on around them. She nodded. It was time to dance in the silver rain. This day was going down in history.

"Everyone listen!" A woman with long brown hair shouted. "Stop!" Graham looked at her. She looked excited, but with all the music and laughter, most people were ignoring her.

"Quiet!" the giant named Mot yelled. Everyone stopped and looked at him. He nodded to the woman. It wasn't easy to ignore a giant.

"Friends and neighbors, look!" The woman held out her hand and an orb of light appeared in her hand.

"Sela has magic!" someone exclaimed next to Graham.

"I can do magic!" Sela yelled.

Graham rubbed the goosebumps on his arms as chaos erupted. People who hadn't had magic were all trying to do magic. Orbs of light sprung up throughout the crowd. So many people were talking at once that nobody was listening.

"Fire!" someone yelled as a nearby tree went up in flames. Graham ran to the tree and put the fire out before it could spread.

"Everyone stop!" Mot yelled, grabbing their attention again. The crowd turned to him once more and Dovin stood up on a crate.

"Friends!" Dovin said, drawing their attention. "We did not foresee this happening. It appears the silver eclipse has given everyone magic!" Some people cheered. "Yes, it's an amazing thing, but you must be careful. We cannot have so many people trying unknown magic without proper guidance. Please refrain from using magic until you are properly instructed."

Wren tilted her head and looked at Graham. "Do you think everyone in the world that didn't possess magic got it, or just the people in Boztoll?"

"The silver eclipse was supposed to reset the weather for the entire world. My guess is everyone has magic now," Graham said.

Brake came up behind them and put his hand on Graham's shoulder. "This is going to cause a lot of problems we weren't expecting. All the people are going to require training."

"Who gets that job?"

"There are plenty of people that can help. Most people have family that can instruct them. We just need to make sure everyone isn't experimenting at the same time. I sent Zera a message. She's going to spread the word as fast as she can and tell people to be patient and wait for further instruction."

Wren looked thoughtful. "I wonder if this happened when people did the silver eclipse the other times."

"Do you think it's because it had the golden dust from the cave?" Graham asked. "It only took a small bit to make Mali magic. I guess we didn't need to go there. She would have gotten magic anyway."

"I bet it is from the dust," Wren said. "I wonder if only people who were outside when it happened got magic. Maybe they had to get rained on?" They looked at all the people streaked in the silver rain.

"Anyone who was inside probably came out to investigate, so my guess is, everyone is magic," Brake said. He pointed to a glimmering puddle of silver. "I'm sure everyone will want to touch it."

"I wonder if it washes off," Graham said. "If not, there are a lot of people with ruined clothes."

"I doubt anyone cares," Brake said. "In fact, it wouldn't surprise me if people save the clothes to mark this moment in history."

Graham nodded. It wasn't a bad idea. It would be something neat to show future generations.

"What now?" Tal asked, joining them. Ming Li was right behind him.

"Our part is complete," Wren said. "Now it's up to all the governors to decide how they want to handle things in the different cities."

"Yes," Brake agreed. "We will follow the governor's guidance and see where that takes us."

"You have to follow the governor," Ming Li grinned. "If you don't, she could make your life miserable."

"That's for sure," Brake agreed with a huge smile. "Lucky for me, Zera always has good ideas."

"It's time to conduct one last meeting of The Silver Eclipse," Graham said. "Then we all go back to life."

"Last meeting?" Wren asked, biting her lip. "Like forever?"

Graham nodded. "Hopefully. The Dark Cloud isn't a threat anymore, and the sky looks beautiful. Look at that moon." He glanced up and smiled. It was nice to see some natural light.

"It sounds sad to say it will be the last meeting."

"We can still see everyone. And now we won't all be stressed all the time. We can go back to school and do normal things that teenagers do."

"Yeah, and we can watch Jaaz in his new popular role," Tal said, grinning. "Isn't that something you want to see?"

Wren smiled. "It sounds too weird."

"It will be great," Graham assured her.

"I bet it's uncomfortable to go back. Everyone will talk about us."

"In a good way. We just saved the world. We can do school."

"So everyone has magic?" Wren asked three days later. The Silver Eclipse members were all gathered together in the uncomfortable parlor in Flordillia.

Zera nodded. "Everyone we have heard of."

"Even people who were inside?"

"Yes. And people on the other continent as well. It sounds like everyone who observed the eclipse saw the same thing, and heard the loud boom."

"It is amazing something could be seen and heard by all," Brog said from his seat on the floor.

"Did it affect the giants?" Graham asked. "And what about the trolls and the goblins?"

"We are not affected," Brog said, tilting his head thoughtfully. "Giants already have our own magic. Not like human magic, but we possess some."

"Like the way you grow food?" Ming Li asked.

"Yes. And all giants can do magic. I have never met a giant that couldn't."

"And the trolls and goblins?" Graham prodded.

"They seem to be the same," Zera said. "I think it only affects humans."

Drew leaned forward in his chair. "I heard Graham got a message from the goblins?"

"Yeah," Graham said. "Vork was so happy about the weather. He said he'll have berries from the maze sent to me regularly ... for a small price."

Ming Li clapped. "Hallelujah! The sick world is saved!"

"They would've been saved anyway," Graham said. "It just would've tasted bad." Wren smiled. She loved how excited Graham got when he talked about healing people. Now he would have time to learn more.

"Can I go find my family after this?" Sen asked. "I'm not sure if I want to stay on Earth, but I want to see them. I know my dad told Wren he would come for me, but I'd rather go now."

"It might be hard to find them," Wren said.

"That's okay. I've nothing better to do."

"I'll teach you to teleport to different worlds," Dovin offered. "Then you won't need to rely on Wren and her portals."

"I can give you the map to the spot I took your family," Wren said. "Your dad sounded like the village wasn't far from there."

"Can you teach all of us to go to other worlds?" Tal asked.

Dovin winked. "Perhaps. I'm not sure I trust you running off to other places."

"Funny."

"What about me?" Dree asked. "I have magic now, but I still don't want to go home."

"You can come with me," Sen offered. "I can teach you how to use your magic."

"I'm still not sure I want to do magic."

"I can teach you enough to not hurt yourself by accident."

Dree nodded. "And you'll bring me back if I don't like it there?"

"Yes."

"Alright. Thank you."

Brake rubbed his chin. "There are other options as well. You are welcome to stay with us if you don't want to go to Earth."

"Thank you, but I think I'll go with Sen for now," Dree said, with no hesitation.

"Are there any changes with Zalliah?" Austra asked. "Is she still claiming amnesia?"

"She is," Dovin said, running a hand through his hair. "The day after the silver eclipse, she wouldn't talk to anyone. Now she's back to claiming she doesn't care because she remembers nothing, anyway. She keeps asking to talk to one of these five, but I don't think that's a good idea."

"Why would she want to talk to us if she's claiming she doesn't remember anything?" Wren asked.

"Who knows?" Dovin said with a heavy sigh. "I'm sure she's busy plotting something."

"There's no way she can escape, though. Right?" Tal asked.

"Not without a lot of help," Drew said. "Those cells are secure. That one, especially since I fixed it so the sewer can't open."

"One of us should talk to her," Wren said. "She might say something."

"I doubt that's a good idea," Valeena said, pushing back her curls. "She probably wants to place doubt in your mind. If she can keep some fear of her alive, she still has some power."

"What if it's just for five minutes?" Graham asked. "I'm curious about what she has to say."

"I will allow it if one of us listens in," Zera said.

"And then everything goes back to normal," Brake said.

"Do you guys even have a normal?" Ming Li asked.

Hamble laughed. "Not really. Perhaps I'll go back to teaching school. It's been a long time."

"And I hope to become a part of the fleet," Austra added.

Drew draped his arm over her shoulder. "You'll win for sure."

"Will you still be our science teacher?" Wren asked Dovin.

"No," he said. "My work there is finished. I can't help thinking I could've helped you all more than I did. I will not fail like that again."

"What do you mean *again*?" Brake asked.

"I am well versed in prophecies, and I see people's auras. I know the next group I need to help, and I'm going to help them before they are left to figure things out on their own."

"It all worked out for us," Wren protested.

"Yes, but if I had gotten you all together earlier, things might've gone more smoothly."

Zera tapped her chin. "I hope you will not leave until we train the newly magical people in Akkron."

"I'll stay for that, of course. I am an excellent teacher, after all."

"Thank you," Zera said, looking relieved. "I will feel much better once people stop accidentally causing chaos."

"Has it been bad?" Wren asked.

Drew chuckled. "Pretty bad. Zera told everyone not to do magic, and still everyone thinks they can figure it out on their own."

Zera nodded. "There have been a few fires. Most people only managed to hurt themselves. We are ready to start training tomorrow, and then things should settle down."

"I don't know why people want to do magic," Dree said. "I would be happy to avoid it forever if I could."

"It can be convenient," Graham said. "Like with healing. It's amazing how much more I can heal with magic."

Dree shrugged. "I guess."

"What will the giants do?" Austra asked.

"Nothing has changed for us," Brog said. "We are still working towards combining the giants at Meegore and the sand giants. It is a slow process, but it will be beneficial to all."

"So this is it?" Wren asked. She was happy they had succeeded, but she was going to miss seeing everyone regularly.

"For now," Brake said. "If there's one thing I've learned over the years, it's that there will always be evil. We've stamped it out for now, but more will always arise."

"But now it's time to be a regular teenager," Drew said.

"Is there anything you want to tell us?" Wren asked her dad. He had said nothing about asking Austra to marry him and she hadn't had time to ask.

Drew looked at Austra, and she nodded. "Austra and I are going to get married."

"Finally!" Hamble said, pumping his fists in the air. Congratulations came from everyone. Drew and Austra stood as people shook their hands.

Wren stood and hugged her dad. "I'm happy for you."

"Are you?"

"Yes."

"Thank you."

"Welcome to the family," she said, giving Austra an awkward hug. It was going to take time to feel normal about this, but she was willing to invest in it. Austra hugged her back and wiped away a quick tear. Everything was going to be new, and Wren was going to make the most of it.

Chapter 20

"Wren, good to see you," Zalliah said, looking up from her book. Wren crossed her arms and frowned at the woman in the cell. Zalliah looked a lot better. Her color had returned, and she was sitting on a wooden chair. Her green dress was clean, so Governor Zera must treat her prisoners better than Governor Briggs had.

"So, you aren't even going to pretend amnesia anymore?"

"Oh, I have amnesia," she said. "It's too bad. It sounds like I've made quite the impression on the world."

"Not really. No one is talking about you except as a failure."

Her eyes narrowed, but she smiled. "That won't be forever. Someday you will all regret not following me. It might not be soon, but it will happen. I'm a very patient person, and I always get what I want."

"How do you know what you want if you only remember being sixteen?"

"I'm a stable person. What I want now is what I'll want fifty years from now."

"Why did you want to talk to me?"

"I just wanted to congratulate you and your friends. That eclipse was amazing. I watched it through the bars. I'm sure you are all pleased with yourselves. It's nice to see people succeed at things."

"Even when they mess with your plans?"

She tilted her head and studied Wren. "Since I don't remember my plans, I don't see any reason to be upset."

"Everyone knows you're faking," Wren said. "What's the point?"

"Why would I fake?"

"I'm sure you're the only one who knows."

Zalliah smiled. "I'm sure you'll understand me someday. I won't be in here forever, and then I'm hoping we can get together for a reunion."

"I don't imagine you'll ever leave this place. Maybe you should work on becoming a better person."

Zalliah threw her head back and laughed. "Thank you Wren. That's what I'm going to do. You are so inspirational."

"I'm done," Wren said, walking to the door. There was no reason to be here.

"Goodbye Wren. We will meet again."

Wren hoped not. She left the room and walked outside with Austra, who had been listening at the door.

"Why did she want to talk to me?" Wren asked. "She said nothing worthwhile."

Austra pushed her long black hair behind her ear. "Zalliah has always been one to like her own voice. I think she wanted to make you nervous. She can't escape. Don't dwell on her anymore."

They teleported to Wren's house. Drew was pacing the hallway, waiting for them.

"What happened?" he asked.

"Not a lot," Wren said. She told him everything that Zalliah said.

"I agree with Austra," he said. "She just wanted one last chance to get in your head. It's time to move on. Start worrying about things like school and boys."

"You want me to worry about boys?" Wren asked with a grin.

Drew shook his head. "Not really, but it's better than dwelling on that woman. Graham's a good kid. I don't disapprove of you liking him, but I will have you watched."

Wren could feel her eyes twinkle. "Oh yeah? By who? Brog went back to Meegore."

"Oh, I have someone, don't you worry."

Wren just shook her head. He was probably bluffing. She changed the subject. "I had a dream the other day. It was about my mom."

"Oh?"

"It wasn't a normal dream. She was really there. Strangely enough, so was Governor Briggs."

"Governor Briggs?"

"Yeah, it was odd. It was really short, and she gave me some advice for summoning the silver eclipse. It was good of them to come. I don't remember her, of course, since I was so young when she died, but it was good to get to see her and get a memory of her."

Drew and Austra both watched her like they weren't sure where she was going with this. Wren had gone through this conversation in her head a few times before, and it always went a lot smoother.

"I just want you to know that I'm happy to possess that one memory of my mom, but I still have room for another ... I don't know. Another mother type figure in my life, I guess. I'm going to try to make things work, Austra. I don't want you to worry about whether I'm going to accept you."

"Thanks Wren," Austra said, with misty eyes. "I do worry."

"No more worries," Drew said, drawing them into a group hug. "We're going to be happy. Just you watch."

Graham ignored all the curious eyes and whispers that followed him through the school. He didn't blame people for being curious. He would feel better with his friends, though. Graham hadn't been in school long, but it felt nice to be back.

"Graham!" Wren called through the crowded hallway. He stopped and waited for her to catch up. Ming Li was only a few steps behind her. If anyone wasn't staring before, they were now.

"Where's Tal?" he asked, taking Wren's hand.

Ming Li looked at the ceiling and shook her head in irritation. "He's signing his name on people's bags and arms. We had a whole army of nerdy kids following us around. He's enjoying it way too much."

"Hey guys!" Jaaz said, joining them. "I see you're holding hands."

"You're very perceptive," Ming Li said, rolling her eyes.

"It's good to have you all back," he said, pulling a notebook from his bag.

"Good to be back," Graham said. "Where's Solia?"

"She has an early morning club she runs," he said, writing something in his notebook. "Holding hands in the hallway," he muttered.

"Why did you write that?" Wren asked.

"No reason."

Ming Li snorted. "Taking notes? I would think Solia would tell you everything you are supposed to do."

"She's not as bossy as she used to be," Jaaz said. "After she got rid of my lame clothes, she stopped telling me what to wear and stuff. Turns out I just needed a little guidance. She's still bossy about some things. It really annoys her if I use my sleeve as a handkerchief, but really what am I supposed to do? Let snot run down my face? Shirts get washed every day, so I don't see why it matters."

"Believe me, it matters," Tal said, joining the circle.

"I already got the lecture," Jaaz said, rolling his eyes. "Solia made me a bunch of handkerchiefs and made me promise to always carry one."

"That was nice of her," Wren said, hiding a smile.

"Yeah, she's really nice sometimes. She's still Solia, but way better than she used to be," he said, writing in his notebook again. "Rubbing thumb against hand."

Graham's eyes narrowed. "Are you writing what we're doing?"

"Me?" Jaaz asked. "That's silly. Why would I do that?"

"I have no idea."

"So now you guys are back, we can hang out, right? I mean, we've kind of been through a lot together now."

"Sure," Tal said. "Things aren't boring when you're around."

"That's what Solia says. She said sometimes she wishes I was more boring."

"Where are you living now?" Tal asked. "Are you still staying at Zera's old house?"

"No. They proved my parents really belonged to The Dark Cloud, so it looks like they're going to stay in prison forever. That made their money transfer to me. Since I'm over sixteen, I could buy a house. I could have rebuilt, but that would take too long. I bought a small house so I don't have to clean much. Cleaning isn't one of my priorities, so why have extra space?"

"I see the sense in that," Wren said, smiling as she linked her arm with Graham. Jaaz scribbled in his notebook.

"You are writing what we're doing," Graham said, taking Jaaz's notebook from him.

"I'm just getting ideas," Jaaz said, snatching it back.

"How much is my dad paying you?" Wren asked.

"Your dad?" Jaaz asked, looking confused. "Which one was your dad again, and why would he pay me?"

"Now you're just being pathetic," Ming Li said, shaking her head. "Remember how you aren't going to lie to us anymore?"

"You want us to trust you, right?" Graham asked.

"Alright, fine. I told Wren's dad I wanted to be a spy, and he asked me to tell him everything you and Wren do when you're together."

Tal laughed. "Just for future reference, spies don't write things in a notebook while they're talking to the people they're spying on."

"I've got a lot going on. If I don't write it down when it's happening, I'm never gonna remember later."

"You'll have to work on that. Spies have to remember things."

"I guess."

"I'm okay with you practicing on us," Wren said, smiling. "I'd rather know who my dad's spy is."

"And bonus," Graham said. "Jaaz doesn't have Brog's hearing."

"Great!" Jaaz said. "I thought about being a matchmaker first. I figured Graham and Tal were pretty good teachers, so I would be able to do it. That turned into a disaster. Spying will be much more interesting. I guess if I'm telling everything, I also told Valeena I'd watch Tal and Ming Li."

"I can't imagine my mom paying for that," Tal said, grinning.

"I'm doing it for free. After Drew talked to me, I asked Valeena if she wanted me to inform her. I thought she was going to say no because she laughed a lot, but she said that would be great."

Tal raised a mischievous eyebrow. "Write this in your notebook," he said. He grabbed Ming Li and dipped her, kissing her in the middle of the hallway.

"Oh wow," Jaaz said, scribbling in his notebook. "This is pretty good stuff. I think I'm going to enjoy being a spy."

Graham smiled as Tal stood Ming Li back up on her feet. He wasn't sure, but it looked like Ming Li was blushing. Jaaz was going to make a terrible spy, but it was going to be fun. Graham didn't notice they had an audience until people started clapping. He looked around at all the kids in the hallway that were smiling and watching them. How long had they been there?

"Alright, everyone to class!" Hamble said, poking his head out of a classroom.

"Looking good, Hamble," Ming Li said as the crowd dispersed. "Very professional."

"You think so?" Hamble asked, pulling at his shirt. He ran a hand over his bald head. "It's been a long time since I taught school. I'm a little nervous."

"You're going to be great," Wren said.

"Professor Hamble?" a short girl with blonde braids said shyly.

"Yes?"

"I don't have your class, but my mom was wondering if she could have your autograph?" She held out a piece of paper. "She said you helped save the world."

Hamble's entire head turned red. "Yes, of course," he said, taking the paper. "Come into my classroom and I'll use my special green pen." The girl followed him in.

Tal laughed. "Hamble's going to be okay."

"Has anything happened between him and your mom?" Wren asked.

Ming Li tilted her head. "Valeena was probably just messing with him."

"That's what I thought." Tal said. "But now I'm not so sure. She's been talking about him all week."

"That is a couple I would never have come up with," Graham said.

"Hamble's kind of shy about that kind of thing," Tal said. "It would be nice if my mom settled with a nice guy like him. She deserves someone good."

"I guess I could help with one more matchmaking attempt," Graham said. "But just because I like Hamble."

"We can start planning today," Tal said. "There's no way it can be as fun as Jaaz and Solia. That was one of the most hilarious experiences of my life."

"Why hilarious?" Jaaz asked.

"Uh ... It's hard to explain," Tal said. Graham smiled. Tal must have forgotten that Jaaz was standing with them.

"Did you see the statue they built for Hedder in the history hall?" Wren asked, coming to Tal's aid.

"Yeah, it's huge," Jaaz said.

"The plaque Dovin donated was nice," Tal said. "Maybe too nice. It didn't sound like it was about Hedder at all."

"He deserves it," Ming Li said. "He helped us a lot. Without him, we might not have figured out how to perform the silver eclipse."

Graham nodded. "It was too bad he didn't get to see it. My mom said that they got permission from the goblins to put a monument to him at the base of the goblin mountain as well. We should probably put a plaque there that says, 'The place where Hedder died, after defeating a member of The Dark Cloud.' He would like that more than if we gave it a real name."

"Probably," Wren agreed.

"I heard they're also naming the hill by the side of the stream after him," Tal said. "Hedder's Hill."

Wren smiled. "I'm glad. It's good to know he'll be remembered."

Wren patted Asalee's back and smiled as Graham did the same. The alicorn nuzzled into Wren. She could sense Graham's unease. "We don't have to fly."

"I'm trying," Graham said. "It isn't easy for me to be around animals."

"Just because I like to fly doesn't mean you have to."

"I want to do things you like to do."

"But I like to do lots of things. If you still hate flying, we can do something else."

"Once we take off, I think it's fun. Sort of."

"It's so exciting to own an alicorn. Did Tal take Zebra home or did he leave him with Brog?"

"He took him home and Zebra freaked out when she saw the alicorns and the pegasi, so he took her back. She likes the island, just like Walter."

"So you're going to leave Walter with Brog?"

"Yeah. He loves it there, and he loves Brog. I've always tried to be comfortable around animals, but it isn't easy."

"Ben likes you now."

"We've come to an understanding."

"Ben's happy to be home. He's pretty adaptable, but he loves our house."

"So, are we going to fly?"

"Only if you really want to."

"Let's do it."

Wren mounted gracefully, and Graham climbed on about as awkwardly as he imagined was possible. "I'll try not to take off as fast."

"I'm fine," Graham said, holding on tight. Asalee trotted across the dirt and Graham closed his eyes. His stomach flopped as he felt them lift off the ground. It wasn't as bad as last time. He opened his eyes and watched as they broke through the fluffy white clouds. It was beautiful up here.

Graham's mind wandered over the events that had occurred since he came to Akkron. So much had happened and so many relationships were formed. Now he had his parents that loved him and let him know it. He had good friends that would do almost anything for him and that he would do anything for. And he had Wren. The Dark

Cloud had been defeated, and the world was basking in beautiful sunlight. It might not always be this way, but for today, he was going to enjoy the view.

ACKNOWLEDGEMENTS

I would like to start by thanking my readers. I appreciate your support. If you enjoyed it, I would love to have a review from you! Reviews are important for future readers.

I want to thank my family for their support. They always let me bounce ideas off of them and are willing to read things multiple times.

Thanks to Michelle. I know making countless hours of edits isn't always fun. Mary, I appreciate the name help! Special thanks to everyone else that has been so supportive! I feel the love!

About the Author

Kristy Dixon graduated with a degree in English. She started writing stories when she was seven and has been writing ever since. She started writing The Silver Eclipse at the urging of her children. She has ten children and six chickens. If she isn't writing or playing board games with her kids, she is probably eating cookies or wishing that she were eating cookies. You can contact Kristy at kristydixon35@gmail.com and find her website at www.kristydixonbooks.com.

Books by Kristy Dixon

The Silver Eclipse Book #1: Akkron

The Silver Eclipse Book #2: Boztoll

Coming Soon

More Than Once Upon a Time

Jenna, a skeptic of happily ever afters, is catapulted into a whimsical fairy tale realm where she becomes the reluctant protagonist. Trapped in a land of make-believe, Jenna must navigate through one story after another against her will. There she meets Jerron, a fellow captive whose belief in love has dwindled with every scripted romance.

Bound by a shared desire to return home, they discover that happiness holds the key to their escape. Jenna and Jerron embark on an adventure that changes their views of love and destiny. As their connection deepens, they hope to rewrite their own fairy tale endings. It soon becomes apparent that the fairy tale world is not as innocent as it seems.

Made in the USA
Monee, IL
19 November 2023

46752809R00204